THE BUDAPEST TRADEOFF

THE BUDAPEST TRADEOFF

Robert Carroll

HSP HARWOOD-SMART PUBLISHING

First published in Great Britain in 1976 by
Harwood-Smart Publishing Co. Ltd.
18 Coulson Street, London SW3 3NB
also at
Wessex House, Blandford Heights,
Blandford Forum, Dorset DT11 7TS

ISBN 0 904507 14 9

Reproduced and printed by photolithography,
and bound in Great Britain at The Pitman Press, Bath

FOR DONNA—WHO KNOWS

PART ONE

1 HUNGARY, APRIL 1957

The villages they sped through were ghostly, lit by full moonlight. No one on the cobblestone streets, hardly a light showing in the houses.

"How did you get the car?" she asked.

"Borrowed it," he said.

"From whom?"

"What does it matter?"

"But how will you return it?"

He shrugged. She could just barely make out his profile as he held the wheel with rigid hands.

"You stole it," she said.

"All right. Isn't it better that way?"

"Why?"

"You ask idiot questions," he said. "They'll find the car, and if it belongs to a friend, he gets in trouble. This way . . ."

"Whose is it?"

"I don't know."

"I'm frightened. If we're caught . . ."

"We won't be."

"How are you so sure?"

"Be quiet," he said. "It's not far now."

The car's headlights lit up a road sign that said *Köszeg.* He slowed the car to a crawl.

"We can't go through the town," he said. "The AVOs have a checkpoint at the other end. But there's a dirt road. Look for it on the left."

"Here," she said.

It was more a pathway than a road, and it ran between two farm houses that loomed on either side.

"Yes," he said. "This must be it."

He switched off the headlights, and now there was only the moon to guide them. The little Topolino squealed and groaned over the caked mud ruts. The houses were gone, and fields now lay on either side. At the end of the fields on the right, she could make out a ridge line; on top of it squatted several shapes like turtles, but the turtles had long, thin snouts.

"Russian tanks," he said.

"Can they see us?"

"Not likely."

"Can't we walk from here?"

"Not yet. The river's five miles off."

The river, she knew, was the border. She was a good swimmer, but the water would be icy. She already felt the numbness; and how would she manage with the heavy knapsack on her back? It was all a mistake. She should not have let him persuade her.

"I want to go back," she said.

"Are you crazy?"

They had left Budapest two hours before. She had made an excuse, telling her parents and her brother that she was going to Buda to study with a girlfriend. In a cul-de-sac in the old quarter, he had been waiting with the two knapsacks. She had been shivering, not so much from the cold, for the April night was fairly warm, but because, on her way there, an AVO sitting in the back of the trolley, had kept his eyes on her all during the ride. The dress she wore, and the light coat over it, came only to her knees, and it was her legs he had seemed most interested in. She had been afraid he might follow her. Her legs were good, she knew. Already, at sixteen, she had been approached and indecent suggestions had been made to her, sometimes by the Russians. She was more afraid of the Russians than of the AVOs; polite enough by day, they were made bolder by drink at night, and she knew of girls who had been raped, although it was something you were never supposed to talk about.

He had hugged her to him, and his warmth had made her feel better. "You're up to it?" was all he had asked, and she had said, yes.

He had led her past apartment houses, a few chips in the stone façades the only reminders of the snipers' bullets of the previous year. Two blocks from where the trolley had let her off, a car had been parked by the ancient sidewalk.

"Get in," he had said.

Now, with those tanks squatting so ominously near, the full awareness of her decision to leave with him caused tears to flow. What, she wondered, was she crying about? Leaving her family, yes, but more than that—she was weeping for her own death. It seemed certain to her. Very soon now, she would be dead. She began reciting a prayer she had learned before prayers had been forbidden to her. *Our father, who art in heaven . . .*

"What are you chattering about?" he asked.

"I was praying."

"Praying!" He gave a growl of derision. "Think of Vienna," he said.

Vienna. He had talked to her over and over of Vienna. Of the bright lights, of the absence of Russians, of good food, of a chance to live. In a year, he had said, she would be a dancer at the opera, she would have the best teachers, he would see to that. He was only nineteen, but he had a confidence in himself that was close to arrogance, and he had to leave, because he knew soon enough that *they* would know he had fought in the uprising, and it would be prison for him, if not a firing squad. "If you love me," he had said, "you will go with me." He had kept at her about it, and her family must have sensed something, because they had forbidden her to see him, saying he was a bad one, and made for trouble.

It had seemed easy enough, the way he had talked about it. The way to the frontier would be simple, because these days everyone, out of fear to be seen at night, took to their beds early, and the security was lax because, if no one was on the streets, what was there to watch for? North of Köszeg was a branch of the Danube that formed the Hungaro-Austrian frontier. There they were building watch towers. They would make the crossing at an uncompleted section. Across the river was woodland, relatively unguarded because it was only recently that the Russians had left Austria, and there had been little reason for tight security at the border. He knew the safest place to cross. All it took was to cut through some barbed wire near the river bank, and he had the wire cutters with him.

Ahead of them now was a small copse. He left the road and ran the car directly toward the trees, then cut the motor.

"From here we walk," he said.

He helped her shoulder one of the knapsacks. It was surprisingly heavy.

"I can't swim with this," she said.

"Don't worry about it," he said, "and shut up."

He led her by the hand, through trees, across a field smelling of newly turned earth. It seemed like an hour they walked. Suddenly, just ahead of her, he kneeled down and motioned her to do the same. She peered where he was peering, and after a while she could make out the faint sound of water, the gentle sound of a current. She could not yet see the water, but she did see something faintly dark, like a fence.

"The wire," he said.

She crept forward with him. The snap of the wire as he cut made sharp cracks in the night. Did he have to make so much noise?

A stab of light suddenly shone, picked them out.

"Stop!"

She couldn't see who it was behind the light, but she knew that now it was the end. They would be shot. They would both lie there by the wire, rotting. Her impulse was to run, but her legs were too weak, and she could force no movement from them.

"I see you," the voice said. "Stand up, both of you, and don't move!"

Then came a loud report, so loud it made her ears ring, and the red flash came from him. The light changed direction and came from the ground, and she heard groaning. He ran and got the flashlight, switched it off.

"Now," he said. "Through the wire."

Barbs tore at her as she followed him. Whole pieces of her coat and dress were ripped off. The barbs cut her legs. From far off she heard a motor start up.

"Take off everything!" he commanded at the river's edge. He grabbed the knapsack from her and opened it. Inside was a large can. He ripped off its cover and plunged his hand into the can, began smearing some evil-smelling substance over her face.

"Grease," he said. "It will keep you warm."

She stripped to her panties and smeared the grease over her cold skin.

He had stripped too, and soon his whiteness disappeared beneath the grease. A light, more blinding than the flashlight, began moving up and down the bank.

"Into the water," he whispered.

She slid down, her feet meeting mud, and, gripped by fear, she kept her head under water for what seemed minutes but was probably not more than a few seconds. Then she began swimming, literally for her life.

He was beside her.

"You all right?"

"I think so," she said.

The frenzied activity of the swimming had made her somehow braver.

"Let the current take you," he said. "The further it carries us, the better."

"How much farther?"

"A hundred meters. No more."

More and more lights gleamed on the water, tracing criss-cross patterns.

"If the lights reach you," he said, "dive under. Are you all right?"

"Yes," she said.

But all at once she couldn't move her right leg; it was as though something had gripped it.

"I have a cramp," she said.

"Give me your hand."

She reached out, and his hand gripped hers. With her free arm, she swam, but she would have floundered if he had not forced her ahead with him. Her toes touched bottom.

"We're there," he said. "We crawl from here."

She slid herself along the muddy bottom, encountered weeds, small stones. Then he pulled her up onto firm ground.

"Lie flat," he said, "on your stomach."

She lay beside him, gasping for breath. Her chest heaved. She was nude, except for the grease and the blackened panties, but she felt warm. It was several minutes before the lights on the opposite bank snapped off, one by one, but she could still hear distant voices, carrying across the river.

"The bastards got Otto," she heard a Hungarian voice say.

"Toward the trees," he said peremptorily. "Now. Run."

She ran with him, into the shelter of the woods.

2 PARIS, MARCH 1974

By the time the wall clock in the lobby of the Plaza Athenée showed fifteen minutes past five I was sure something was terribly wrong.

I had been nearly a half hour late in getting back from the business lunch, and at first I'd thought Caryl had grown impatient waiting for me to meet her in the lobby, as we'd prearranged, and had gone back to the room, or wandered outside, delaying getting back, perhaps in pique, or as a kind of punishment for being late. But she hadn't done anything like that before, and when I'd checked our room she hadn't been there, and the doorman hadn't remembered her going out. ("Yes, I remember the lady, and I keep a careful eye on who goes in or out. But, no, monsieur, I have not seen her, not since one, when I came on duty.")

Damn that long-lasting lunch at Fouquet's. The aperitif, the hors d'oeuvres, the fish course, the meat course, the wines. I had paid my respects to the good food and drink, but I'm not a heavy eater, particularly at lunch. Still, I had my job to do. As Ben Graham's lawyer I could hardly cut out of the concluding phase of the deal he was making with Compagnie Dassault. And it was a coup of sorts, the importation rights to some hitherto unexported bottlings from the Côte du Rhône, early maturing reds of breed and quality at a price that would ensure their salability.

Finally, though, there was a formal shaking of hands with Eduard Lassally, president of Compagnie Dassault of Paris and Lyon, and Pierre LeBrun, my French counterpart. Outside, in a faint sprinkle of cold March rain, Ben was in a good mood, almost as though those forthcoming shipments of ten thousand cases were already filling him with a rosy glow.

"Don't forget," he said, "you and your wife are to be my dinner guests before I leave town."

Town! Paris, even under a lowering gray sky, could hardly be called a town. Ben had the heavy physique of a football tackle, which, indeed, he had once been; he had moved into the family liquor distributing firm, which had only recently gone into French wines, and he admitted to having had to take a crash course to learn the ins and outs. My own expertise in the field had led to my being given the Paris assignment. Perfect, from my point of view, being able to combine a business trip to Paris with the pleasures of a new marriage.

I said I'd check with Caryl back at the hotel and call him at his, the Meurice. Taxis in this weather were scarce, and I hurried back to the Plaza Athenée by foot. I was without a raincoat—the sky had been clear when I left the hotel—and my outer coat was damp by the time the doorman swung the revolving door for me and I looked for Caryl among those sitting in the lobby's plush-covered chairs. No sign of her, so I used the house phone and called our room. And no answer.

That was the first alarm.

Well, she'd have left a message for me at the desk, wouldn't she? No, she hadn't. And our room key was in our box, which meant she'd gone out.

Now, why?

She knew how damned important the lunch was.

It was a new marriage, and I hadn't known Caryl very long before it, but one thing she didn't have was a temper. Not that I'd seen. Still and all, I'd kept her waiting, so I was at fault.

But she'd have left me a message, wouldn't she?

In the room, then. I got the key and went to the room, which was on the fourth floor. Her perfume hit me as soon as I opened the door. She used a French scent called Cabochard, and I'd surprised her with a two-ounce bottle of it the day before, after leaving her alone for a couple of hours for a business meeting. I knew she didn't like being left by herself, although she accepted the necessity for it, and I'd bought the perfume to make up for it, in a way. One reason she didn't like being alone was that, when walking in the streets, she would get an occasional attack of dizziness. She didn't know what caused it, she said, and it hadn't happened in New York. We were going to check it with a doctor, and it occurred to me that maybe that was where she had gone.

I looked for a message. Nothing on the round, marble-topped coffee table, nothing on the chest of drawers, nor on the bedside table.

I began feeling peevish. Inconsiderate of her. She knew I'd worry.

The room was undisturbed. On the bed was a dress she'd taken from the closet, the one she planned to wear for dinner. It was a sheathlike dress of black silk jersey with a low neckline, and it was one of my favorites—it did nice things for her figure. I'll admit I got a kick out of the way men stared when she came into a room or a restaurant; and it reinforced the feeling that she was mine, that—call it pride or ego—I had won the woman I wanted, and that she also wanted me.

My first wife had died—tragically, I suppose, is the word for it, shocking, horrifying, too—and it had somehow held me back from marrying again, though I'd met appealing others. But now I was thirty-seven and unwilling to face a bachelor future. And so I had leaped, as had Caryl, who was thirty-two and was perhaps having similar qualms about a lonely future.

But it was not as though each of us were settling for someone pleasant and tolerable. It was much, much more than that. Each of us brought our experiences, memories, and knowledge of others, and yet lovemaking was as fresh and exciting as though we were encountering the varied possibilities for the first and exploratory time. In fact, with the lowering sky and the cold mist falling on the way back to the hotel, I'd had in mind forgetting about a museum expedition and closing the drapes and curling up in that soft French bed. Lunch had finished with cognac, and cognac tended to make me feverish.

In the room, the drapes were drawn back and I could see across the wide avenue to the row of buildings on the other side. Lights were already on in some of the rooms, and I could see people moving about in offices and workrooms.

Her scent was still in the bathroom, with its two washbasins. Her toothbrush was in its holder, and in the soap dish was a hypoallergenic soap she used. Hanging on a door hook was her nightgown—a vivid Pucci print. It was traditional, she said, that a bride should have new underthings and nightclothes, and I'd insisted that she use my Saks charge card (handy for gifts) and that she go wild. This trip, although mainly business, was to be our honeymoon, too, I said. She had replied, with only the faintest of smiles, "But haven't we already had a couple?" It was at Saks, too, that I had bought her the matched Vuitton luggage, two cases, now on the luggage rack.

She had not been that anxious to make the trip—in fact, had been more than hesitant about it. "Why not?" I asked her. "Because it's business?" Partly that, she said. Was it anything else? Well, she had to close down her own apartment, decide which of her possessions to keep and which to dispose of. She still had time to go on her lease, and she ought to try to sublet—silly to keep paying rent on it. But I insisted, said I didn't want to leave her, even for a week. I knew why, though I didn't tell her the reason; she would have said I was being superstitious.

The last time I had seen my first wife, Sybil, was when I left for a trip of a week. Sybil had wanted to go; I was the one who refused. And the awful thing had happened while I was away. I did see her again—but not alive. She was in her funeral casket.

I returned to the lobby and waited, on edge. I damned myself for not having broken away from the lunch and gotten here at three. The hands of my watch hardly seemed to move. People came in, people left. I wouldn't have been able to describe any of them, because I was watching only for Caryl. I remembered to leave word at the desk that I was to be paged if any calls came through for me. And I asked them again: were they *sure* they had not seen her leave or return? Were they *sure* she had left no message? They answered with polite but distant concern. Madame was undoubtedly delayed. The traffic these days, especially when it rained, was incredible.

When my watch showed it to be four thirty—it was as though the hands had suddenly jumped a half hour—I was getting mental pictures of such clarity that I felt physically sick. . . . Of Caryl fainting, falling to the pavement, hitting her head. Or . . . crossing the Champs-Elysées, filled with crazed French drivers of Renaults, Citroens, Peugeots, blasting their horns at her as she paused in dizzy confusion. . . . The sickening thump, Caryl prone, traffic halted, angry horns blaring, policemen running.

Now cut it out, I told myself. She's late. There'll be an explanation. She'll come hurrying in, that lovely face filled with concern for me. Oh, my darling, forgive, forgive me. You see, I . . .

Didn't realize it was so late. Or, *you were late, so I . . .*

What?

I had left her in the room a little after twelve. We'd spent a leisurely morning, had breakfast side by side in bed. I read the *International Herald-Tribune.* She did her nails. Then there were phone calls, and while I spoke she lay in a hot tub in the bathroom. I went in, and she said: "Would you soap my back, darling?"

I soaped her back, and she laughed as I soaped her breasts. She splattered water on my face. "Would you like to dry me?" she asked.

I dried her with the hotel's large towels, and then, in the bedroom, I told the operator we wouldn't take any calls for a while, and we made love.

"Aren't you glad we came to Paris?" I asked her.

"Oh, yes," she said. "Oh, yes."

"Have you made love in Paris before?" I asked her, jealously.

"I won't answer that without counsel," she said.

"I'm your counsel."

"Let's never, ever speak of those things," she said.

When I left for my lunch appointment, she was dressing, drawing nylons up over her slim legs.

"I'll be back no later than three," I said. "What'll you do?"

"Some shopping, maybe. I need a pair of walking shoes. I'll be waiting for you in the lobby. Try not to be late."

I was late. And now she was late, terribly late.

The ugly thoughts persisted. She walked along the Rue du Bac, window browsing. (I remembered her telling me there were furniture shops on that Left Bank street, and we ought to go there, on the chance we could pick up some unusual pieces for our planned refurnishing of my apartment.) A car slid to the curb, a man got out, came up behind her, grabbed her arm, twisting it. His hand clapped over her mouth before she could scream, and she was forced into the rear seat of the car. And, even if anyone had noticed, how would they know who she was, or where she was from?

Or, suppose, leaving the hotel, she was followed? The Plaza Athenée was a *luxe* hotel, patronized by monied people. An attractive, well-dressed woman leaves the hotel, her handbag an inviting target. There were muggings in Paris, too.

I couldn't stand the waiting any longer in the impersonal lobby. If she was delayed, if she had been taken ill, she would be trying to call me.

I went back to the room and got the operator, asked her if there were any calls.

"No, monsieur. Wait. Just one moment. I have a call for you now."

A click and I was put through.

"Caryl!" I shouted it into the phone.

"No, Steve. It's Marge. Were you expecting Caryl?"

"Yes," I said dully.

The relief that had flooded me for a moment changed to a feeling of heaviness, as though I were wearing shoes with lead weights. I wanted to cry out to Marge that Caryl was not here, that she should have been here, that I was in an agony of waiting, but I held back. Marge and her husband Norm were good friends. Norm I knew back from my prelaw days at Columbia. But I didn't want to alarm them about something that was yet intangible and might be easily explained.

"Your voice sounded funny," Marge said. "I'm just calling to remind you we're expecting you here at seven."

"I know."

"You have the address?"

"Yes."

"We're looking forward to meeting Caryl."

"So is . . ." I choked over it. "Marge, I'm expecting Caryl to call any second."

"Oh, I'll get off the line, then."

15

The room wasn't that warm, but I was perspiring. I went to the window and scanned the street in both directions, looking for Caryl, who would be hurrying toward the hotel entrance. I saw a woman in a tan gabardine coat much like the one Caryl wore (for it was not on its customary hook in the foyer) and my heart gave a couple of extra beats. But it wasn't her. My jaws ached, and, wondering why, I realized that my teeth were clenched.

What in hell do I do if she doesn't come?

Now the daylight was beginning to fade. Snow sparkles mingled with the falling mist. It was fifteen past six and I was sure of it. Caryl had disappeared.

3

The first time I saw Caryl was in my own office. "A Miss Batory to see you," Marie, my secretary, announced over the intercom. She came in, carrying her coat—it was January—and removing a small, floppy wool knit hat. I looked up from checking a dictated letter that Marie had typed and noticed her fluffing the feathery brown curls that clung to her head. "Sit down a moment," I told her. She took the chair across from my desk, and it was then that I noticed her eyes. In the light from the desk lamp, they looked more violet than blue, and they were unusually shaped, slightly uptilted at the corners, as though someone among her forebears had been oriental.

She had come to pick up some documents for translation from Hungarian to English. Ben Graham's firm, Madison Liquors, was importing some Hungarian specialty wines with names like Egri Bakaver and Soprani; my law firm was handling the contracts. The chore came to my desk, because I was regarded as the house wine expert. It was Marie who had located an outfit called Internation Services that specialized in Eastern European translations.

She glanced over the documents, nodded as though familiar with their stamps and notarization seals, and asked when I needed them back and how many copies.

"Three or four days?"

"Yes, I can do it."

"And just one carbon," I said, "because we can Xerox the others."

She nodded and was about to get up to go when I said: "I can't quite place your accent. You're Hungarian?"

"Yes, but I left a long time ago."

"And you're employed regularly by Internation?"

It was clear that she sensed my interest in her, and it was almost as though she waited to find out if I would make some kind of approach. She was certainly attractive—more than that, a beauty. Her small nose had a suggestion of an uptilt, and her lips were full and nicely shaped, but her eyes, more than any other feature, made her stand out.

"I'm sort of freelance," she said. "I know several languages."

I could employ her again, since we had international contacts. "What others?"

"German," she said, "French, and Italian, though I'm weakest in Italian."

"Been in this country long?"

"Nearly five years," she said. "I'll be a citizen soon."

"And before?"

"England . . . France . . . why do you ask?"

"I suppose I'm just making talk."

"I see." She smiled, but without flirtatiousness. "I'll have these back on Thursday."

"Could you make it three o'clock? I'd like to look at the translations and just make sure they're clear."

"Of course," she said. "Three o'clock."

As she left the office, I took notice of her slim, firm figure, and after she closed the door behind her I kept staring at it a moment, thinking, even that early in our acquaintance, that this Miss Batory was a woman I would like to know very much better.

On Thursday, promptly at three, Marie buzzed me. "Miss Batory is here. She has the documents with her. Do you want to see her?"

"Have her come in."

She came in, this time hatless, her face glowing from the chill outside, and, unbidden, took the chair opposite me. From a briefcase she took a large manila envelope and handed it to me.

"Have much trouble?" I asked.

"Not really," she said.

I opened the envelopes and saw that she had typed the translations on legal size sheets. I looked them over, hoping to find something that needed clarification, but there wasn't a thing wrong. They were precise enough to stand up in court, if need be.

"They seem fine," I said.

If anything, she had grown more attractive.

Her remarkable eyes full on me, she said, "Will that be all, then?"

"For the moment," I said. "I just want to say that we'll very likely be able to use you again soon. Shall I contact Internation or you, personally?"

"You can contact me personally. I'll give you my card."

She found a small card in her briefcase and handed it to me. It read: *Caryl Batory, translations.* Her address was on East Fifty-fifth Street, and there was a phone number, too.

"An odd spelling of your first name," I said.

"Not so odd in Hungary," she said, rising. "If you should call, I'm more likely to be there in the mornings. But there's a service."

"I'll be sure to call," I said.

"Very good."

She got up, and I would have liked to hold her longer, then and there, but it seemed just too out of place. This was an office, after all, and she had come on a business matter. And there was something about the firm of Jackson, Pryor, Marek, and Mayer—of which not long ago I had been made a partner—that encouraged propriety. And, anyway, I had her card.

I happened to be the only member of the firm, junior or senior, who wasn't married. Old Charlie Marek, a traditionalist if there ever was one, regarded the state of marriage as a guarantee of respectability and responsibility. I was a widower, of course. I'm sure he chose to think of Sybil's death as a tragic accident, and whatever the gossip about it might have been in the offices, it never got back to me. I rather suspect it was his dictum. Somehow, in the wood-paneled, wall-to-wall-carpeted atmosphere of our offices on Madison Avenue, I felt a pressure to remarry. And it was made quite tangible the year before when my senior partnership had been celebrated with a champagne office party. Charlie Marek's hand had fallen on my shoulder, and he said jovially: "I guess you'll be thinking of marrying again one of these days and starting a family. Have to have someone to leave it to, you know." It was his way, also, of reminding me that my new salary now included a profit-sharing arrangement.

My bachelor state was not for want of opportunity. Other members of the firm saw to that. I was invited to dinner parties where, invariably, there was an extra woman. Flora March, for one, a heavy-hipped and exceedingly bright lawyer in her mid-thirties. We went out several times and had an affair, but, though the flesh was willing, the spirit was not. "You're not in love with me," she said, one early morning in her bed. "I'm very fond of you, though," I said. The wrong words. And there were others. Francine Gordon, who designed and manufactured artificial flower arrangements. She was a former actress who believed in having two or three affairs at once, had already gone through three marriages. My masculine ego was not quite strong enough to allow me fully to accept the sharing arrangement she tacitly proposed. There was a dewy-eyed publisher's assistant of twenty-four I saw for a while. She smoked pot and insisted I try it, and couldn't understand my lack of enthusiasm for Bob Dylan and Neil Diamond, whose recordings she played constantly in her small apartment. It was as though the more women I met and saw, the fussier I got. And, I *had* been married once. A private hell it had turned out to be, both during and after. I wasn't ready, I wasn't mentally set to try again. That is, until Caryl came along.

Late that afternoon I took out the card she had given me and wondered what graceful words I could say that would account for my calling her so soon. How the hell could I put it? I didn't want to come on like a horny stud making a pass at a woman who has struck him as an attractive possibility. Wasn't it that, though? Well, I was intrigued by her, certainly enough. By a face and a figure, or more than that?

Marie went home at five; I faced an empty evening. The Knicks were on television and I could watch the game. I could put some Mozart on the stereo system in my apartment in the east sixties, less than a mile from where she lived. There were a few women I could call, and undoubtedly I could find one willing to see a movie on Third Avenue, and probably induce her up to my apartment afterward. But five years of bachelordom can make a man a little weary of that kind of thing.

Oh, why the hell not? I thought, and I dialed her number on my outside line. The receptionist was still there, and you were never sure if she listened in.

"Yes?" she answered.

"This is Steve Parrish," I said.

"Oh." A hesitation and she said, "You found something wrong?"

"No. I'm calling because I wondered if you happened to be free for dinner this evening."

Silence on the line, and I was about to add, this is sudden, I know, and it's just that you seemed someone I felt I wanted to know better. . . . But I didn't have to say any of that kind of bilge.

"Yes, I am," she said quietly. "Where?"

I was absurdly grateful for her taking me off the hot seat. I picked a favorite restaurant, Jimmy's La Grange, where I was known and could count on service and attention. The owner, Jimmy, catered to his regulars and would be courtly to someone as attractive as Caryl.

And so it proved. She was appreciative of Jimmy's time-tested specialties, and the wine I chose, Musigny, was soft and velvety. Jimmy hovered over us, as though he were aware this was an important occasion. When he noticed our heads bending closer together, though, he retreated, with a lift of his eyes at me that implied I chose food, wine, and women well.

Her eyes had a glow of approval, but I sensed her reserve. She had to know me better, much better, before she was ready for revelations about herself. It was only after I'd told her a good deal about myself that I was able to glean anything about her background. She had left Hungary when she was sixteen, had escaped across the border with a young friend. It had been a year or so after the Hungarian uprising in 1956, a bad time, she said, with the Russians everywhere. She had stayed in Vienna for a while, then had gone to England to live with relatives. She had wanted to be a ballet dancer, but had lacked the time and money she needed for thorough training. She had gone to a secretarial school, developed facility with languages, and had worked in London, Paris, and Marseilles, mainly in the import-export field. Eventually, she had assisted a young English documentary filmmaker. I saw a look of pain cross her face. She had been his fiancée. A little more than five years ago, he had died. "Killed," she said. "Ian . . ." Even to say his name was painful to her. "He was killed in a car crash, in the south of France."

"How long ago?" I asked.

"Five years. No, a little longer. I couldn't stay there. In France, or England. I decided to start over. Here."

"You don't wish to talk about it," I said.

"No. And yours, too. So we won't. Looking back does no good. You can't change anything. Better to look ahead."

"All right," I said. "Let's look ahead."

But I didn't go into what I was already looking ahead about. I thought of asking her to my apartment for a nightcap but was afraid it would seem I was rushing things. At her apartment door, she hesitated, as though considering whether to invite me in, but she merely said: "Thank you for a lovely evening."

There were three locks on her door, and she inserted a key into each.

"You believe in security," I commented.

"There have been robberies in the building," she said. "I don't care for intruders."

She held out her hand. I thought of kissing her, but I didn't, because I knew I hadn't been given that kind of signal. What I did do was take another kind of plunge. I told her I was leaving Saturday for a two-day skiing trip to Vermont. Did she ski?

"Yes," she said, "and are you asking if I'll come with you?"

"I was about to ask that."

"I think I'd enjoy it," she said. "What time Saturday?"

"Early. Eight o'clock."

"I'll be in the lobby."

She made it simple and clear, and, with her beside me in my three-year-old Mercedes, I felt that I floated all the way up to Stowe. She'd like the Lodge, I was sure, where I had booked separate rooms. I didn't know how experienced a skier she was, so I took her first on the easy slope which ran practically to the snow-covered lawn of the Stowe Lodge. But the moment I saw her jam her poles into the hard-packed snow and whoosh off ahead of me with complete confidence, I knew we were in for a fine weekend. The late afternoon was clear and cloudless. After that run, we drove a mile or so to the foot of Stowe Mountain, where a chair lift took us five thousand feet up. At the summit, in the small hostel, we had steaming cups of hot chocolate to warm ourselves, then took the seven-mile trail that spiraled completely around the mountain to its finish. About five miles down, one of her skis caught a low pine branch hidden in the snow, and she fell. I helped her up, brushed her clean of snow, and held her for a moment.

"You all right?" I asked. There must have been anxiety in my voice, and it was true that at the moment of her fall I had felt a pang of real fear that I would hurt or lose this person who had somehow become very precious. Her eyes fixed on mine, wonderingly, then:

"Yes, catch me."

And she was off again, and I was filled with admiration for her courage, her ability to shake off a fall that might have made most people cautious. I made sure to catch her only at the finish of the trail. She hugged me, her eyes bright and happy. "That was lovely," she said. "It reminds me of . . ." She stopped, tossed her head, and finished, "But this is so much better."

At dinner, I studied the wine card. The '61 Brane Cantenac I chose was superb, a bottle to rejoice over.

"Luck," I said. "Sheer luck."

"But it means good luck," she said. "Do you know what's in my mind?"

From the glow of her eyes I was beginning to have an idea.

"Tell me," I said.

"What's in my mind is that this is much too perfect a wine to spoil by—sleeping in different rooms. Does the thought bother you?"

"*Bother* me!"

She held her wine glass and stared into the rosy depths.

"You're sure?"

"Yes, but are you sure?"

She clinked her glass against mine and took a sip, swallowed.

"Quite sure," she said judiciously. "A man who chooses a wine like this? Oh, yes, quite sure."

4

Wine was all that Caryl ever really drank, and never more than two glasses, and never alone.

I mention it, because that could not have been said of Sybil. And because I was trying to convince myself that I was not jinxed, maritally speaking. The circumstances were not at all the same. I *knew* that Sybil drank, all too well.

You see, when I had gone off on that week-long trip to Seattle, to handle a court case, she had wanted to come, had begged to come, as though she might have had a premonition. And I had refused. Why? Well, embarrassment. She had embarrassed me before, she would again. And this was business, and business, according to my rules (and, I suppose I should say it, Marek's) had to be kept separate from private affairs.

And, while I was in Seattle, my wife, twenty-six-year-old Sybil, with a pretty face that somehow never showed (when we were with others) her excesses, had drunk herself into a lonely stupor, the half-smoked cigarette in her hand falling to the rug. When they battered down the door of the smoke-filled apartment, she was still alive but in shock, 80 per cent of her body covered with second- and third-degree burns. The police located me in Seattle. By the time I reached Lenox Hill Hospital on Park Avenue, she was dead.

That plane trip from Seattle to New York—five and a half hours that seemed a year. And the years of self-accusation.

I saw the reproach in the faces of her relatives at the funeral: her mother, her sister and two brothers, cousins, aunts, uncles. *You knew she drank,* they all seemed to be yelling at me at once. Their frozen silence said it; their distant manners said it.

Yes, I knew she drank. All too well, I knew it.

Not at first, no more than two or three martinis before dinner. I'd have a couple myself. She was an assistant art director in a small ad agency, and, during the second year of our marriage, she lost her job. I told her it didn't matter; she'd find another. But she blamed herself. On top of it, her father, to whom she was overly attached, had a sudden heart attack and died. She became morose, and she'd sit in the apartment for long hours, a glass of gin on the rocks in her hand. The glass got taller. I said she had to see a psychiatrist. I didn't use the word *alcoholic.* She saw a psychiatrist a few times, but she didn't like him. All he talked about was sex, she said. How did she feel sexually toward me, her brothers, her father? He makes me *sick,* she said. She'd try doing without drinking for a day or two, and would smoke incessantly, lighting one cigarette from the butt of another. There were cigarette chars all over the place. I would get to the point where, instead of understanding, I would substitute blind, unreasoning anger. If I found a bottle of gin, I would pour it down the sink.

At that time I had already begun my wine collection, more as a hobby than for drinking purposes. When we entertained, I enjoyed pulling out a bottle of Margaux '57, or a Mouton Rothschild '54, and watching the faces of the guests. Of course, the prices were a lot lower, then. There were special bottles I put away. A Château Yquem, a Romanee Conti, and other burgundies like Musigny and Bonnes Mares. She got into them. I suppose it was a little like a child whose playmate has just destroyed the electric train set you've always wanted and finally gotten. It wouldn't have been his fault, and it wasn't Sybil's. Nor was it merely the price of a Romanee Conti. It was being saved for some special occasion, not as a substitute for a cheap bottle of gin. I reacted. I slapped her, hard. She went into the bathroom and wouldn't come out for nearly two days. I begged her to at least allow me to give her some food. She could stay in the damn bathroom. But at least *eat* something. She didn't need food, though. She had had the foresight to fill one of my barber-size hair tonic bottles with gin.

Well, there was more of it, a lot more. Anyone who's lived with an alcoholic knows the story. How you don't want the friends and neighbors to know, as though that's the most important of the priorities.

I knew that the Seattle trip was bound to take at least a week, because the court calendar date wasn't firmly fixed. She wanted to know why, if I was going to have time to myself, I wouldn't take her. She didn't want to be left alone, she promised not to touch so much as a single drop of anything, except water. I said no, the case was important. It involved a large fee for my firm. I needed to concentrate. True, but not strictly true. I left her home, locking my wine cabinet and checking to see that no bottles were hidden anywhere. I asked her mother and sisters to look in on her. (They didn't; they were too busy.)

And she burned to death.

Does that explain why I insisted that Caryl come with me? And why, when she hesitated, that I promised her we'd take an extra week after the business was finished and go skiing in Saint-Moritz or Cortina, if the snow conditions were favorable? That, she couldn't resist. Perhaps it explains something else. My absolute determination not only to find Caryl but to clear up completely whatever it was that was keeping her from me now. For, in an almost paranoic way, I was beginning to try to fit together certain hints, even the very lack of hints, that would explain her absence.

5

Marcel Caille, manager of the Plaza Athenée, was a smooth-faced, dapper man in his mid-forties. He wore a dark blue pin-striped suit, a white shirt with starched collar, a plain blue tie. His gold-linked cuffs protruded one-half inch each from his jacket sleeves. He shot the cuffs as he rose to greet me.

"Yes, Mr. Parrish, in what way may I assist you?"

He didn't look as though he were all that anxious to assist me. His face had a mildly pained smile. He had had to contend for years with irate guests, with ruined room rugs, broken arms of elegant furniture, with maids who stole and porters who complained of penurious tippers, with water taps that made whistling noises and toilets that wouldn't flush. And, I was sure, with stolen jewelry and guests who would not give up their rooms on specified dates. He was a much put-upon man, but it was his job to pacify guests who paid sixty and more dollars a day.

I took the chair he offered me. I explained that my wife was now more than three hours late in returning to the hotel to meet me. I feared she had been taken ill or had had an accident, and I wanted appropriate police action taken. "Not the local *poste,*" I said. "I want police equipped to locate a missing person."

His eyes took on a guarded look. One thing he plainly did not want was the police nosing around his precious domain.

After a few murmurs of sympathy, he cleared his throat, shot his cuffs again, and pointed out, unnecessarily: "This is a very large city. And it's not unusual for people to fail to keep appointments. It's incredible, the traffic jams these days. A wife quarrels with her husband, she . . ."

I was doing my best to keep myself under control, but my voice came out snappish anyway. "We didn't quarrel. We had no reason to quarrel. If my wife has been away this long, I know something serious has happened. I don't intend to sit around and wait and do nothing."

"I was about to say," he said soothingly, "the police would not take action this soon. In the morning, perhaps."

"Then what do you suggest I do?"

"What would you do in New York?"

"Notify the police. Call hospitals."

"The last I can do at once," he said, looking relieved. "Mrs. Parrish has an American passport, of course?"

"No," I said, "British."

"You are British?"

"No," I told him, exasperated. "I'm American. We were just married. My wife carries a British passport. We didn't have time to change it."

"I see. Then we will first call the British Hospital in Levallois."

"Her name on the passport would be Caryl Batory." I spelled it out for him and gave him a brief physical description.

From a list on his desk he picked a phone number and dialed it, tapping a ballpoint pen on his desk top as he waited. He spoke to someone who came on at the other end. He mentioned who he was, and said he feared the wife of one of his guests had been taken ill or suffered an accident. He gave whomever he was talking to Caryl's single and married names. Then: *"Il faudra que vous nous preveniez si quelqu' un de ce nom devait être admis—ou si vous obteniez d'autres renseignments. Oui, merci. Je repetez mon nom, Monsieur Caille, le Plaza Athenée. Ou, Monsieur Steven Parrish, chambre 412, a la même hôtel. D'accord. Merci, madame."*

After hanging up, he said, "No information about her there, so I will try the American Hospital in Neuilly. If the police found her, they would take her to one or the other."

The American Hospital had no information about Caryl, either.

"Now, the police," I said.

He sighed, looked up another number on the list, and, as he dialed, said: "Best to call the Prefecture directly." When an answer came on the line, he asked to speak to an *inspecteur*, explaining that it was an important matter concerning a guest at the Plaza Athenée. Whoever he got took down much the same information he had given the hospitals. Then he listened for a while, said, *"D'accord,"* and hung up and turned to me.

"It's as I said—they can't take serious action until the morning. Meanwhile, they will check all major hospitals in the city area and report to us immediately if anything turns up on the case rosters. So, we have done what we can. I profoundly hope that by morning we will have no need of the police. If you wish a doctor, I will have one visit you immediately."

"Why would *I* want a doctor?"

"To calm yourself, Mr. Parrish. I understand the strain you are under."

"Forget the doctor," I said. "I'll be in my room. Please make sure that the people at the desk and your phone operators notify me at once if there's any word."

"Of course," he said. "Of course. I do regret the . . ."

I nodded, thanked him briefly, and went back to the room, now, with night fallen, emptier than ever. I called the American Embassy on Avenue Gabriel and got the night desk. The consular officer on duty, when I told him of my missing wife, said the best he could do at this hour was notify the Paris police. They were already notified, I said, and wouldn't do much of anything until morning. Well, if I was in touch with the French police. . . . He gave me the name of someone to see in the morning, but not before ten. No help there. It seemed to me I was moving in circles.

A knock came on the door. I raced to it and found a waiter standing in the corridor, holding a tray. On the tray was a half-pint bottle of Courvoisier, a bottle of Perrier water, a plate of small sandwiches, a white china coffee pot, and a cup and saucer. "Compliments of the manager," he said.

I had him place the tray on the low, glass-topped coffee table, and he asked me if I required anything else. I found a few francs in my pocket and gave them to him.

The bottle of brandy brought back a recent memory. On that second skiing trip together, to Stowe, we had after-dinner brandy.

I was about to order Remy Martin when she said: "I prefer Courvoisier, *fine champagne.*"

"Can you tell the difference?" I asked.

"Oh, yes. It's what I sometimes used to drink."

"When?"

"Oh, a long time ago."

"Where?"

"I forget."

"You don't want to tell me."

"That's right. I want to forget everything and everyone but you."

How considerate, how thoughtful of her, I'd thought at the time. But I wished I'd insisted, asked for more details. I poured some of the brandy and was warmed by it, but not enough to quell the quivers in my stomach. I was scared. I didn't know quite what of, other than the fear of never seeing Caryl again. Unless it was fear of this sprawling and ultimately strange city. I couldn't keep my mind from racing through possibilities: car accident, robbery, rape, kidnapping, desertion . . . Ridiculous, the last. She wouldn't walk out without a cause or a reason, or giving some notice. Hardly two weeks after marrying? A woman apparently as much in love with me as I was with her? After a morning spent in lovemaking? It was a happy, satisfied woman I'd left earlier in the day, drawing stockings up over slim legs. . . .

* * * *

"What did you say?"

She asked the question almost idly, as though I'd made a remark about the weather.

I knew what I'd said. I kept my eyes on the road, my hands firmly on the wheel, because there were icy patches, and I hadn't bothered to switch to snow tires. We were returning from that second trip to Stowe.

I could see her reflection in the windshield; she, too, was staring straight ahead. We were approaching Brattleboro, and the Monday morning had turned cloudy. The bare trees were black and stark against the moody sky. I already knew what I wanted.

"I said: I'd like to keep this going—permanently."

"For the rest of our lives?"

There was a mocking tone in her voice, and I stole a glance at her. Now she was looking directly at me, and in this light her eyes were more violet than blue.

"You don't think I'm serious?"

"No. I think you *think* you are, but you don't know me."

"I know enough."

She sighed. "Not yet, Steve. Not yet. Please don't rush me."

"If I ought to know more, tell me."

"Years," she said. "Years and years and years. Do you want each year, or each month, or each day?"

"Whatever you feel I ought to know."

"There's Budapest," she said.

"You were born there, you were raised, went to school, took dancing lessons, had a boyfriend, I suppose."

"You make it sound so simple. What about the Russians? Suppose I was raped by the Russians?"

"Were you?"

"No, but I was afraid of them."

"After you escaped, you went to Vienna."

"Yes, Vienna."

"What about Vienna? You went there with—who was it?"

"Zoltan," she said.

"And in Vienna he was your boyfriend?"

"In a way, yes, in a way, no. I don't like talking about it, Steve."

"We won't talk about that. Then it was London?"

"Yes, London. And after London, Paris. And then, other places. But it's all so boring now."

"Well, New York. Five years in New York. Will I meet your friends?"

"If you'd like. I don't have many. There's an old man I play chess with sometimes. You'd like to meet him?"

"Of course."

"And I've had other men friends, Steve. And I didn't play chess with them. Does it bother you?"

"No. I've had women friends."

"But I don't want to meet your women friends. So, let's make a bargain. You won't meet my men friends—except Oskar—and I won't meet your women friends."

"Except Marie," I said. "She's my secretary, and the most helpful person in the world. You'll have to meet Charlie Marek, and a few other partners. You're lucky. My mother lives in Minnesota, and one of my sisters in Seattle, and another in San Diego. They have husbands and children. One of these days maybe you'll meet them all, and that would be it."

"It sounds dreadfully like marriage."

"Anything wrong with marriage?"

"You're in a hurry. Why?"

"I feel I'm getting on," I said. "I'm thirty-seven—and I don't want to lose you. Five years age difference isn't bad, is it?"

"No, it's quite good."

"At thirty-two," I reminded her, "you shouldn't wait much longer."

"Gruss Gott!" she exclaimed. "Already the dear man is thinking of children. All you suggest is that I change my entire life."

"Changing your name doesn't have to be that drastic."

She remained silent and thoughtful; we were passing through Brattleboro, and at an intersection I debated on which route would take me most directly to the New York State Thruway.

"My name would be Parrish," she said, as though musing.

"That's right."

"Mrs. Parrish."

"How do you like the sound of it?"

"I don't know," she said. "I don't know."

We were past Albany, the Mercedes humming along smoothly at seventy on the Thruway, when she asked: "Where would we live?"

"My apartment, I suppose."

"Is it safe?"

I glanced at her. There was an expression around her eyes that was close to pain.

"The elevators are always manned," I said. "You have a thing about security, don't you?"

"I like lots of locks," she said, with a smile and a shrug. "I like to feel that I'm snug and private, and no one I don't want is ever going to intrude on me. I like fireplaces, and deep chairs with soft cushions. Don't you ever have that feeling?"

"Sometimes, I suppose. My fireplace works, and you can change the furniture. And, as far as I know, the Russians in the consulate a few blocks away have never intruded on anyone in the building."

"Why Russians?"

"You said you were afraid of the Russians in Budapest."

"I'm being silly," she said. "I like your apartment. All it needs is softer chairs and lots of cushions." She moved closer to me and breathed in my ear. "For making love."

She moved in my arms and moaned. Somehow I was closely entwined with her and yet observing her from a distance. Was it her perspiration I felt, or mine? "I'm afraid," she whispered. "Don't let them find me." Who? I asked. Find who? "Turn it off," she said. "It's hurting my ears."

It was a jangling sound, repeated, insistent. Startled into wakefulness, my forehead clammy with sweat, I realized it was the telephone next to the bed and what had been so vivid a moment ago was a dream. I had fallen asleep in an armchair, and my neck felt stiff, as though I'd twisted it. I had been determined to stay awake through the night, but morning light now streamed through the wide windows. I was still dressed as I had been the day before, except I'd removed my shoes. The Prices' dinner! No, I'd canceled it.

"Yes?" I barked into the mouthpiece. My voice had turned hoarse, and I was aware of a throbbing head as well as a stiff neck.

"Reception desk, sir. Some police are here to speak with you. May they come up?"

"Yes," I said.

The voice on the phone had been respectful, solemn. So, they had found Caryl and she was dead. I was certain of it.

6

The knock came, and I swung the door open. The two men who stood there were mismatched. The older one was short and heavy; the other, his junior by at least fifteen years, was tall, with hulking shoulders.

"Inspector Delahaye," the older one said, perfunctorily waving a wallet at me, with the police identification showing.

"Gazin," the other one said. "Assistant inspector."

"You've found her?"

Delahaye's expression was patient, a little tired. His scraggly mustache was gray, as was his short-cropped hair. His shirt collar was tight, and a fold of neck flesh hung over his badly knotted tie.

"Your passport, please," he said.

"Is she *alive?*"

I had raised my voice, and he held up his hand, as though to soothe me.

"You'll allow us?"

I stood aside, so they could enter the room. Gazin pursed his lips as he studied the Louis XVI furnishings.

"So she hasn't contacted you," Delahaye said.

I shook my head, feeling a certain amount of relief. They, at least, seemed to know as little as I did. The inspector repeated his request for my passport, and I handed it to him. What he could learn from it, other than my place and date of birth, I didn't know. It was relatively recent and showed no other visa stamps other than the one on entry into France. He examined it without comment and gave it back to me.

"Your wife had her own passport?"

"Yes," I said, not liking his use of the past tense. "Now, would you tell me what you're doing to find her?"

"Please," Delahaye said. "We are here to get the necessary information, but I can assure you that all accident reports are being examined, and arrest lists for the past twenty-four hours. I take it your embassy has been notified."

"Yes."

"What possessions did she take when she left?"

"The clothes on her back," I said. "But that was reported to you. Her other clothes are in the closets. Those are her bags over there. So, obviously, she hasn't gone anywhere. She's here in Paris. There was no reason for her to leave. The point is, do you have people searching for her?"

"Where would they search, Mr. Parrish?"

I felt helpless. "At least in the area of this hotel. She wouldn't have gone far; she was supposed to meet me less than three hours after I last saw her. She may have gone shopping. She was in good health, except . . ."

"Except what?" Delahaye asked quickly.

"She complained of occasional dizzy spells while walking."

"Then she might have taken ill?"

"Yes, that's possible."

Delahaye walked slowly around the room, glancing at objects on the mirrored dressing table, then looked out the windows. "You've called the hospitals, of course?" he asked.

"Of course."

I thought: good God, he's like a comic detective in a movie. He turned to me and said, almost idly. "You perhaps quarreled?"

"No."

"And she has not been gone the entire night . . ."—he cleared his throat—". . . before this?"

"We've been married two weeks," I said.

He nodded sympathetically. "Most upsetting, naturally, but we must not be alarmed. We will find the explanation. You have been in Paris for how many days?"

"Five," I said. "We've been together except on business occasions. I'm a lawyer. Why don't I just line up the facts you need?"

"Very good."

I gave them the chronology: date and time of arrival at Orly, reasons for our trip to Paris, the people—relatively few—we'd seen, the nature of my business here, our not-too-definite plans to ski. She was of Hungarian nationality. She was familiar with Paris but had not visited the city, so far as I knew, for about ten years. She had not mentioned knowing anyone here. She had once lived and worked in London, but that was also a good many years ago.

"When did she leave Hungary?"

I noticed that Gazin had taken out a notebook and now had pen poised.

"It was about a year after the uprising. That would make it 1957. She was a refugee. I don't know the exact date, but she was sixteen at the time."

"Do you have a picture of her?"

I showed him the snapshot of Caryl I had taken in Stowe.

"Most attractive," he said, and passed it to Gazin, whose heavy eyebrows lifted.

"You will allow us to take this for the time being?"

"Just so I get it back." I went on to say that others I'd taken in Paris would soon be developed.

"The question, Mr. Parrish," Delahaye said regretfully, "cannot be avoided. Is it possible your wife has admirers in Paris, that she knows, or at one time knew, other gentlemen?"

"Let's forget that line," I said, unable to keep the annoyance out of my voice. "We're newly married. I assure you our relationship is close. You can see for yourself she left everything behind—even her toothbrush is here. Now, a woman doesn't walk out just like that."

Delahaye's expression remained patient.

"I am merely asking the indicated questions. Please bear with them. Does your wife, by chance, have mental problems? Are there unusual medications she uses? Drugs, perhaps?"

"No," I said, bleakly. "None of that."

"But you've not known her long."

"Long enough."

Gazin had noticed the cognac bottle on the tray that had been brought the night before. He held it up.

"Nor does she drink," I said. "An occasional glass of wine, that's all."

If it had been Sybil, I couldn't help thinking, that would have been my first thought, and it was probably common enough that a disappearance could be blamed on a prolonged bender. But not Caryl. One thing she distinctly was not was a lone drinker.

"I must ask this, too," Delahaye said. "Your wife, I take it, has no record of any kind, nothing that would have involved her with the police."

I hesitated and saw that Delahaye's eyes had narrowed in his round, smooth face.

"Well, at the time she escaped Hungary, it could have gotten to the attention of the authorities."

"But that would be sixteen years ago, and she has not visited the country since, or—perhaps had contacts with relatives there?"

"By letter only."

"Did she write letters while here?"

"None, so far as I know."

"Curious," Delahaye said, almost a murmur.

"Why curious?"

"That she would be so isolated, except for you?"

"I don't find it curious," I said, a little stiffly. "She does have friends in New York. Now that I'm married, I don't spend much time with anyone else."

"Very well," Delahaye said, with a nod. "If you'll just add more details to the description we already have, we will go to work."

Gazin read me from his notebook what he had, and I mentioned a brown leather handbag, quite large, she habitually carried and that was not among her possessions, that the brown buttons on her gabardine coat matched the color of the bag, that she had mentioned needing shoes for walking, and that she still lacked some items for a skiing wardrobe.

"We'll hope for the best," Delahaye said. "She hasn't been gone that long, and there could be several explanations. Generally, within forty-eight hours on these cases we get word of some kind." He handed me his card, which showed him assigned to Police Headquarters on the Rue des Saussaies, number eleven. "If you should receive word or information, kindly notify me or my assistant at once."

He held out his hand, which was fat and soft when I shook it. His breath had a faint odor of garlic.

At the door, he said: "One more thing. Did she carry large funds, airline tickets?"

I told him she would have had something in the neighborhood of five hundred dollars in American Express checks, with perhaps one check converted to francs, and that I had our return tickets. She also had an American Express card in her maiden name.

Both gave me a little salute as they left. I scratched the stubble on my face, trying to trace a random thought I'd had while he was questioning me. Yes, letters. So far as I knew, she had written none, but she might have, and there might be letters she had received without my knowing.

I went through the bureau drawers and others in the dressing table. Nothing.

I opened one of the matched Vuitton traveling bags I'd bought at Saks Fifth Avenue for her. Not much in it. With a slight feeling of guilt that I was impinging on her privacy, I felt with my fingers in the inner pockets and found—sanitary napkins. I opened the other bag. Everything had been removed and placed in closets and drawers except for a small sewing kit and a leather case not unlike the kind used for carrying shaving articles. It had a lock on it, though, which required a key. I didn't hesitate. I took out my pocket knife and pried the lock open. Inside was some costume jewelry, a string of cultured pearls, and a small cardboard box that rattled when I shook it. The flap came loose and something hard and metallic dropped to the rug.

I picked it up, feeling queasy. It was a bullet, quite small, brass jacketed. The box contained five others, and it was only half full. Twenty-five caliber, I guessed, bullets for a small pistol.

The chill traveled straight up to my scalp.

7 AUSTRIA, JULY 1957

The former troop barracks were located three kilometers from the village of Krumau. She shared a room with two other women, Hungarian escapees like herself, and, like them, had been given a temporary visa. This allowed her to visit the village with Zoltan, who was in another part of the barracks. The building was three-sided, two stories high, each side facing a compound where, she was told, SS recruits had drilled during the war. She knew about the war, and she also knew the SS were worse than the Russians. Their presence, though, had been all but obliterated. The Austrian refugee authorities had planted flowerbeds and placed wooden benches on the former parade ground. Still, this was a disappointment for her after what Zoltan had promised, although he kept assuring her that one day soon they would leave for Vienna.

She had been interviewed a few times, once by a woman, twice by a man, and she had been questioned about relatives who could provide her with financial aid. She said her relatives were all in Hungary, except for an aunt and uncle in England. Did she want to go to England? No, she said, she preferred Austria. Why had she left Budapest? The Russians, she said, the Russians frightened her, and she wanted an education, and she wanted to be a ballet dancer. They were kind enough to her, although the woman interviewer advised her to contact her relatives in England, because that might be a better place for her to go. So she wrote them a letter, and she also wrote her parents in Budapest, assuring them she was in good health and happy.

But the truth was, she was homesick. More often than not she felt empty and drained in the pit of her stomach, and she had begun to be certain that she had made a mistake in leaving. The days stretched on, and she occupied herself by improving her German.

Zoltan disappeared sometimes for two and three days. He

was seeking work, he explained, and, once he found it and could prove that he could support himself and her, they could leave. "You must say you are my fiancée," he said, "and that we plan to marry." He dropped his voice to a whisper, saying, "I've already been to Vienna and I have prospects, good prospects."

His air of confidence reassured her. Other escapees trickled in to the refugee center and were provided with clothes and fed their three meals a day. The food was plain but substantial, and she heard that much of it was provided by a nearby American army unit. And, sure enough, in the big kitchen where the food was prepared, she saw stacks of large, olive-colored cans labeled *beef stew, vegetable soup, powdered eggs.* They ate on long, planked tables with bare wooden benches attached, and she realized that, in a way, it was like being in the army. And, reassuringly, too, refugees left the center, some for other countries, some for cities—Linz, Vienna, Salzburg. A bulletin board posted job offers; most were for maids, kitchen help, carpenter's assistants, and a few for more specialized occupations, like skilled machine-tool workers.

"Next week we leave," Zoltan told her one day early in July. "I have a job. I am to assist a banker."

"A banker?"

Zoltan was capable, but what did he know about banking?

"Yes," he said, "but don't tell anyone else. I've already told the people here that I'm taking a factory job. Polishing marble tabletops." He grinned. "Can you see me polishing tabletops?"

With work permits in their pockets, they set out a few days later for Vienna, seventy miles away. Just outside Krumau, a coal truck stopped for them and took them as far as Baden. After a few hours of waiting at the roadside, an American soldier in a jeep gave them a lift the rest of the way. She liked the American and decided that one of the first things she must do in Vienna was to learn English.

Their first night in Vienna they stayed in the banker's apartment. His name was Otto, and he did not fit her idea of what a banker should look like. He was in his mid-twenties, with an acne-covered face that reminded her of a fox. The apartment had little furniture, and most of that rickety, and it had a bad, garbagy smell, though not as bad as the persistent odor of disinfectant in the refugee center. Otto took it for granted that she and Zoltan would sleep in the same room, which had only one narrow bed. "How can we sleep?" she asked, knowing what it meant and resigned to it. While in Budapest, she had not let Zoltan take her virginity, but once having decided to go with him, she knew what must follow. But in this room, with the pervading bad odor?

"Can't we wait?" she asked.

"Why?"

"I don't know," she said, vaguely. What she meant was that she wanted it to be better and nicer than this, and not between sheets that were almost gray from lack of washing.

But then, pressed against him in the bed, the closeness and the warmth of his body released feelings in her, profound and urgent, and she responded to his own vigorous motions. There was only the one sudden, sharp pain, and after that a flood of continuing pleasure.

"Isn't it good?"

"Oh, yes," she sighed.

"You'll be a good woman," he said, "because you like it."

"Yes."

"Do you love it?"

"Oh, yes."

"Do you love me?"

"Yes," she said. "Yes."

In the morning, when she awoke, she saw Zoltan's gun on a chair that held his clothes. He was still sleeping, so she picked it up and examined it. She smelled the barrel; it still had the acrid odor of gunpowder, and she knew why. She gave a shudder. She didn't like to think about it, but during the nights especially, she would hear again the loud sound and see the orange flash.

"Put it down," he said.

Zoltan was awake.

"You still have it," she said. "You told me you threw it away."

"Put it down. It's loaded. I'm going to sell it."

"I don't like your banker," she said, putting the gun back on the chair.

"Otto? He's not the chief banker, but I work through him."

"What will you do?"

"It's simple," he said. "Easy. Nothing to it."

"If it's so simple, explain it to me."

"The banker gives me a wad of money, and I exchange it for American traveler's checks. That's all."

"But why give away money to get money?"

"Don't be stupid," he said. "The traveler's checks are worth more. You can exchange them anywhere. For a fifty-dollar check I give sixty dollars in schillings. Of the profit, I keep twenty per cent as my share."

"If you give more, how is there a profit?

"The traveler's checks are worth seventy dollars in schillings, if you sell them in Paris, or Rome. This is international banking."

"Do you have an office?"

"Not for this kind of banking. You do it on the streets. You meet people who have traveler's checks, like businessmen and American tourists."

"Is it honest?" she asked.

"Sure it's honest. Everyone does it. Would you rather I polish marble tabletops?"

"I don't know."

"You'll have to trust me. I told you I would take care of you, and I'm going to. We'll get along."

"I don't like this room."

"Don't worry, I'll find you a room."

He got up to dress and shave and, when she was alone in the room, she found herself crying. She wasn't sure what she was crying about, but Vienna was not what she had expected it to be.

8

During the morning hours that followed, it seemed to me that I was living partly in a dream, that all would soon be as before, with Caryl walking in the door and explaining why she had spent the night away from me and making perfect sense of it and, oh, the gun, yes the gun, well, she had this fear of intruders, and so she was in the habit of carrying it, although of course she'd never shoot anyone, it was only to scare away the robber, the mugger, the intruder. . . . But it was the reality that was even more unlikely, for the phone kept ringing. First, Ben Graham, reminding me of an afternoon appointment with LeBrun, at his offices, to sign the papers, and there was nothing to do but to tell him, my own words sounding bald and improbable.

I hardly heard his words of shock, his saying, by God, we'd get the Paris police on it, and LeBrun probably knew someone in the Sûreté, and he, personally, would call the embassy, because they had investigative people, and please, please call on him for any kind of help whatever.

After that it was Marge Price, asking if Caryl was all right now and could they set another date for dinner, and I told her, too, and she began crying, and I said I'd keep her informed, the police were handling it, and if I needed help. . . . Then a call came from one of the partners in New York; I'd left a case behind that needed some immediate action, and somehow I managed to tell him what to do about it, and didn't say a word about Caryl. Any minute now she would be walking through that door. And, how could I say that Caryl had a gun with her, and hadn't told me about it? I supposed I'd have to tell Delahaye about the bullets I'd found. But suppose she didn't have the gun with her? Suppose it was still here in the room?

It was while I was searching through her clothes, pockets of suits and coats, another of her handbags, and a small beaded evening bag, that a polite knock came at the door. I raced to open it. There was a porter with a maroon-wrapped package and a bulky envelope. I tipped him hurriedly. The label on the package was addressed: Mme. Steven Parrish. I ripped off the paper, opened an oblong box, and found—a pair of shoes. Brown shoes, with low heels. The label had the address of the shop from which they had come; it was on Rue du Faubourg Saint-Honoré. The envelope was from a photo shop and contained the pictures we had taken in Paris. I glanced at them only briefly and selected one that showed Caryl smiling, full faced, putting it in my wallet, the remainder in a pocket.

I stayed in the room only long enough to call the number on the card Delahaye had left with me. When I got some uncomprehending policeman who made absolutely sure to misunderstand my French and spoke almost no English, I left him my name and asked him to have the inspector call me later at the Plaza Athenée.

Outside the hotel, I took a waiting taxi away from an outraged South American couple and was at the shop, La Belle Chausseurie, in ten minutes. There were no customers inside, only an elderly woman and a girl of about twenty. I chose the older woman, opened the package, and showed her the shoes. "Do you remember who bought these?"

"Pardon, monsieur?"

She beckoned to the girl, who examined the shoes.

She spoke English.

"I sold them. Yesterday. They don't suit madame?"

"You sold them to a Madame Parrish?"

"Yes, certainly. I sent them to the Plaza Athenée. They fitted very well, sir."

I pulled out my wallet and extracted the picture of Caryl; it had come out sharp and clear; she had worn the gabardine coat.

"Was this the lady?"

"Yes."

She looked up at me with a touch of alarm. My voice and manner must have struck her as accusing. I tried to make my tone more matter of fact.

"Can you tell me what day and what time she bought these?"

"Yesterday," the girl said. She turned to the other woman, and, in French, checked it with her. "Yes, early afternoon, perhaps around fourteen hundred hours. A little earlier, I think. I came back from lunch at the half hour, that would be *treize heures et demie,* and she was my first customer. Is there some complaint?"

"No complaint," I said. "Now, she paid for the shoes—how?"

"With a traveler's check of one hundred dollars. I remember very well. The price of the shoes is one hundred francs, forty—they are very well made." Obviously, she worried that I might be here because I felt cheated, and she added: "I gave her the proper change."

I didn't stand on ceremony.

"My wife," I said, "has been missing since yesterday."

The girl caught her lower lip with her teeth. I wished to hell I didn't have to tell people, friends or strangers, that stark fact. It wasted time. They wanted to ask questions. Sympathy, I could well do without. Almost breathlessly, the girl conveyed what I had told her to the older woman, who, I gathered, was her employer. Now both stared at me: this American had walked into their shop and involved them in something of which they were innocent and had no knowledge.

"What I want to know," I said, "did she seem ill when she came in? Did she look as though she was in trouble?"

"No, monsieur. It was quite otherwise. She seemed quite happy. She liked the shoes very much, said that they were what she was looking for."

"You saw no one waiting for her outside the shop?"

"No one."

"Did you notice which direction she went in when she left the shop?"

"No, monsieur."

"Do you remember anything she said, anything she talked about?"

"She was going to continue shopping. Yes, she asked about sweaters. She wanted a heavy sweater, I believe it was for skiing."

"Did you suggest a place?"

"I thought a department store best. I mentioned the Trois Quartiers, and the Galeries Lafayette. I remember she looked at her watch and said she wasn't sure she had the time."

The Trois Quartiers was the nearest, close to Place de la Madeleine, but it would be an endless task for me alone to go through that huge store in search of someone who might have seen Caryl. I had learned this much: that an hour or so before she was to have met me, she had been well, apparently cheerful, and knew that she had an appointment to keep with me.

I left the shop and, on Rue du Faubourg Saint Honoré, looked for a taxi. When I found one, I heard a motorcycle start up, quite near, and I wondered why I had noticed the sound. By the time I remembered that I had heard the same sound when I'd left the hotel, the taxi had swung into Avenue Franklin D. Roosevelt. A look out the rear window only confirmed that a couple dozen motorcyclists were swarming amid the heavy horn-blowing traffic.

Imagination, probably, that I was being followed by someone on a motorcycle, unless it was Delahaye who had put someone on to observe my movements. *Naturally,* he would purr, *I must explore every possibility.* I hadn't yet looked through all the photographs, but now, with mingled pain and longing, I examined each of the twenty color prints, taken with a small Rollei with a short-focal-length lens. Most of them had come out sharp and clear.

Caryl smiled at me as she stood in front of a small restaurant we'd found not far from Saint-Germain-des-Près. Two others I'd taken as she sat at the sidewalk terrace of the Deux Magots. Three of me, taken by her, which I thrust in my coat pocket. A near close-up of Caryl in front of the American Express office on Rue Scribe. Something odd about the expression of her eyes. They were wide open and alert, and her head was slightly cocked, as though she were looking over my shoulder behind me as I held the camera. Her hand was on the shoulder strap of her bag, the same one she had with her wherever she was, and I noticed the tightness of her grip on the strap. If she had a gun with her, it would be in that same bag. The more I stared at the picture, the more it seemed to me that her expression was one of an indefinable fear. Why there, on that busy corner? We had gone inside to register our names, a precaution I took in case someone wanted to reach me and didn't have my hotel address.

I had written on the register: *Mr. and Mrs. Steven Parrish, Hotel Plaza Athenée, Avenue Montaigne, Paris.* Was that fear in her eyes of someone learning our whereabouts? Anyone, of course, was at liberty to look at the register. I noticed again how tightly she gripped the strap of her bag; her knuckles were white. Why, why, had I left her alone the day before?

Back in the lobby of the Plaza Athenée, a man, squat as a fireplug, rose laboriously from a chair. It was Delahaye, looking as though he were about to preside at a funeral service.

"Mr. Parrish," he said, gripping my hand. "I must take you to the hospital. An identification must be made."

The woman's face was bruised and swollen; a net had been pulled over her brown hair. Her eyes were open, but seemed sightless as they looked at me and through me. I shook my head, idiotically relieved. Her eyes were brown. Delahaye had told me little as we rode in his black Citroën to the American Hospital in Neuilly, only that an accident victim, semiconscious, had been picked up in the Bois de Boulogne at dawn. What words she had been able to speak had been in English, and it was natural that the police should take her to the American Hospital. She carried no identification. Her handbag was missing, and with it, her passport.

As we left the hospital, he said, "She doesn't know who she is—yet. A sad case. Raped, by more than one. She is still in shock. I am sorry, but it was necessary to make the identification. This is very hard on you, I know."

He held open the door on the passenger side of the Citroën for me. I got in, and, as he turned the starter key, I heard, at almost the same moment, the coughing sound of a motorcycle starting up. A policeman accompanying Delahaye? Through the windshield, I got a glimpse of a man, helmeted, a visor over his face, speeding around the curve of the hospital's driveway. If he was a policeman, he was in civilian clothes.

"Do you have someone following you?" I asked.

"No, why?"

"Or me?"

"For what reason?" he asked, giving me an odd glance.

"Just wondered," I said. Then I asked: "Didn't they tell you the woman had brown eyes?"

"They were closed at the time the report came through. My apologies. After leaving you, Gazin paid a visit to the morgue—two females brought in during the night, one a prostitute, the other a sixty-year-old suicide. No need to trouble you."

"Inspector," I said, "there's something more I should tell you." On the ride to the hospital, I had told about the shoes and visiting the shop, although it had seemed a little superfluous when we were on our way to identify an injured woman who might have been Caryl. Now I told him about finding the bullets in her luggage, locked in the jewelry case.

He digested the information, his fat hands clutched carefully on the wheel.

"So you think she carries a gun," he said, almost sighing, as though the case was now growing truly difficult.

"I think so," I said.

"Why?" He asked it softly.

"I don't know. I only know—well, I don't know—but I *feel* she's afraid."

"And what makes you feel that?"

"I took some pictures," I said. "I have the prints. There's one. I'll show it to you back at the hotel."

"And you'll let me have the bullets?"

"Of course."

"Later," he said, "after I check out with Gazin the shop and Trois Quartiers, we'll have a talk. I think we must take some time and have a talk."

9

Delahaye met me at nine the next morning in the hotel's restaurant. His puffy eyes were sleepy, and the first thing he did on sitting down was to light a Gauloise Filtre and take a few deep puffs.

"So," he said, "how are you feeling?"

I wanted to say, "Lousy," but I shrugged. How to say: heavy-hearted, depressed, at a loss. The previous evening at the Prices' hadn't helped much. Ben Graham had dropped by, and I told him and the Prices what I knew and what was being done. I'd left early and tried to get some sleep. At the hotel there had been Delahaye's message, saying he would see me in the morning.

I had the small box containing the bullets with me, and I gave it to him. He held it on his lap to keep it from the prying eyes of waiters and other breakfasters, opened the box, extracted one bullet, and fingered it.

"Beretta, most likely," he said. "Small, but lethal. She didn't register it on entry?"

"Hardly," I said. "I'd have known about it."

"Presumably no New York license?"

"I wouldn't know."

"We are looking, then, for an armed person. A serious matter, Mr. Parrish."

"We're looking for a decent, frightened woman, who is also my wife," I said sharply.

The waiter was there, wishing our orders. Delahaye wanted only coffee, white, and a brioche with butter. I ordered the same. It came quickly enough, and Delahaye, maddeningly, carefully poured hot milk into his coffee, unwrapped three lumps of sugar, dropped them in, stirred, then broke off a piece of his brioche and heaped it with butter. I wondered if he'd ever heard of cholesterol.

"A frightened woman," he said. "What makes you say that?"

I had the picture of Caryl in my pocket, and I showed it to him. His eyes narrowed and focused on it, as though he was taking an X-ray.

"Yes," he said. "A curious picture. There's something else that's curious."

His lips opened, the buttered piece of brioche went into the round cavity of his mouth, he chewed and took a gulp of his café au lait.

"Your wife was seen the day before yesterday."

"The Trois Quartiers?"

He wagged his head negatively. "Gazin had three men going through the place. No one saw her, which means nothing—a crowded store . . . But . . ."

Again he buttered a piece of brioche, then, as though aware he was keeping me on tenterhooks, said: "On Rue Pierre Charron, off the Champs-Elysées, there is a small café called Bar des Champs-Elysées. Gazin had assigned two men to make inquiries at such places on either side of the avenue. Bars, restaurants, bistros, on the assumption your wife would have had lunch. In any case, the bartender at this place recognized your wife from the picture you gave us."

"When?" He had left out the important detail. "Exactly *when?*"

"Between fourteen and fifteen hundred hours, the day before yesterday. One could almost trace her path if we assume she left the shoe salon, did not go to the Trois Quartiers, but instead, walked along Rue du Faubourg Saint-Honoré toward Place Goyen. Between there on Pierre Charron and the Champs is this bar. You told me yesterday your wife knows no one in Paris?"

"Other than those I mentioned. What are you getting at?"

"According to the bartender, your wife, if it is the same woman, was seen at a table with a man."

I felt my stomach muscles contract, almost like a cramp.

"Who?" I asked idiotically. "What kind of man? A description?"

"The bartender was vague. An ordinary man, maybe thirty, maybe forty, wearing, he thinks, a brown leather jacket, a workingman's jacket, and dark glasses of the kind aviators in old movies used to wear. His words. Your wife and this man talked, for perhaps twenty minutes. They seemed to know each other well, again according to the bartender. The man left, and the woman, your wife, left, after paying the check. Now, can you explain that?"

"Do you think it's a positive identification?"

"Gazin tells me he seemed certain. I haven't spoken to the man myself."

"No," I said. "I can't explain it."

"Perhaps," he said. "You could ask for another brioche."

I beckoned to the waiter and gave him the order.

"Since you're American," Delahaye said, "everything goes on the expense account, yes?"

I ignored the question and said gloomily: "It doesn't sound like Caryl. I don't think it was."

"A curious thing," Delahaye said, staring at the butter, as though he might consider trying it without the brioche, "but so often, in these cases, we find it's a matter of drugs. We inspected your room, by the way. You don't mind?"

"I expected you would. And so you can discount the drug theory. I'm not all that blind." I had once lived with an alcoholic, but no reason to tell him about that.

"I'm not assuming your wife is an addict. But if, in the bar, it was your wife—what do we have? She enters, then a man enters, they know each other, they have a chat, he leaves, then she leaves. What does it look like?"

"I don't care what it looks like. Do you have someone watching the bar? Let's find out who the hell came in and talked to her."

A platter filled with brioches was put on the table. Delahaye seized one and buttered it. He refilled his coffee cup. My stomach was beginning to turn.

"Another possible angle," he said. "The political. She escaped from Hungary. How?"

"They got across the border somehow."

"They?"

"With a friend," I said.

"This friend—who was he?"

"His name was Zoltan something. Anyway, that was a long

time ago. Sixteen years. Why would the Hungarians, if that's what you're thinking, be interested in him or her now?"

"But it's something to look into, don't you think?"

"I don't care what you look into," I said. "Just find her, get her back."

"We've had political kidnapping cases here," Delahaye said. "I hesitate, at this point, to bring the Sûreté into the matter. If another country is involved, it could be delicate. And then there's the other thing . . ."

"What other thing?"

"The possibility that, without your knowledge, your wife is an employee of a certain branch of your government. You understand me?"

Oddly, at that moment, I suddenly remembered the three locks Caryl kept on her apartment door. And, before we left for Paris, she'd wanted me to have a set of those keys, but insisted I keep them in a safe place. They were in my office desk now, in New York. What was so important about the apartment that it had to be kept securely locked without her being there? She'd said she was afraid of intruders. . . . No, it was her sense of privacy.

"That's nonsense," I said. "Pure nonsense."

"Can you say with absolute certainty that nothing I have mentioned is possible?"

I hesitated.

His moon face creased into a small smile, to be immediately replaced by a look of discretion.

"And, Mr. Parrish, if none of those possibilities I have mentioned fits the situation, then there is one other."

"I know," I said, dully. "She met someone, this man in the bar, and ran off with him. I'll consider it, but I won't believe it."

"I understand," he said. "But you agree, we must find the man."

I nodded slowly, disheartened. If it were a man, I'd just as soon not find her.

Outside the hotel, the day was clear and cold; the damp weather had been replaced by a wintry snap. After Delahaye went off in his car, I walked in the direction of the bar he had mentioned, noting the time it took. Fourteen minutes with my long stride, longer if Caryl had walked the distance. If, from the bar, she had started toward the hotel, it was these very streets she would have been on, and somewhere between the bar and the hotel she had disappeared. But I wanted to be certain she *had* visited the bar.

Facing the entrance was a long, high, copper-covered counter, on it a huge coffee-making machine. Few patrons occupied the wrought-iron-backed chairs at the plastic-covered tables. The *patron* read his newspaper at one end of the counter. A much younger man wiped glasses. I told him what I was there for.

"Ah, you're the gentleman," he said in English, his sharp eyes alive more with curiosity than with sympathy.

"Is this the woman you saw?" I asked, showing him the full-faced close-up of Caryl, and another in which she wore the same gabardine coat she would have worn when she left.

"Yes," he said. "I'm certain. She sat over there, at the third table from the window." He pointed to his right. "She asked for a *café filtre* and I brought it to her."

"She came in alone?"

"Yes, alone, but . . ." His voice grew careful.

"A man joined her?"

"Yes." He looked a little relieved that I had brought it into the open. "I looked up and saw the man with her. I had not paid much attention to him when he entered, an ordinary fellow, but then I paid attention because he was not someone I would have thought a woman like that would—you understand? Meet at a café? I am trying to say he looked a rough sort, while the woman, your wife, had definite refinement."

"Can you describe him?"

He tapped his forehead a few times as though to get his memory in better working order.

"I noticed the leather coat, it came to here." He indicated a spot a few inches below his hips. "Dark glasses, aviator size, black hair, bushy on the sides, as I remember, pale face. Medium height, perhaps thirty-five or a little older."

"And they seemed to know each other?"

"Yes, quite well, I would say. They talked in low voices for maybe ten or fifteen minutes. He would tell her something, she would nod, she would say something, he would nod. I thought to myself, forgive me, sir, a liaison is being arranged. Pardon my saying so, but that definitely was my impression. I even remember thinking: that woman could do a lot better for herself. Still, you get used to things like that in a place like this. I, myself, you see, am studying to be an actor—I'm only working here temporarily—so I make it my business to notice people."

"And your *patron* there? Did he see them?"

"He wasn't here at the time." He lowered his voice. "He bets on the horses. He went out to place his bets."

"What did the man order?"

"Coffee. I looked their way from time to time, in case he wished to order something more, but they were busy talking. So I did not interrupt."

"They left together?"

"No. He left first. Then she sat for a little while, perhaps five more minutes. One other thing. She did not touch her *café filtre.* That is why I assumed she had come here to arrange a meeting. She did not want the coffee."

"She paid for it?"

"Yes. She left some franc pieces on the table."

I extracted a fifty-franc note from my wallet and handed it to him, asking him his name. It was François Gonnet.

"If she should come here again," I said, "or the man you saw with her, would you notify me at once at the Plaza Athenée. If I'm not there, leave word for me."

"Certainly," he said. "I am to do the same thing for the police."

"Of course," I said.

I thanked him and, before leaving, went over to the table that he had pointed out. Last seen, Caryl had been sitting at the table. My eyes smarted.

Back at the hotel, I stopped at the lobby desk to ask for messages. None. Someone tugged gently at my sleeve. I turned and saw a young man, fair-haired, thin-faced, wearing large glasses with thick lenses.

"Mr. Parrish?"

"Yes."

"Eric Sutton," he said, sticking out a hand. "Do you have a few minutes?"

10

He was a newspaperman, an American, working for the Paris office of the *International Herald-Tribune.* There had been an item, he said, in *France-Soir,* something to do with an American woman missing from her hotel. An inquiry at the Commissariat de Police of the eighth arrondissement had led him to me. He wanted the story.

"No," I said.

"You want your wife back, don't you?"

I glared at him, then saw that he hadn't meant to be insulting but had something in mind. And he saw from my own expression that I'd at first misunderstood him.

"Get it into my paper," he said, "and someone might pop up with information. I'm sorry, I should have . . ."

I brushed away his apology.

"You're offering help?"

"O.K., put it that way."

"It won't help my wife or me to have this thing sensationalized, but a picture of her, asking for information—that might bring a response."

I knew his paper was distributed throughout Europe, even in some of the Eastern countries.

He looked dubious. "It would have to be up to my editor—the news desk. Couldn't promise."

"How about trying?"

"O.K."

I selected one of the snapshots from the pack in the envelope. It showed Caryl seated at the terrace of the Deux Magots; she'd worn the gabardine coat that day, the same one she would still be wearing. Sutton looked at it and gave a low whistle. "She's quite a beauty," he said lamely. "See what I can do."

A nice enough fellow, young and anxious to prove himself a news hawk. Maybe he'd do it and maybe he wouldn't. He offered to buy me a drink, but I said I had things to do.

I went to the room to make some calls. There were a few loose ends left to tie up for Ben Graham, and although I was hardly in the mood for business, I couldn't very well leave his deal hanging, even though he'd offered to get hold of a substitute lawyer. But all that left my mind as soon as I opened the door to the room. The hall closet doors were wide open, as though a careless maid hadn't bothered to close them. A couple of the drawers of the chest were part way open, too. And one of Caryl's bags was on the floor, instead of the rack.

My first thought was that whoever had searched the room for Delahaye hadn't bothered to conceal his work. But at breakfast he'd said the search had already been done. That meant that in the intervening few hours someone else had been in the room. Who? The condition of the room looked as though the intent had been robbery. The drawers holding my clothes were a mess. Whoever had done it had been in a hurry. Nothing, though, appeared to be missing.

I spent a half hour doing a kind of inventory, going over my belongings and Caryl's. My gold cufflinks, worth something, were there in a small black case on the top of the chest of drawers. Caryl's jewelry case had been opened—bracelets, earrings, a string of cultured pearls, were in disarray, but, as far as I could tell, nothing had been taken.

But, whoever the intruder was, he or she had been looking for *some*thing. I dumped all my small items on one of the bedspreads. I went through all the pockets of my suits in the closet, and whatever I found I put on the bedspread. What was missing? I went over the things, item by item: my checkbook, folders with traveler's checks, credit cards. The one thing I could not locate was a small leather-bound address book. I'd left it in one of my suits, in an inside pocket. It was gone. I checked all through my pockets. Yes, it was gone.

Now, what the hell did that mean?

Delahaye's man might have taken it; after all, they'd be checking on me as well as Caryl. I called his number. He was out, but Gazin was there. He came on the phone, and I told him that at some time between nine in the morning and noon my hotel room had been ransacked. Was it his or Delahaye's doing?

He assured me it was not. He personally had conducted a search the previous afternoon, and all had been left as it was.

"How about my address book?" I asked him.

"I examined it," he said. "It was replaced."

"Well, it's gone now."

"You're certain? Such things are easily misplaced."

"I know damn well someone took it."

"I will send a man immediately to the hotel to question the help."

"That's all you can do?"

"Monsieur Parrish, what would you suggest?" His tone implied that he was a patient man, dealing with someone unreasonable.

"Well, will you inform the inspector about it?"

"Of course."

"And maybe," I said, "it wouldn't be a bad idea to put someone on this floor to see who gets in and out of my room."

"But you said nothing of value was taken."

"Someone," I said, "wants to find out something about me. It's not exactly pleasant, and it might have something to do with my wife's disappearance."

"The inspector should know about this."

"Yes," I said, and gave up with him.

It was now close to one, which would make it nearly 8 A.M. in New York. Caryl hadn't wanted me to inquire too closely into her past life, but there were things I had to know. My mood had turned stubborn as well as grim, and there was a source of help in New York. Marie, my secretary. She lived in Brooklyn, an hour's subway ride from our midtown offices, and she'd be up getting ready to leave her small apartment. I knew her number well enough, since I often had to call her at home. I got the call through fairly quickly.

"Where are you calling from?" she asked cheerfully.

That meant she hadn't heard anything yet about Caryl.

"Paris," I said. "Now hold on tight. I've got some bad news."

I filled her in briefly, but when she started to commiserate I cut her off. I said that I wanted her help, and that I wanted it all kept quiet until some definite word came through.

"But it must be so awful for you," she said, and I could

almost see the tears welling into her eyes.

I told her that it was a shock, and that I'd had a hell of a couple of days, but that so far it appeared she was alive. The problem was to locate her, and that meant I had to keep my head clear so that everything that could possibly be done would be done. The Paris police were looking into it, but, being a foreigner, I'd have to take my own measures, too.

"Are you O.K. now?" I asked.

"Yes."

"First, has anyone been around asking about me or Caryl?"

"You mean, in the office?"

"Yes, the office."

"Just a few people who were wondering when you were coming back."

"Anyone strange?"

"No."

"All right. When you get to the office, you'll find a set of keys in the bottom drawer of my desk on the right. The one that we keep locked."

"Yes."

"Those are the keys to Caryl's apartment. She hadn't moved most of her things yet to my apartment. Now, get past the doorman somehow and go to her apartment. I want you to look through it carefully—letters, papers, address books, anything that might give us clues to who she knows in Europe, family, friends, anything at all. Whatever you find, bundle it up and take it to the office and go through it. Then I want you to phone me and tell me what you've got. Do you understand?"

"Yes."

"And you'll keep it quiet, until I tell you otherwise?"

"Yes. Has she done something wrong?"

"I don't think so. But we don't want to overlook anything."

"And you haven't any idea . . ."

"No, Marie. Do you think you can do it?"

"I'll do it," she said. "Do I call you at the Plaza Athenée?"

"Yes, and if I'm out leave word for me to call you. Keep cool, and let's both try to handle this like sensible people. O.K.?"

"I'll do my best."

And she would. I could count on her, I knew. Marie was tiny, hardly an inch above five feet, but she was as capable a secretary as I'd ever had. She had a knack for organization, and, lacking a steady boyfriend, she had quietly, in a sense, attached herself to me. It had taken luck to find a secretary like Marie; there was no way of buying one.

If I had Marie here, I thought . . . and then I thought, why not?

11 VIENNA, JANUARY 1958

Her room was heated by a small, cylindrical stove ornamented with turquoise tiles. It was a colder than usual Vienna winter, and the Grünewald was blanketed with several inches of powdery snow. The heater, as much as she plied it with shiny hard lumps of coal, didn't give off enough warmth. She had to wear two heavy sweaters, but even so she felt the chill in her fingers and her toes. Each day, except Sundays, she spent three hours in the ballet class, after which she would do some shopping for food and prepare a supper for Zoltan, who would come in the evenings, stamping his feet for circulation. He spent much of the day on the street, doing "business," as he called it, and he always had enough money for her, for the room rent, for the shopping, for her classes. He asked for nothing in return; it was as though, in a way, she were his ward. After a while, he would tell her, there would be more money, a lot of it, and they would be able to dine in the best restaurants, and go to the opera and the Burg Theatre whenever they felt like it. He had brought her a bicycle—he had one, too—and she kept it, locked with a chain, at the bottom of the stairwell in the old building on Garnisongasse, near the Votivkirche, which she sometimes visited, more because it was quiet and peaceful than for religious reasons. Then, too, it reminded her of the time, many years before, when her mother used to take her to church on Sundays in Budapest.

Then, one day, he came in the middle of the afternoon, pounding on her door. When she opened it, he was out of breath, as though he had been running, or bicycling hard. He said he didn't have much time, he was going away for a while—there was some trouble. He pushed some money into her hands and gave her the name and address of a woman she was to see; the woman, whose name was Grete Kellner, would help her find some work. He brushed away her questions, said he had no time, but he would be back one day.

Meanwhile, if anyone asked her about him, she was to say nothing and, above all, not to say that he came here, or that he ever gave her money. She had never seen him so nervous or so pale; he would go to the window, look out, and tell her not to worry. Grete would look after her; she was a good friend of his friends; and she had promised. He pressed her close to him, and there was a look of pain on his face. When he left, no more than five minutes after he had come, she felt lonelier than she had ever felt before.

A few days later, with the money beginning to disappear, she went to see Grete Kellner in the Lehargasse, which was very near where she took her ballet classes. Grete was older than she by four or five years, strikingly pretty, her blonde hair tinted a harsh yellow. She was tall, and it could be seen at once that she had dancer's legs.

"So," she said, "you're Caryl, and you dance and you need work."

Grete's apartment had two rooms, heated like hers with tile stoves, but it was much warmer and comfortable looking, with some low couches and dozens of tasseled pillows. A record player was on, and she recognized Marlene Dietrich's voice, singing sad German songs.

"Your boyfriend," Grete said, offering her a cigarette, which she refused, then lighting one for herself with a slim gold lighter, "got himself in a pile of trouble. You heard?"

She shook her head.

"He exchanged some dollars for a package of schillings," Grete said. "An old trick. He was foolish. The package had paper in it. But the fellow had connections with the police, who are out looking for your boyfriend. Let's see you dance."

She looked at her dumbly.

Grete put another record on the player. It was a song called "Patricia," popular on the radio, and the arrangement of it had a suggestive kind of rhythm.

"Here, like this, little one," Grete said, and began dancing slowly across the room, then back, with exaggerated swings of her hips and mincing little steps and waves of her arms above her head.

"Try it," Grete said.

To the beat of the music, she imitated Grete, a little shocked when she swung her hips, because she knew it was sexy. Grete clapped her hands to the beat of the music and urged her on, then stood before her, grinding her hips. Then Grete nodded and took the needle off the record.

"I could teach you," she said. "Have you danced without your clothes before?"

She shook her head.

"Would it bother you?"

"I think so."

"You could do it with veils," Grete said, thoughtfully. "It would be artistic. Since you're so young, the boss might go for it. But he wouldn't pay you more than three hundred schillings a week, unless you sat and drank with the customers. I don't think you would do that."

"No," she said.

"We might even try you," Grete said, "wearing ballet slippers. So, you come to the club tonight and watch, and I'll have you meet the boss, and we'll see what can be done. All right?"

"Where do I come?"

Grete gave her the address and told her not to come until ten o'clock. The boss wouldn't be there before then. "If any of the musicians try to paw you," she said, "just give them a good hard slap. Good and hard."

"Is Zoltan in a lot of trouble?" she asked.

"Oh, is he in trouble!" Grete said, with a hard laugh. "He was out to gyp his own people. You can't be in much more trouble."

She felt sick, more for Zoltan than for herself.

12

I spent most of a day visiting more hospitals and, toward the close of the day, the morgue. Gazin accompanied me. "Necessary," he snapped, not happy himself about what he regarded as chores. I saw several female bodies. I saw accident cases. Thank God, none of them was Caryl.

During the course of the day, I learned Delahaye was pursuing his own lines of investigation.

"What lines?" I asked Gazin, in the car back to the hotel.

"He's at Interpol headquarters, Saint-Cloud."

"What's there?"

"Files," he said.

"What files?"

"One never knows," Gazin said, and whistled tonelessly.

He was an irritating fellow, and I felt a little better back at the hotel, rid of him. I wasn't due back at my offices in New York for another week. That gave me time, but enough time? A New York call had come for me, I was informed at the desk. It was a Brooklyn number, Marie's home phone.

I called her back from the room.

"I got into her apartment," Marie said, her voice surprisingly clear over the thousands of miles.

"I took the day off," she said. "You didn't want anyone to know, you said."

"Did you find anything?"

"You see, I charmed the doorman, sort of, gave him a story about Caryl's wanting something, and her being in Europe . . ."

"Marie," I said, "did you find anything?"

"I collected everything that was loose—bills, a few letters, check stubs, canceled checks. I went through it. You wanted me to go through it, didn't you?"

"Yes."

"Well, it all seems very ordinary to me."

"What about the letters?"

"One has to do with her citizenship papers; it's from the State Department. One was from you, sort of silly . . ."

"Forget about that."

"And the other is from someone who lives in Greenwich Village, wanting to know why she hasn't come to the Chess Club."

"That's all?" I said, disappointed. "You looked everywhere? All the drawers, closets, her clothes?"

"Yes, except for one thing, a kind of file box, metal. It was locked."

"Did you try to open it?"

"I couldn't. There was no key anywhere. It's too large to walk out with. What do you want me to do about it?"

"Figure out a way to get it open."

"All right."

"Do you think you can?"

"I'll try."

"When you open it, if there's anything I should know about, call me."

"But what are we looking for?"

"I don't know. Use your judgment."

"I will," she said.

She'd get that file box open, I was quite sure.

I had dinner sent up to the room and spent a good part of the evening carefully packing Caryl's clothes into her bags. I gathered up her toilet items and packed them neatly into their cases. Her underthings and blouses in the drawers shed a faint fragrance, and her perfume was in the room, hanging suspended in the air like an intangible presence. I stored the bags in the hall closet. Now I had the room to myself. I was alone. It was my way of facing having to live a life without her.

I drank some brandy and, after considerable tossing in the bed, I managed to get to sleep, in a confusion of dreams and nightmares. In one dream I ran through the musty corridors of an ancient hospital, opening the doors of room after room, hoping to find Caryl. A nun stood by the door before one of the rooms, a large gold cross on her chest. She opened the door for me and motioned me inside. A single bed was in the room, and on the bed was a form covered by a white sheet. I lifted the sheet and saw the horribly burned face of Sybil. I awoke in a sweat. I went to the window and stared out at the wide, quiet street. Up the street a way, I saw a motorcycle leaned against a tree. I watched the motorcycle for a while, wondering if its owner would come to claim it. No one did. I returned to the bed, tried for more sleep, and got up again as dawn's light came through the windows. I stared outside again. The motorcycle was gone. I shook my head. Meaningless. All of it—meaningless.

Normal life took over. At eight o'clock, a tap came on the door and the waiter entered with his own key, carrying my breakfast tray, along with the hotel's complimentary copy of *Le Figaro* and the customary *Herald-Tribune.* I flipped through the latter's meager number of pages, and, on page 5, Caryl stared at me. Sutton had gotten it in, and mentally I sent him my gratitude. A caption above the picture said: MISSING. And below it was a brief item: *Mrs. Caryl Parrish, wife of Steven Parrish, lawyer, of New York City, has been missing since March 4. The Parrishes arrived in Paris on February 28 for a one-week residence at Hotel Plaza Athenée. Paris police are investigating.*

The phone rang a half-hour later.

Delahaye sounded annoyed.

"I take it you arranged for the item in the *Herald-Tribune.*"

"A reporter came to see me. I thought it might be a good idea."

"I would have preferred your consulting me first."

"I don't see anything wrong."

"This means additional work for us. A hundred crazy people will call the police to tell us they've seen your wife—on a train, in a car, robbing a bank. . . . And we'll have to check out every one, which, I assure you from past experience, will most likely be a waste of time. Add to that the fact that already your wife's photo has been sent to every place it should go—by which I mean those qualified to investigate."

He was very definitely annoyed with me. But it wasn't his wife who was missing; it was mine.

"I'll see those hundred crazy people," I snapped back at

him, "or get someone else to do it, if necessary."

"Also," he went on, as though I hadn't said anything, "it was not necessary for you to complain to your embassy."

"I notified them," I said. "If there were complaints, they probably came from Mr. Graham, who is naturally concerned about this."

"What I'm asking," he said, "is that you place more trust in me. I expect to have results very soon."

"What results?"

"I'm on the track of something quite interesting. You'll see."

"For God's sake," I almost yelled at him. "If you know something, tell me."

"Later, Mr. Parrish. *A toute à l'heure.*" He hung up.

I spent a good part of the afternoon arranging for a tourist visa for Hungary, then hurried back to the hotel. Delahaye had promised results very soon. How soon? I was in hopes of a message from him when I stopped at the desk in the lobby. "Ah, Mr. Parrish," a concierge said. "Yes, there *is* a message for you." His expression conveyed that it was something of import and that he was pleased to be able to transmit it. "A call came from Milan while you were out," he said, and he handed me a folded message slip.

"Milan?" I said. I didn't know anyone in Milan.

The message was from a Signor Torelli, and it gave me a Milan telephone number to call. The scrawl at the bottom of the message slip was handwritten in French. It translated to: "Concerning your wife."

I took a deep breath; I'd felt a momentary dizziness.

"Who took the call?" I asked.

"I did, sir."

"And that's all he said?"

"I did try, sir. I asked him for more information, but he insisted he speak to you personally. It was an hour ago. I kept calling your room. He will be at this number all afternoon."

"Will you get me a line to Milan?"

"Of course. At once. Five minutes, no more. I will insist the operator put you through at once."

"I'll take it in my room."

The phone in the room was already ringing when I got there.

"Your call to Milan, sir," the operator said.

"Pronto?" an Italian voice said.

"This is Steven Parrish," I said. "Am I speaking to Signor Torelli?"

"Si."

"Do you speak English?"

"Uno momento. Prego."

Someone else came on the line. "Mr. Parrish? I am Torelli's friend. I speak English." The Italian accent was heavy, but it was definitely English he spoke.

"You have information about my wife?"

"Si. Yes. Very definitely."

"Well, what is it?"

"You are missing her?"

I mentally cursed him but kept my voice relatively even. "Yes. What do you know about it?"

"My friend Torelli has seen her."

"When?"

"Very recently."

"Where?"

"There is a reward, yes?"

"Yes. Where did he see her, and when?"

"Mr. Parrish . . ." The man sounded regretful. "You must come to Milan."

"Why? Is she in Milan?"

"I am sorry, Mr. Parrish. Torelli will only speak to you in Milan."

It could be a hoax, I thought. Someone who had seen the picture and the item in the *Tribune* and saw a chance for quick and easy money.

"I'll absolutely guarantee a reward," I said. "But if this is some kind of game, the police will hear about it."

Maybe, I thought, I shouldn't have said that last. There was no sound at the other end of the line, and for a moment I was afraid I'd lost the connection. Then the voice came on again, mild and a little regretful.

"No police, Mr. Parrish. This is a personal matter. Torelli assists you, and you will give him the reward." A pause. "One thousand dollars."

"All right," I said. "If the information is genuine. . . ."

"In Swiss francs," he said. "The current exchange rate. Torelli has seen your wife, and for one thousand dollars he will tell you where. Agreeable?"

"Agreeable," I said. For the first time, I could hope.

PART TWO

13

No one waited near the information booth. "I am to meet a Signor Torelli here," I told the girl in the booth. "Is there a message for me?"

"Your name, please?"

I gave it to her.

"Yes," she said, and gave me an envelope with my name on it.

Inside was a paper folded in half; scrawled on it in English was: "I meet you near taxis in blue Fiat 120." It was signed, "Torelli."

I followed the signs that said *Taxi* and went outside to the arrivals platform. Drivers in waiting taxis beckoned me. I kept going to the end of the taxi line and saw the small blue car. It was a Fiat. Two young men were waiting in the front seat. Why two?

The one on the passenger side spoke to me. "Signor Parrish?"

I nodded.

"Get in please."

"Are you Torelli?"

"My friend is Torelli. He speaks no English. I am here to help."

I hesitated. "Where are we going?"

"Not far. In back, please."

I opened the rear door of the car and got in. Torelli, at the wheel, started the car and drove from the airport area onto a main road that signs identified as leading to Milano. A few minutes later we came to a cluster of houses and a crossroad. Torelli turned onto that road and drove about a half mile farther. The houses were small and close together; it had the look of a working-class suburb. He stopped the car in front of a café with a red neon sign that flashed on and off: *Cinzano.*

"We will talk here," said the man in the passenger seat. As

I got out, he saw that I was carrying my overnight bag with me. "Leave it in the car," he said. "No one will take it."

I left the bag on the floor of the rear of the car, and Torelli locked the car doors as though to reassure me. He was tall, lean, with a bronze complexion and a thin, hawklike nose. I judged him to be in his mid-twenties. The other was shorter and plumper, about the same age. He wore glasses with thick black rims. Both shook hands with me formally, and I followed them into the café. The bar had a huge espresso machine that hissed and gasped as the proprietor filled coffee cups for the men sitting on stools. Heads turned to look at us as Torelli led the way through a beaded curtain to a small back room with round tables. We had our choice of the tables, for the room was empty.

"May we offer you a coffee?" the one with the glasses asked.

I accepted. He left the room for a moment, and Torelli and I examined each other. He smiled at me ingratiatingly and said haltingly, "I—no—speak—English."

"I understand," I said.

The one with the glasses returned and seated himself between us. With a businesslike manner, he said, "Torelli asks if you have the Swiss bank notes—one thousand dollars at the current rate."

"Yes," I said, "but first I have some questions to ask."

"Of course."

"Si," Torelli said, having understood.

"Signor Torelli claims to have seen my wife. Would you ask him to describe her?"

He repeated this to Torelli, who nodded and spoke for a full minute to the friend.

"Yes," the one with the glasses said. "He judges her to be one meter . . . no, in your measurements it would be . . .," he mentally calculated, "five feet, five inches. Correct?"

"Go on."

"Brown hair, short, with little curls. Age, perhaps thirty. Slim, nice body, very attractive."

"That's not enough," I said. "He could have told that much from the picture in the paper."

"You doubt him?" The smaller man looked hurt.

"No, but I must be sure."

He spoke again to Torelli, who gave him more information in Italian. Then, back to me. "He mentions the eyes, most extraordinary, the shape. A little, how do you say? Oriental? And blue. He noticed her eyes particularly. Not an ordinary blue, but——" He sought for the English word. "Viola?"

"Violet?"

"Yes," he said, with relief. "Violet. In Italian is *viòla.*"

I nodded, all but giddy with a kind of relief myself.

"Where did he see her?" I asked.

"First," he said, apologetically, "the reward. We must trust each other."

"I'd like him to look at these pictures."

I handed Torelli some snapshots of Caryl, watching his expression carefully.

"Definito!" He snapped. "Is the same. But . . ." He explained in Italian something about the pictures.

The friend said: "He says the clothes she wears in the pictures are not the clothes she wore when he saw her. He wishes to make that clear. The hair, yes, the same, but not the clothes. Otherwise, he makes positive identification."

"Did he speak to her?"

Again a moment for translation.

"He did not speak to her, but he heard her speak. In English, but it was not like your English."

"An accent?"

"Yes, a little accent. So he did not at first take her to be American."

"French?"

"No, not French."

Torelli said something to him, and the friend translated.

"He is not certain of this, but he has feeling she is Yugoslav, maybe Romanian. Is it possible?"

I was convinced, and I didn't want to use up any more time. I took the envelope with the franc notes from my inside pocket and handed it to Torelli, who quickly rose and went through a door marked WC.

"He wishes to examine, to make sure all is correct," the friend explained. "A formality. You understand?"

"I understand," I said, controlling impatience.

The coffees came. I tasted mine, found it black and faintly sweet. Torelli returned, smiling and nodding to me.

"So," the friend said, "we will talk. You wish to know where Torelli saw your wife. He has told me. It was at Saas Fee."

"Saas Fee?" The name meant nothing to me.

"In Switzerland," the friend said, while Torelli nodded vigorously. "A ski resort, very small, very high. You know it?"

"No."

"You know Zermatt?"

I nodded. I hadn't been there, but I had a good idea where it was.

"Well, over the mountains, from Zermatt, on the other side, is Saas Fee. Very good skiing."

"All right," I said, "Saas Fee? When did he see her?"

"Yesterday. He left Saas Fee yesterday for Milano, he saw her yesterday morning, he also saw her the day before. Three times he rode on the same cable car with her."

"She was *skiing?"*

"Yes. Your wife, he says, is good skier. Torelli is very good, himself. Close to champion. He tried to speak to your wife. He did not know, of course. . . . But, nice-looking young woman. She spoke back in English. He also heard her speaking to a woman, sometimes in English, sometimes German."

"The other woman," I said. "What did she look like?"

"Also attractive, blonde, typically German. A little older than your wife."

My puzzlement must have shown on my face, for Torelli looked chagrined, as if he had not provided sufficient information for the money given him. He spoke to the friend, who said to me: "Torelli wishes to know—has he helped you?"

Almost to myself, I said: "It doesn't make sense."

"Torelli says the truth," the friend said, hurt. "The two women skied together. They took one run, he took another. Then at the bottom he saw them again, talking."

"Where were they staying?"

"He does not know. There are thirty, perhaps forty lodges in Saas Fee."

"They could have come from somewhere else, just for the day."

"We do not think so. One does not reach Saas Fee easily."

"How do you get there?"

"Only by car. There is no train to Saas Fee. You can go to Visp by train, but from there you must take a car. There is a road from Visp that goes up and up. . . ." He made a spiraling motion with his hand. It is near the mountain called the Dom, higher even than the Matterhorn, maybe forty-five-hundred meters high. A beautiful place. Sometimes you can ski there until June. Torelli, who is an excellent skier, likes it best of all."

An excellent skier no doubt, I thought, sizing him up. A lover of the easy life, and women. And he had found a way to make a little easy money.

"How did he see the picture?" I asked the friend.

"This morning, he took the plane from Geneva to Milano. A man sitting next to him had the newspaper, and Torelli saw your wife's picture and he asked the man to read to him what the print said, and that was how he knew to call your hotel in Paris."

"From here," I asked, "how long would it take to reach Saas Fee?"

They conferred. One way would be to fly to Geneva, if a flight were available at this hour. From there a car or train to Visp, from Visp another hour or two. Better to take a car from the airport and drive by way of the Simplon Pass. They calculated seven hours for the trip. "But it is late," he said. "Better to wait for morning."

It was 9:30 P.M., I saw by my watch, and I certainly wouldn't be able to sleep.

"Will you take me back to the airport?"

"Of course." But, before getting up, the friend put a sympathetic hand on my arm. He had a question, they were both curious. I saw a slightly mocking look in his eyes behind the black-rimmed glasses. "Your wife has run away from you?"

"It's beginning to look like it," I said, and to my own ears my voice sounded harsh.

The rented Lancia held up well, and took innumerable hairpin bends with ease. In Saas Fee I parked near the Information Center—closed because of the early hour. Now, how to go about finding Caryl? Ask for her at every one of the lodges and hotels? The town was full of them, far more than the thirty or forty mentioned by Torelli's friend. If she was here, she would have registered, presented her passport, filled out a police identification card. Swiss regulations were as strict as those in France. The identification card would have gone to the police.

When I got out of the car, my ears started burning from the cold. Above me, gleaming whitely, loomed the Dom. No cars ran the cable at this hour. The police *poste* was only a block away from the Information Center, identified by a blue lantern.

"Do you speak English?" I asked the policeman on duty behind a desk.

He nodded.

"My wife came on here ahead of me," I told him. "But I don't know her hotel. Could you help me find her?"

"You wish me to place calls to the hotels and lodges?"

"It would save time if you looked up the address on her identification card."

"Not possible," the policeman said, shaking his head. "I'm not permitted to give such information."

I had with me the page from the *Herald-Tribune* showing Caryl's picture. I unfolded it and showed him the photograph and caption.

"As you see," I said, "I am attempting to trace her. She may be in trouble. Someone saw her here in Saas Fee as late as yesterday morning. Surely your regulations would allow me to locate my wife."

"Your passport, please."

He examined it. "Your wife's name is Caryl Parrish?"

"She would have possibly registered as Caryl Batory. You see, we were recently married, and she hasn't yet changed the name on her passport."

He thought for a while. He looked at the passport, looked at me, then shrugged and went into another room. Through the door I saw him pull open a file drawer. He came back with a card. I wanted to physically wrest it from him, but I held back.

"There is a Batory," he said. "American passport. What is her place of birth?"

"She was born in Hungary," I said.

"And she comes from New York?"

"She would have come from Paris."

"It says here, New York."

"Yes, both of us come from New York, and we stopped in Paris. Where . . ."

"The Hermitage," he said, abruptly. "Up this street three blocks, turn right, one more block. You'll see it on the left."

I let out a deep breath, and for a moment I felt dizzy. I was less than a half mile from Caryl. She was here, she was in good health—or else she wouldn't have gone skiing. My knees turned weak from a kind of fear—that I would learn something from her that I didn't want to learn.

I ran to the Lancia, kicked the starter into life, and drove to the Hermitage, barely managing to avoid a skid from the icy surface as I turned a corner. The Hermitage was a concrete lodge, three stories high, wooden beams at a slant patterning its walls. The hotel's parking area had been cleared of snow. A flight of wooden steps mounted to a glass-enclosed veranda. The entrance gave into a large, hall-like room. Off it was the small reception office. A porter was on duty, half asleep in a chair. I saw a bell on the counter and I banged it. He came alert with a start.

"Sir?" he said.

"My wife is here. Caryl Batory. Her room number, please."

"You wish to register for a room?"

"No. I want to see my wife. The police say she is here."

"The police?"

"Just look up her name in the register," I said.

I must have sounded ominous, for he opened a large guest register and scanned names.

"Her name?" he asked.

"Batory. Caryl Batory. Or possibly, Mrs. Caryl Parrish. She uses both names."

He turned a page, and his finger moved down the list of names.

"Yes," he said. "Batory."

"Her room number," I said.

"But she has checked out, sir."

The weak feeling came again. I had to lean on the counter. My eyes teared, from lack of sleep, from the profoundest kind of disappointment.

"When?"

"Yesterday afternoon."

14

From the register the porter determined that Caryl had reserved her room for a week, and that she had arrived three days before.

"Did she say anything? About where she was going?"

"Not to me, sir. I helped put her bag in the car."

"What car?"

"I believe, sir, it was a Peugeot. As I remember, a Peugeot five-oh-four, with a French license plate."

"You definitely remember a French license plate?"

"Yes, sir. And her friend, the blonde woman, left at the same time, in a Porsche."

"This friend, the blonde woman, was also staying here?"

"No, sir. Are you a police officer?"

"I told you," I said wearily, "I'm her husband."

"And she was to meet you here?"

"No, that's not it." I was too tired to explain, and what good would it do to explain anything to this dull man, who wanted to finish his night tour and get back to sleep.

"Did she have skis with her?" I asked.

"No, sir. I would have seen them on the car. She must have rented them here."

"And the blonde woman?"

"Yes, she had her own skis, fitted on a rack on the Porsche."

I got what details I could from him. About four the previous afternoon, she had suddenly checked out, had paid her bill. In the parking area the blonde woman was waiting in the Porsche. Then, the two cars drove off. The blonde woman had presumably come from another hotel, although he had observed the two women at dinner together in the dining room the evening before last. They kept to themselves, he had noticed. Why had he noticed that?

"Because of the men here," the porter said. "They were attractive ladies, and there is dancing here in the evenings, but they would not dance with anyone. They sat by themselves and talked."

"Do you think anyone here would have talked to them?"

"I don't know, sir. Starting at seven, breakfast will be served. You could inquire of some guests. The waitresses could point out her table."

It was twenty minutes to seven.

"Can I get some coffee now?"

"Yes, sir, if you will take a seat in the dining room, I will bring some."

I made sure to hand him some French francs.

In the empty, wood-paneled dining room, I took a table near a window. Outside, I could see that the cable cars were now running. In the early morning light the ski trails could be discerned. I found myself blinking. I needed sleep.

The porter brought me a thick mug and a metal pot with a spout, I poured the strong black liquid into the cup. I drank it boiling hot, and in a few minutes I felt more alert. I tried to put it together. Caryl had a car with a French license plate. That would have meant she had rented it, and, in all likelihood, in Paris. From Paris to Geneva was a four-hour trip along good roads. Her bags were back in the hotel room in Paris; therefore she had stopped somewhere and bought luggage and ski clothes. If she used traveler's checks or her American Express card, sooner or later the bills and checks would turn up, and places and dates and items could be checked. That was something, anyway. But it told me nothing that I needed to know. She had left here suddenly—why? If she had seen her picture in the paper. . . . That much snapped suddenly into place. She would have known that someone sooner or later would recognize her here, and that led to only one supposition: that she did not wish to be found, and apparently by me.

It was dishearteningly clear to me now. She had run off, to get away from me. The simple, ugly word for it was desertion.

But I was damned well going to find her and find out why.

Early morning skiers filtered into the dining room. A waitress came up to me, wearing a black sweater and red dirndl skirt.

"You have just arrived?" she asked, cheerily.

"Yes," I said, and lied: "I was supposed to meet my wife here. But there was some mistake, and she left suddenly. A Madame Batory."

"What a shame!" she said, overflowing with sympathy. "I waited on her myself. At that table." She pointed out one a few tables from where I was sitting.

"Unfortunately," I said, "she failed to leave word for me. I wonder: was she friendly with anyone here?"

"Mostly, she dined alone. But one night, I think the evening before yesterday, she had a guest."

"A blonde woman," I said. "Would you know her name, or where she stayed."

"No, sir, but . . ." She suppressed a giggle. "One of the men said he recognized her."

"Who would that be?"

"Herr Dittersdorf."

"And he knows her?"

"Well . . ." She seemed hesitant. "He said he saw her once in Munich, in a nightclub. He said he saw her do a strip dance."

"A strip dance!"

"Yes, sir, he was sure of it."

I leaned an elbow on the table and rested my forehead on my palm. I could understand Caryl's knowing a dancer at some time in her past life—she had trained for a while as a ballet dancer—but a *stripper?* It was maddening.

"Are you all right, sir?"

"Yes. This Dittersdorf . . . is he here in the dining room?"

"Not now. Your wife is also—a dancer?" She was staring at me with curiosity.

"No," I said, "she's not. But when this Dittersdorf comes in, would you ask him to join me at this table?"

"Yes, sir. Would you like some eggs and toast?"

"No, nothing."

She hesitated, looking at me dubiously, then left.

Dittersdorf was outfitted for skiing, in tight, form-fitting black wool pants and a heavy yellow cable-knit sweater. He turned out to be Swiss, from Zurich, about forty, and a little paunchy, with heavy features. I kept it conversational for a while, then gave him the same story about arriving late for a meeting here with my wife.

He nodded, with familiarity. "I understand. A family matter. The waitress has already explained to me. How can I help?"

"You recognized, so the waitress said, the woman she had dinner with."

He nodded, with a faint smile and a shrug.

"You know how it is at a small place like this. People talk, they gossip, they wonder who everyone is. Naturally we wondered about Madame Batory—your wife."

"Parrish," I said.

"Of course. She is a liberated woman. So she uses her maiden name."

"Very likely," I said. "But this other woman, the blonde . . ."

"I looked at her," Dittersdorf said, "and I said to myself, I have seen that woman somewhere before. Now, where?"

"Yes," I said, urging him. "Where?"

"About a year ago I was in Munich, on business, without my wife. . . . I went into a few bars, the kind that feature naked women—you understand?"

"Go on," I said.

"And one, a large blonde with—" He gestured. "With magnificent bosoms, you call them bosoms? caught my eye." He paused. "She sat with me, for a bottle of champagne, which cost me plenty—and bad champagne at that. Look, between two men, I made a little offer of money. . . . She refused. That was it. So, when I saw her here with—your wife—I waited until they had finished dinner, and afterward I went to her and said: 'I know you from somewhere.' She looked straight through me. At first I thought: well, I've made a mistake. A lot of these ladies look alike. But the more I looked at her, the more I was sure. It was the same woman."

"Do you remember her name?"

He scratched the side of his head. "That's what I have been trying to remember. That type of woman doesn't give her name, but sometimes her first name. I have a memory that, in the Munich bar, she told me her Christian name. Of course, they use different names. Could it be Gretchen?"

"Could it be?"

"I think so. The more I think about it, the more I think so."

"Gretchen," I said. "From Munich."

"These ladies," he said, "travel from place to place. I remember talking with her about that. This one mentioned that she traveled from London all the way to Beirut, wherever they have these strip places. It's a circuit. Sometimes they do three or four clubs the same night in one city."

"You're well informed," I said.

"Well, you sit with them," he said lamely, "you have to talk about something. They don't understand my business, stocks and bonds, though I'm sure they would like to."

"And my wife seemed to know her well?"

"Yes, quite well. What, may I ask, is your wife's profession?"

I had figured, sooner or later, he would ask that.

"She's a translator," I said.

"An odd combination, then."

"What is?"

"A stripper and a translator."

He started to laugh at his wit, then, when he saw my sober expression, stopped abruptly. He rose, shook hands, said he had to be off, because he was to meet someone at the T-bars. From the look on his face, I gathered it was not his wife.

I used the Hermitage's washroom to freshen up and went back to the police *poste.* Another policeman was on duty, and I explained my situation and said I was looking for a German woman, whose name possibly was Gretchen, and could he help me?

"This woman, you say, is a friend of your wife's?"

"I think so. If I can find her address, she might have information about her."

"Her last name is?"

"I explained, I don't know her last name."

"You wish me to look in the files and find everyone whose name is Gretchen?"

"She would probably have arrived here in the past week."

"I am not permitted to do that, sir."

"What would permit you to do it?"

"That would require authorization from Geneva."

His face was set hard and adamant, and I knew I wasn't going to get anywhere with him. Best to return to Paris and ask Delahaye to intercede for me. Anyway, I was wasting time. In Paris, Delahaye would be able to have car rental agencies checked, and that might lead to something.

It was a long, long drive to the Geneva airport, where I turned in the Lancia.

A stripper and a translator! My ears burned.

15

While waiting for Delahaye to meet me in the café next door to the hotel, I put a call through to Marie at our offices in New York.

When I got her, she said she had opened the file case in Caryl's apartment.

"How did you manage it?"

"My brother has carpenter tools. I borrowed a hammer, a chisel, and a large screwdriver. I ruined the case, but I got it open."

"What's in it?"

"Mostly letters. Bundles of letters, close to a hundred of them. I have them here in the office."

"Good girl. Did you read them?"

"Well," she said, hesitating, "a few of them."

"Only a few?"

"Some of the ones in English," she said. "But most were in other languages, French, I guess, and German, and Hungarian. I couldn't read those."

"What about the ones in English?"

Again she hesitated.

"They seemed to be love letters, Mr. Parrish."

"Who from?"

"Someone called Ian. Ian Cameron."

"I know about him," I said. "Her former fiancé. He's dead."

"Oh."

"Where are the ones in foreign languages from?"

"All over. Budapest, and Munich, and Vienna, and Berlin. West Berlin, it looks like."

"Who's that one from?"

"Someone who signed herself 'Grete.' There's no last name."

"Marie," I said, thinking *Grete,* not *Gretchen.* "Do you have a passport?"

"No."

"Find out how fast you can get one. I want you to bring all those letters here to me in Paris. The office will issue you a check to my account for the fare. Cable me here your time of arrival. If I happen to be off somewhere, there'll be a room reserved here for you at the Plaza Athenée."

Her voice betrayed her excitement. "I'll be there as soon as I can. What do I tell people at the office?"

"That I'm giving you a vacation, that I'm going to be delayed in Europe. O.K.?"

"O.K.," Marie said.

When I entered the café from the hotel's inner entrance, I found Delahaye already there, in front of him a large cup of hot chocolate with a dollop of whipped cream floating on top. A bit of white froth was clinging to his scraggly gray mustache.

In view of the hour, 5 P.M., I asked for tea.

"So," he said, wagging his head sympathetically, "you've had a long trip, and it cost you money, and you learned . . . what? That your wife has left you."

I had called him from the Geneva airport, told him what I had learned, and asked him to attempt to locate the agency from which she had rented a Peugeot.

"Any word on the car?" I asked.

"Not yet, but I expect it soon." Again he wagged his head commiseratingly. "Frankly, it looked like desertion from the beginning."

"You wanted to see me to tell me my wife has left me?"

"Perhaps you should have a whiskey," he said. "It would help the nerves. I have some further information. Technically speaking, since your wife appears to have left the country, it is no longer my case. However, there are now additional elements."

"Such as why my room was ransacked," I said.

He held up a chubby hand.

"Yesterday," he said, "on your behalf I spent some time with the Interpol files at Saint-Cloud, as well as seeing to it that a missing persons bulletin went out over their Telex system."

"And those files," I said, "of course revealed that my wife is an international dope smuggler."

"Ah," he said, looking owlish and ignoring my sarcasm, "one comes across surprising names in those files. Yes, I poked into the files on fraud, drug traffic, counterfeiting. . . . But only after the name of Caryl Batory turned up in the master file."

I must have paled, for he said: "Really, Mr. Parrish, allow me to order you a whiskey.

I didn't resist. Caryl, my wife, was in the Interpol files, and now Delahaye, like a fat foxhound, was on the trail of something.

"Yes," he said, his eyes on me sympathetically, "there it was, the name. It startles, you know—a routine check, the name rolls up, and with it a cross-reference. You mentioned, didn't you, that your wife left Hungary with a friend named Zoltan?"

I nodded glumly. Maybe it was all hopeless, maybe I was better out of it, before I learned something more devastating. The scotch came, and I gulped it neatly. The lawyer in me emerged. She could have been a witness in some case or other. Being in the files didn't necessarily mean you were a criminal.

Delahaye drew his notebook from his pocket. He flipped pages.

" 'Zoltan Czepel,' " he read. " 'Alias Dmitri Karpov. Refugee, Hungary, 1957, age twenty. Jailed, London, 1963, five to ten years, after conviction cocaine smuggling, France to England. Released, 1968. Jailed, Marseilles, 1968, illegal possession traveler's checks. Released, February 1974.' " He looked up. "Approximately one month ago, that would be." He continued reading. " 'Of interest to Hungarian authorities, charges unspecified. See Caryl Batory, drugs, inactive.' "

I swallowed what was left of the scotch. I said: "Go on."

"So," he said, "in those files I find the following: 'Arrested, British airport customs, upon entry from France, 1963. Found in possession six kilos cocaine. Charges dropped when Zoltan Czepel confessed to having employed her as dupe. Of interest to Hungarian authorities. See Zoltan Czepel, also Julio Alvarez, Fraud section, inactive.' Interesting, yes?"

"I'll have another scotch," I said.

"Evidently," Delahaye said, "your wife failed to mention any of this?"

I shook my head.

"In 1963," he said, "six kilos of cocaine would bring, roughly, more than a hundred thousand British pounds on the wholesale market. But she was duped. What about, then, this Julio Alvarez. Is the name familiar?"

I shook my head.

"I happen to be acquainted with it," he said. "In fact, it involved me, in a way. The case concerned a bad bunch we only knew as the Marcel group. Very clever. We got on to Alvarez when Belgian police, some ten years ago, apprehended a woman found cashing a large bank draft in Brussels. To save herself, she gave a tip to the police. Her boyfriend, Julio Alvarez, had given her the check to cash. We went to pick him up in a hotel here, and he chose to shoot it out. Unfortunately, he was killed."

"Why unfortunately?"

"Because his was the only name we had that might have led us to the Marcel group. From the woman's description of his activities, it appeared he was one of them. So, at Interpol, I looked up his dossier. Sure enough, your wife's name."

"You're saying my wife was the one they caught in Brussels?"

"Not at all. It's quite puzzling, really. In going through his effects, a list of names was found. Some had numbers after them. Your wife's name was on the list, and after it a number: 72-A-4759. The assumption is that it referred to a secret bank account or safe deposit box. However, it was never located. I would very much like to ask your wife about that number and about Julio Alvarez. Does it mean anything to you, Mr. Parrish?"

"Not a thing."

"But this does complicate matters, you can see that?"

"It appears to me," I said, stiffly, "that she may have known a couple of unsavory characters who used her. The cocaine charge was dismissed. Why assume anything about this other thing?"

"I assure you, my mind remains open," Delahaye said, "but I must ask you a personal question: how much are you worth?"

"What's that got to do with her disappearance?"

"Kindly answer the question."

"All right. Salary fifty thousand a year, plus bonus, plus pension fund. Also some stock holdings, depressed at the moment, some tax-exempt securities. Say a few hundred thousand, all told."

"The pension fund—does it pay a death benefit?"

"Of course."

"And that amount?"

"Prior to retirement, I suppose you mean? One hundred thousand."

I already knew what he was getting at, but I waited for him to make it plain.

"Have any of these securities, funds, bank accounts been put in your wife's name?"

"The pension fund, yes. A savings account has been made out in trust for her. And one checking account I've made joint. It has seven or eight thousand at the moment."

"If she wished to, she could draw on that account and also run up bills in your name?"

"I suppose so, until I put a stop to it. But there's been no sign of that, inspector."

"Follow me," he said. "Your wife meets a fellow in a bar, runs off, joins a woman, a stripper, in a remote ski area. Meanwhile, your room is entered, searched—for what? Checkbooks, perhaps? An address book is taken, with names —important names for anyone interested in perpetrating a fraud involving you. You mentioned you thought you were being followed by someone on a motorcycle. So, I must come to the conclusion that persons known or unknown are attempting to set you up. For what, we'll leave open."

He sat back in his chair and folded his hands across his large stomach, surveying my reaction.

"I don't believe it," I said.

"Why not?"

"One reason. My wife."

He shook his head sadly. "I see you're in love."

"I know her," I said.

"But not much about her, apparently. You Americans sometimes surprise me. We French are much more cautious in these matters. You meet an attractive woman, after six weeks you're ready to marry. She accepts. You go abroad, and the woman disappears. Why be naive?"

"I just won't believe it," I said stubbornly.

"I have some advice for you," he said, "but I doubt you'll take it."

"What is it?"

"Return to New York and take immediate steps to annul your marriage."

"What grounds?"

"Abandonment. You have proof that no physical harm has come to her. And you can now be assured of my interest in locating her."

I shook my head.

"I didn't expect you to follow my advice," he said, with a shrug. "Gazin will keep an eye on you for the moment—for purposes of protection. If I can give you further advice or help, feel free to call on me."

He got to his feet and thrust out a pudgy hand. I shook it. *"Au revoir."*

"Good-bye," I said, and, after he had lumbered out, I ordered another whiskey. A few minutes later, Delahaye came back into the café.

"I omitted one other fact," he said. "Something you should know. I inquired at the Hungarian Embassy for information concerning the escape. There is a good reason for their interest in Czepel and your wife. A border guard was shot; they have reason to believe it was Czepel who did the shooting. Did your wife also neglect to tell you that?"

He patted me on the shoulder and left me with the whiskey.

16 VIENNA, NOVEMBER 1958

Sometimes, at three or four, even as late as five in the morning, Grete would bring a man back to the apartment with her, and on those occasions she would sleep on the cot in what was supposed to be the maid's room, although there was no maid. When Grete didn't have a man with her, she used the bedroom for sleeping. The room had a small extra bed, which was narrow and hard, but sometimes Grete would not come home at all, and then she could sleep in Grete's bed, which was large and soft, with fluffy pillows and a satin-covered blanket that she could roll herself up in and feel warm and safe and far, far away from the club where she worked.

She was grateful to Grete for having taken her in and providing her with money for clothes and shoes, but when she'd thank Grete, she'd be told she had nothing to thank her for, because money was coming in mysterious ways from Zoltan, wherever he was, and it was meant for her.

Grete had taught her some dances. One of the numbers had her in the briefest of ballet costumes, and she did the dance *en point* to the music of *Swan Lake,* played on the club's record system. The idea of the dance was that she was appearing in a dream to a sleeping man, and every time he would rise and try to reach her, he would grasp one of her filmy scarves, but that was all. Each scarf that came off would reveal more of her thighs and arms, but, just as the man would finally grab her and hold her, about to remove the last of her garments, the house lights would go off, and she would disappear backstage. None of the numbers she did, however, satisfied the customers, who jeered rather than applauded, and finally the club manager said she couldn't be part of the show anymore unless she agreed to let all her clothes be removed. It would be only for a second or two, then the lights would go off.

She wasn't ashamed of her body, not at all. Her breasts had

grown full, and her hips had rounded, and everyone said she had the best legs of any of the dancers. But the small stage on which she danced was right up next to the tables, and she was aware of the way the men feasted on her body with their eyes, and it repelled her. She tried to ignore them, to imagine she was dancing all alone, and then would come the jeers, and in the crowded dressing room, overwarm with girls' sweat and stale perfume and cigarette smoke, she would sit, shivering with embarrassment, by herself, until it was time to go on again.

So, when the manager came in to tell her she'd have to dance nude or not at all, she said she wouldn't dance anymore. "She can handle the cloakroom," Grete told the manager, and he said all right, if she'd sell cigarettes and cigars, too.

One of the waiters at the club was only a year older than she was, and he seemed nice enough. His name was Anton Duringer. She would meet him during the daylight hours, and he would take her to a café where older men sat reading newspapers and drinking tea, and some playing chess. Anton taught her chess, and some of her most pleasant hours were spent with him, poring over a chessboard, though she rarely won a game.

Anton wanted to make love to her. He couldn't understand why she wouldn't, since she seemed to have no other man in her life. But she said, yes, there was, a dear friend who was away on a lengthy business trip, and she had promised herself to him. Anton was dubious. Someone who would leave her for so long a time, weeks and months on end. Surely he could come back for at least a day or two. Stubbornly, she refused to talk about Zoltan. One day he would be back. He had promised. Sometimes her body seemed to ache for him.

A few letters reached her from her brother and her parents in Budapest. In them was the implicit warning that she should not try to return—and she had to admit to herself that sometimes the thought of going back had come to her—that her trouble there was grave and that they would appreciate not hearing from her, because it would cause them trouble, too. She interpreted this as meaning she should send news of herself to her relatives in London and this, in turn, would be relayed to her relatives in Budapest.

One night, in the early hours, after she finished at the club, Anton offered to walk her home to Grete's apartment. In the courtyard he asked: "Is she home?"

Knowing what was in his mind, she said: "What difference would it make?"

"She wouldn't mind," Anton said.

"Mind what?"

"I love you," he said, his eyes suddenly wild. "It's not fair to me."

In the darkness of the courtyard, no lights in any of the windows above, she felt his arms about her, and his lips were seeking hers.

"No," she said, "no," trying to twist out of his binding arms. If he was going to be insistent like this, she would have to stop seeing him. Suddenly, a shadow loomed in the courtyard, hovered over both of them, and Anton was torn away from her as though by a giant force. She heard a thud, the sound of a fist against bone. Anton fell to the ground, and the form over him was kicking him as he lay prone.

She started toward the street for help, heard the peremptory call, "Stay!" Zoltan's voice. She froze.

Anton was trying to sit up, clutching his head. Zoltan grasped him under the armpits and dragged him to his feet.

"Don't," she cried.

Zoltan's fist thudded into Anton's stomach, and Anton gasped and seemed to bend in two. Then, crouching, he ran from the courtyard. Tears scalded her eyes.

"Slut!" Zoltan said. His clenched fist menaced her, and for a moment she expected she would be hit, too. Then his hand relaxed. "Who is he?" he demanded. "What was he doing here?"

She told him Anton was a friend from the club, just a friend, someone nice and pleasant, and she had been surprised by his advances.

"I took risks," Zoltan said, "to come to see you, and I find you with that piece of shit. Where is Grete? I pay her to look out for you."

"Out with a man," she said.

"She's a whore, too."

But she understood why Grete did it. "I'm no hooker," Grete once told her. "I pick clean guys who I'd like to roll around with anyway, and I make sure that they have plenty of cash, and I ask for a little gift, that's all. And I put it away, because I'm saving. I have plans. I'm not going to wave my ass in front of their faces all my life, I can assure you."

"You've got to get out of here," Zoltan said. "I don't like it. You're going to London. You can stay there with your people, and you'll go to school and get a decent job. Then, when the time is right, I'll come for you. I'll send you some money and a ticket. You start arranging for it. Your relatives will help you get a visa. I'll send them money, so they can promise to support you. Otherwise, they won't let you in."

"Where will you be?" she asked him.

"Different places," he said. "I'm not doing badly. And, whenever I can, I'll come to see you. So, don't ever get funny with anyone."

"What does that mean—getting funny?"

"You know. You're my girl, for always. There's never to be anyone else. You understand that?"

"But I don't like being alone all the time," she said fretfully.

"It won't be for long. I'm arranging it. Why do you think I do this? It's for you, for the both of us. You want to live well, don't you? You'll see how well we'll live."

"In London?"

He shrugged. "Remains to be seen. Anyway, I'll get there soon enough. Don't worry."

"I wish you'd write me," she said. "And I hate what you did to Anton."

"Doesn't it show how much I love you?"

"I don't want it shown that way."

"I didn't kill him," he said, with a grin. "I could have. So just be careful, and it won't happen again. Let's go to your room."

He stayed only long enough to make love to her quickly and

fiercely, and then she crept down the stairs with him to the courtyard, gave him a last kiss and embrace, and he disappeared into the darkness from which seemingly he had come.

It was about a month later that she was on a plane, bound for London.

17

The telephone rang, waking me. From my bed I picked it up and answered, for the moment not sure of where I was. "I am Eva Korbut," a cheerful voice announced in mid-European English. "I am waiting for you in the lobby."

What lobby? My room was narrow and high-ceilinged. The bed was lumpy. Yes, I was in Budapest, in the Hotel Royal, on a wide street called Lenin Korut. I had registered here the afternoon before, gone to the Municipal Touring Office on Roosevelt Ter, and asked for assistance in looking up my wife's relatives. In the morning, I was assured, an interpreter-guide would contact me at my hotel. In spite of the lumpy bed, I had slept soundly, too soundly, for my watch told me it was already a few minutes past nine.

"I'm sorry," I said. "I'll need fifteen minutes or so."

"Then meet me in the dining room. I will be having coffee and reading an American book called *The Valley of the Dolls.*"

She was easy enough to find. She was a small, chubby woman of about thirty, with brown hair clipped in bangs across her forehead.

"Eva Korbut," she said, holding out her hand and closing the book.

Over eggs and Polish ham, I told her I needed assistance in finding a man whose last name was Batory, the brother of my wife, who had left Hungary in 1957.

"An émigré," she said, nodding. "These cases are quite common."

"It's a delicate matter," I said.

"In what way?"

"Because of the circumstances, she has not been in contact with her family for many years."

"I understand."

"Frankly, I don't know as much about my wife as I should know."

She studied me.

"Explain, please."

"Is it necessary?"

"It would help."

I filled her in, telling her that my wife had left me suddenly, and I was in the dark as to why. Already convinced that this woman was in some way connected with the police, or an intelligence branch, I said I was also seeking information about the man with her when she left the country. "His name," I said, "is Zoltan Czepel."

Her brow, under the bangs, furrowed.

"I seem to know that name," she said. "Shouldn't you contact our police?"

"The Paris police," I said, "have already made inquiries of the Hungarian authorities."

"I see you don't want to go to the political police," she said. "You people from the West have strange ideas about us. In any case, I can probably help you. I'll make some telephone calls."

She left the table abruptly. While waiting for her, drinking coffee, I noticed a man in a dark, rather shabby suit put aside his Hungarian newspaper to glance at me. Obvious, I thought.

She was back to the table in ten minutes.

"Well," she said. "It's quite simple. I have already located the brother of your wife. His name is Laszlo Batory, who is quite well known in Budapest. He is a political analyst who often speaks on the radio. He will see you. I have a car outside."

She led me to a small black Moskvich, parked outside the hotel. Handling the car with skill, she drove through the showy, modern section of Pest to a narrow street with older buildings and stopped the car in front of a building dominated by a large iron gate.

"I have explained to him your situation," she said. "He speaks English well. Would you like to be alone with him, or have me with you?"

"I've nothing to hide," I said. "Why not come with me?"

"Very good."

The iron-gated entrance opened on a surprisingly large inner court, with shops on three sides of the ground floor. We climbed four flights up a creaky staircase. Paint peeled from the walls. "Batory works at home in the mornings," Eva Korbut explained, all but out of breath.

Our ring was answered by a lean man of middle height, with thinning black hair. It was hard to detect the resemblance to Caryl. His lips were thinner, his nose more aquiline. Before shaking hands he gave me a quizzical look, then led us into a living room crowded with shabbily comfortable furniture and a work desk. I declined the Russian cigarette he offered me, but Eva Korbut accepted. Was this where Caryl had lived as a girl? I wondered.

"So," he said, "you're Caryl's husband, and she's left you. Why?"

Keep it polite, I told myself. "If it were a matter of her leaving me," I said, "I wouldn't be here."

He shrugged. "Then—why?"

"We're searching for her . . .," I began.

"We?"

"I have help, in Paris. She's missing. We're at a loss to know why. We were recently married, nothing was wrong. She left our hotel more than a week ago and hasn't returned." I couldn't help adding, with a touch of bitterness, "I'd think, as her brother, you would be concerned."

"But you realize," he said, forming his words precisely, "I haven't been in contact with her for many years. She left us, my family, without a word. By doing so she brought us trouble, much trouble. It was in this room that I last saw her, seventeen years ago. Seventeen years is a long time. You're aware of the circumstances under which she left?"

"Somewhat," I said.

"Then you know a border guard was shot during her—escape?" He said the last word reluctantly, and I noticed he gave Eva Korbut a veiled glance. "She told you about it?"

I shook my head. "No, but I've learned about it since. She was with a companion. I assumed . . ."

"The authorities also assumed. Yes, the investigation determined that the companion, Zoltan Czepel, was in possession of a gun. The guard was critically wounded. He eventually recovered. Since she was only sixteen, she has not been listed as an accomplice. But what she put us through! My own career was in jeopardy. My parents thought it best to move to the country. My appointment to the Ministry of Political Education was held up for two years."

"I can understand all that," I said. "But it was a long time ago. What I need to know is, can you help me find her?"

He gave an elaborate shrug and lit another cigarette. "You think she writes me, telephones? I lost her once, too. Maybe that should tell you something."

"All right," I said. "There's her background. I don't know all of it, obviously. I have questions about it."

"I suggest," he said, his expression frozen, "you look more into Czepel's background. She was with him for years. She was also arrested in London for drug smuggling. You knew that?"

"She was cleared."

"And how do you think that happened?"

"Well, how? I want to know."

"My uncle, who lived in London—he's dead now—telephoned me. Naturally, I thought of Zoltan. I reported it to our officials here. They reported it to the London police, and Zoltan was picked up. He confessed, luckily for Caryl. Perhaps he loved my sister, but I've often wondered why he confessed. After all, she was the one caught with the goods. Then it occurred to me. He feared extradition. Better for him to be in an English jail than to be brought for trial here. So, I help Caryl, and what happens? Not a word from her. No thanks, nothing. It was only later, a year later, that I receive a letter from a Viennese friend of hers that she is working in Marseilles, and that she is in good health."

"Marseilles?"

"Yes, Marseilles. That would be 1964, perhaps 1965."

"Do you remember the name of the person who wrote you?"

He shook his head.

"Was it Grete?"

"Perhaps Grete."

"The last name?"

"I don't remember."

"Do you have the letter?"

"I don't keep such letters."

"And you don't seem to care much about your sister."

"And should I?" He got up and paced the room, stubbing out his cigarette. I had succeeded in agitating him. "You don't think I warned her about Czepel?"

His fingers trembled slightly as he lit another cigarette. The peculiar odor of the Russian cigarettes was filling the room. At least the memories were painful to him.

"He lived on this same street. When the counterrevolution began, he was with the fighters. But there were some, like Czepel, without political conviction, who were nothing more than hooligans. So, they shot off guns. . . . Big heroes! He had his eye on Caryl. She wasn't yet sixteen. He had already started at the university, but was thrown out, and for good reason."

I didn't interrupt, but gave him an inquiring look.

"There was in effect at that time," Batory said, "a student saving program. You were given a little book, and each month you bought stamps and pasted them in the book. At the end of a year you could trade the books in for certain goods—foodstuffs, scarce items like—oh—shoes, typewriters." He glanced at Eva Korbut. "You're too young to remember that?"

She nodded.

"Zoltan would buy the books from students for more than they were worth in currency. Then he would trade them for items and sell them on the black market. Actually, he would get someone else to do the trading, so, technically, he kept himself in the clear. But they threw him out, anyway. After the fighting, he told Caryl he had hit a Russian tank with a bazooka shell. He had to leave the country, he said, because soon the AVOs would find out about it. He told her he was certain I would tell the AVOs." Almost involuntarily, he met Eva Korbut's steady gaze.

"If I had believed the story about the tank, I would have. In any case, he persuaded her that his life was in danger. He must have given her a story about the good life she would have elsewhere. Caryl left with him one night. Perhaps they were already lovers, I don't know. But an acquaintance of Zoltan's reported that he had stolen his car. The car was found near the border; a guard had been shot. They came looking for Zoltan, and naturally came to see me. I assured them that Caryl wouldn't know what to do with a gun if she had one. Then, from a camp in Austria, a letter came from Caryl. I saw it had already been opened."

Eva Korbut was expressionless. I had the odd feeling that Batory had told this story before, almost word for word.

"She wanted to know," he went on, "if anything serious had happened on the border. She meant the guard. I wrote her back, saying that fortunately the guard had lived, and advising her—most firmly, I assure you—to return here and put matters straight. But she disregarded the advice. When she wrote next, it was to tell me she had a job dancing. She named the place, in Vienna. I learned it was a cheap nightclub. I wrote her again, telling her this time that if she wasn't returning here she should go to London, where some relatives could look after her. She was my sister, after all." He said, the last as though defending himself.

"She went to London," I said.

"Yes, to stay with the relatives, until Zoltan came into her life again. She had a job, secretarial. He told her he had a better job for her, in Paris. That much I learned from our relatives."

"Do you know where she worked in Paris?"

"She wasn't good enough to inform me," he said, with irony. "Nor did she inform you, I see. But, if she was living in Paris with Zoltan, perhaps she thought it best not to tell you that. A man like Czepel is an embarrassment. I take it you didn't know she was in Marseilles, either. He was arrested there again, you know, several years later."

"I know about that."

"Who helps your research?" he asked drily.

"The Paris police."

"But not your wife. A strange marriage. You don't tell each other anything."

"Czepel is out of jail," I said. "Could she be with him now?"

"There is a saying: your guess is as good as mine. If so, I have some advice for you. Stay away from him. You're my brother-in-law, a member of the family." He gave me a quizzical smile that was not altogether friendly. "If they're together, it could be very unhealthy for you. And, should your researches lead you to that conclusion, I would, if I were you, pack my bags and forget about my sister. As, Mr. Parrish, I intend to."

He was making it very plain that it was time for me to leave.

Eva Korbut started the Moskvich, but didn't put it in gear. "Well," she said. "You've learned enough?"

She was a stout little woman, but not unattractive. It seemed to me I detected warmth in her brown eyes—or was it sympathy?

"Not yet," I said.

I was still mulling over what Laszlo Batory had told me—a few more details than I had known before, the fact that she had spent time in Paris, maybe with Zoltan, and that she had gone after her arrest to Marseilles. How far was Saint-Tropez, where she had been with Ian, from Marseilles? A few hours by car. Caryl hadn't said anything about Marseilles. There were gaps in her life history which she had not even bothered to explain away. "Oh, I traveled around," she said. "I met Ian. He was with the BBC. I worked with him." In Marseilles? And now it struck me that at no time during the talk with Laszlo had Eva Korbut evidenced any surprise. It was as though she had known all of it for a long time.

As she bent to turn the starter key, I said: "I think you're with the police."

"Oh?" She started the car and stared straight ahead. "And what makes you think so?"

"You knew it all, before we went there."

She gave me a gauging look. "You wish me to show you something of Budapest, yes? Perhaps the grand boulevard, the city park. It is very nice walking in the park, or the Horvath Gardens."

"Fine," I said.

In the park, we walked among lemon and orange trees, in bud, but not yet in bloom. When no one was within earshot, she said: "Batory advised you not to go near Czepel. I agree. It would serve the purpose of certain ones for you to locate him, but I like you. You're an innocent. Maybe you're lucky if your wife left you. Think of that. You understand what I'm saying?"

"Not altogether."

"I shouldn't be telling you this," she said, her voice distressed, "but you plan to keep looking for Czepel. Don't."

"What don't I know?" I asked. "There's something else."

I took her hand, and she let it remain in mine.

"Is there something we—I—don't know? We could make a trade." She looked up at me, her brown eyes appealing.

She was cleverer than I was, I began to think. This walk we were taking was not so much to reveal information privately to me, as to extract additional information from me.

"About Caryl, or Czepel?"

"Czepel interests me more," she said.

"What do I get in exchange?"

"A few facts. They won't do you any good, but you should know them."

"Then why should we talk further?"

"Because we're friends now. Aren't we friends?"

"All right, friends. There's a possibility Caryl was seen with Czepel."

"Where?"

"Paris. Someone saw her sitting in a bar with a man. Maybe it was Czepel, maybe it wasn't. I'm going to find out. I've got to know."

"And the bar," she said, "where was it?"

If the Hungarians, I thought, were all that anxious for the information, all they had to do was query Delahaye, unless, it occurred to me, this was too delicate a matter for official contact with the French police.

"You mentioned an exchange," I said.

"This, you never heard from me. Is that clear between us?"

I nodded.

"Czepel killed a Hungarian attaché in Milan in 1962."

"I'm already aware," I said, "that he's not a very nice man. I'll be careful. But you're sure it was Czepel?"

"The gun used was the same as the one that shot the border guard Batory spoke of."

"Then he has political feelings."

"No."

She told me more, and it deepened my depression. It was all so garish and unlikely that Caryl could have been involved in it, and I didn't want Czepel, unless he somehow led to Caryl. I was becoming more and more certain that Caryl had stayed with him for a time out of gratitude, or perhaps involvement in the circumstances of the escape. After 1963, she had had no more to do with him, and until then he had merely used her. But a murder had occurred in Milan, and I had been in Milan, and there I had learned where Caryl had gone. Coincidence, I thought, but I prayed there would not be too many of them.

Eva Korbut said: "In investigating the circumstances, it turned out that our attaché was engaged in financial manipulations. Apparently Czepel was an agent in this. Hungarian currency was being hugely discounted, leaving the country in return for deposits of hard currency in other countries, Switzerland particularly. The attaché was perhaps too greedy and so . . . When Czepel was caught in London, the British refused to extradite him on political grounds. It is a complicated case, and my feeling is that you have merely wandered into it because of your wife. You understand, now, what I'm saying?"

"To get out of it and stay out."

"It's been a nice little walk," she said. "And I hope someday to come to New York, in which case I will take the liberty of looking you up. But now I think I should take you back to your hotel."

18

The man in the black-belted raincoat was waiting for me as I passed through customs at Orly. He was by the gate, and I had already noticed him staring at me. He had even given me a slight nod of recognition.

"Mr. Parrish?"

I stopped. He had the look of police about him. With a practised gesture he flashed an identification card.

"Ferencz," he said. "From the legation. They informed you I would meet you?"

"Who?"

"You have arrived from Budapest, have you not?" He looked a little puzzled, as though I should have known about this, and, somewhere along the line, communication had gone awry.

"Well, what is it?"

I was in a hurry to get back to the city and the hotel. Marie must have arrived by now, and she would have with her those letters that Caryl had locked away.

Ferencz was darkly good-looking, with a long, lean nose, and thin lips. His dark hair was close-cropped; he would have looked more to type in a uniform. Eva Korbut, I guessed, hadn't wasted any time getting in touch with people here.

"A little talk, that's all. We can be of mutual assistance. On the floor above, in the café, we can have coffee. A cognac, if you prefer." His smile was friendly, almost appealing, as though we were brothers of a kind and must assist one another.

"How'd you recognize me?"

"Oh," he said. "Easy enough. I have your description, your time of arrival."

Indeed, it would have been easy. All Eva Korbut had to do was learn the time I left Budapest and telephone Paris. And they, the Hungarians, were acknowledging that I had sources of information they didn't have. But how bona fide was the offer of help? If they only wanted Czepel, good enough; but, if they were after Caryl, too . . . No harm, I decided, in listening.

I followed him to an escalator. We went to the quick-service café, taking a table by the windows that overlooked the ramps and runways. He ordered us coffee.

In the clear afternoon light, I noticed that his bright eyes had large black pupils; I also noticed that when his lips smiled, his eyes did not.

"We wish to make an informal arrangement with you," he said.

"Who's 'we'?"

"Call it a branch of the legation. We don't advertise."

"You're Hungarian."

"Yes, of course. I assumed you knew. We already know a considerable amount about you."

"So, you're following me around?"

"Not exactly. But we keep ourselves informed, because what interests you interests us. You have been to Budapest, but we also know you visited Milan and Geneva. You see? But we don't know the exact reasons for these trips."

They hadn't, at least, followed me to Saas Fee, and maybe that was what puzzled them. Where had I been between Milan and Geneva? Torelli was not one of them, then, and that disposed of the Milan connection.

"I don't think you have much to offer me," I said.

He smiled, but again his eyes didn't smile.

"You're searching for your wife," he said. "We don't want her, I assure you. But we do want Czepel. Very much. You see?"

"I don't want Czepel," I said. "That's your business, not mine. Unless . . ."

"Ah," he said, as though I was at last seeing the light. "That is precisely the point."

The coffee was put before us, and I sipped mine, black and bitter. He left his untouched.

"If," he went on, "her absence is connected with Czepel, whereabouts unknown, then our interests are very much tied together. I thought, perhaps, in Budapest, this would have been made clear to you."

Odd, I thought. Eva Korbut had more than implied that I should give up looking for Czepel. Perhaps she was a friend, after all. She had done her business, her duty, but had thought best to warn me.

"So, you're proposing?"

"Only that we remain in contact. What we learn about Czepel and his whereabouts, we give to you. The leads to your wife, you give to us. You see, that way we work together. No wasted ground. We do the looking for Czepel. You, your wife. Maybe, it is possible, we will find them together. What do you think?"

He looked at me sharply.

"I don't have any reason to think so." Not enough reason, I told myself, not yet. But Czepel had gotten out of prison a month or so ago, and a man called Alvarez had listed her name with a code number, possibly a secret account somewhere. I was beginning to waver, to wonder if Caryl was again tied up in some way with Czepel. If there was money, or valuables hidden away somewhere, it could account for her disappearance. But then, why Saas Fee, and why a blonde woman called Grete? It was as though I had entered a tunnel, only to find myself in a maze of other tunnels. And each one leading to where? For balance, all I had was my faith in Caryl, an intimacy that was closer and better than anything I had known before. Feeling, I thought, against reason. But as a lawyer, I knew well enough how easily the false could be made to appear reasonable.

"I'm suggesting mutual cooperation," Ferencz said. "Quite unofficial, of course. Admitted, I, we, are hampered by diplomatic niceties. But you, not at all."

"I don't see that I have anything to gain. Czepel is a police matter, not mine."

"You're saying you don't want to find him?"

I hesitated. "Only if he can clear up anything about my wife."

"So we have something in common. You've admitted it."

It was as though he was arguing me into a corner. I said querulously, "You haven't told me a thing I don't know. This conversation is useless."

"All right," he said, with a resigned expression. "I will give you something. You've heard of the Marcel group?"

Something made me lie. With a straight face, I said, "No." But Delahaye had also mentioned the Marcel group, and here it was a second time. I waited with a poker face, while he scanned my expression. "What's something called the Marcel group got to do with it?" I asked.

"Czepel," he said, as though imparting information of great value, "is one of them. I assure you, this is an important fact."

"Czepel's been in prison," I said.

"Yes, yes." His voice turned impatient. "We know that. Unfortunately, we did not learn of his release until too late, or we would have been there. He gave us the slip. He's good at it."

"But already he's joined some gang. Is that what you're saying?"

"The gang, as you call it, has existed for many years. Czepel was part of it before. We see no reason why he wouldn't return to it."

"I still don't see what this has to do with my wife."

"She, too, could be part of it," he said.

"The gang?"

Suddenly, with great clarity, I saw it couldn't be so. Caryl part of a gang? Maybe once, unwittingly, but not now.

"The gang, as you call it, is quite respectable. You wouldn't think political people could belong, but they do. To function, they require camouflage."

"You mean, like that fellow in Milan, the attaché?"

I asked the question deliberately. How much did he really know?

"Exactly," he said. "It came out, after his execution."

"Execution?"

"Call it that, from their viewpoint."

"And Czepel was—the executioner?"

"So we think."

I still wasn't sure this man was genuine. And, if he was testing me, I was also going to test him.

"With what reason?" I asked.

"The bullets," he said, "were traced to a certain gun. A gun that was once in the possession of Czepel."

I tired of the game. And I was certainly not going to tell him anything unless I learned something from him I did *not* know.

"I'm afraid I've got to go, Mr. Ferencz."

He held up a hand. "A moment, please. It's possible you'll change your mind. And you'll wish to contact me."

"If so, how?"

"Here is a telephone number." He wrote it on a slip of paper and handed it to me.

At the concierge's desk I learned that Marie had already been checked in and had been given the room next to mine.

She opened the door and for just a moment examined me with the eye of a practiced secretary assessing her boss's mood. Then she dispensed with such protocol, and we hugged each other. After three years of seeing her daily, I knew her wardrobe pretty well, but the dress she wore was new, and she'd had her hair done, and it made her round face, with its pert little nose, quite pretty. It can be said that we were fond of each other, perhaps more than that, and there had been times before meeting Caryl when I'd had the notion that Marie would be a good person to marry. She was bright but not intellectual, and while she didn't make a display of her devotion to me, I always felt it was there. Why not? Maybe we were *too* familiar with each other; neither of us would have had any mystery about the other. She had been born and raised in some part of Brooklyn with row houses, and liked living there now. I always thought about Marie that she would make someone a good wife, and maybe that was the trouble. At least for me.

But that very familiarity, the sense of middle class solidity she brought with her, warmed me now.

"This room," she said, when we went inside. "I've never seen anything *like* it. And I saw what it costs. You didn't have to put me here."

"Nonsense," I said. "Any secretary of mine deserves the best."

I explained I'd been in Budapest for the past two days, that

I'd learned a little more, but only enough to make the puzzle worse.

"What's your feeling?" she asked. "Wherever she is, is she all right?"

"She's alive and presumably well," I said. "That much I know. I've got to face the possibility that she just took off suddenly and left me, for reasons unknown."

"You look tired, Steve," Marie said. "I'd better order some coffee."

I nodded and took one of the brocaded Louis XVI chairs. I might have been in my own room, except that everything faced the opposite way.

While at the phone, she said: "I had your calls transferred to me. That O.K.?"

"Who called? Anyone?"

"Mr. Graham. He's leaving for New York and he wanted to know if he could do anything for you. And, oh, I brought you some of the more important office messages. I can handle them, if you tell me what, and there was a man who didn't give his name. He said he understood you were on a trip to Vienna and Budapest. I didn't tell him anything. Were you in Vienna?"

I shook my head. If it was Ferencz who had called, why would he have asked about Vienna? True, I'd thought of going there, but it seemed too much of a long shot to go around asking about someone called Grete. And, if he was in touch with people in Budapest, he would have known my plane connections. It suddenly struck me that, by being here, Marie was involved, more than I wanted her to be.

"Did he ask who you were?"

"I said I was taking your messages, that's all."

"Marie," I said. "Don't give anyone information without checking it with me."

"But, I didn't," she said.

"This thing is complicated," I said. I was about to add, "and perhaps dangerous," but thought better of it. "And some odd types are poking into it, I don't know quite why."

She gave me an almost scoffing look, as though to say she knew me well enough so that I didn't have to hold things back from her. "You'd better tell me," she said, "what it's all about. Caryl is mixed up in something you don't like, isn't that it?"

"I'd like to get at those letters," I said. I was nagged, though, by the feeling that I ought to get in touch with Delahaye, that he should know I'd been met at the airport by a man who knew about Czepel and who connected him with the Marcel group. "But I should make a call."

"Are you going to tell me or aren't you?"

"Yes, but try this number first, and ask for Inspector Delahaye. How's your French?"

"Good enough to ask for Inspector Delahaye," she said tartly.

But, as she went toward the telephone, it rang. She answered and handed it to me. "Speak of the devil," she said.

"So," Delahaye said, when I took the phone. "What news, Mr. Parrish?"

"Not too much," I said. "I've got a bit more stuff on Czepel, and I was met at the airport by a man from the Hungarian legation. Undercover fellow of some kind. But the reason I'm calling is this: he claimed that Czepel is still part of the Marcel group. Mean anything?"

"Yes," he said, "it does. Will you be at your hotel?"

"Yes."

"Then I'll be there in twenty minutes. The same room?"

"Next door, in my secretary's room."

"I see," he said. "You have a secretary."

He made it sound as though a secretary was something more than that.

19

Delahaye's round posterior made a large indentation on the bed in Marie's room. Gazin stood, his back to the window, covertly looking at Marie, thinking perhaps that this American lawyer knew how to take care of himself with his wife running around Europe somewhere. But it was the Marcel group, more than further word of my wife, that had brought them here in such a hurry. I had told them of meeting Ferencz, repeated the conversation between us with fair accuracy.

"I think," Delahaye said, "we should consider the possibility that this Ferencz has valuable information about the Marcel group."

"I'm looking for my wife," I reminded him. "Not something called the Marcel group. Just what is it, anyway?"

"A clever organization," he said, "headed, so far as we know, by someone called—or who calls himself—Marcel. Sometimes the operations cease, a year, two years, then suddenly it's active again. It's active now. Respectable people, so they seem, show up at banks to cash checks, bank drafts of large amounts, or large sums leave Italy, no one knows how, and suddenly they show up in France or Switzerland. The group handles drugs, too. A large shipment appears in France, from where we don't know. Gold, too. In London, someone has gold to sell that was not known about before. How does it cross borders? Where we've caught people, when we break them, they sometimes mention Marcel, but they don't know who he is. Always, there are intermediaries. We get their names, and they don't exist. Or do they? Where is the business done? How? All we know is that it *is* done, that spectacular amounts are sometimes involved, enough to affect currency exchange rates. So, your Ferencz makes sense. I'd like to meet him."

"He won't have anything to do with the police. He made that clear."

"It also makes sense," Delahaye said, his mustache drooping, his eyes sad, "that your wife could be with them, the group. That she rejoined them. She was seen in Switzerland, in Saas Fee. Last heard from, she was in Geneva. Most interesting, Geneva. A center for many such transactions."

My anger rose.

"If my wife is to be regarded as a criminal," I said, "I want no part of this."

"Material witness," Gazin suddenly snapped. "No charges. Material witness."

"Where do you go next?" Delahaye asked me, his glance at me keen.

"I have a couple of avenues to explore. I'm not sure yet."

"You don't wish to tell me?"

"No."

"Why not?"

"Because I don't want you or your people poking into it and scaring her off."

"Mr. Parrish," Delahaye said, shaking his head, as though I was a man who would simply not listen to reason. "Help us this much. Put us in touch with Ferencz."

"How?"

"Arrange to meet him. I, or Gazin, will be close by."

"You're asking me to set him up for you."

"For our mutual benefit."

Precisely, I thought, what Ferencz had said. Both he and Delahaye wanted me to do their skulking around for them.

"All right," I said. "But I'm not hanging around Paris."

"He gave you a telephone number. Call him now. Tell him you have decided to talk further with him. Arrange to meet him."

"Want me to call?" Marie asked. She actually seemed to be enjoying this; her face was alive with the thrill of what looked to her like intrigue.

"You're staying out of it," I said.

I asked the switchboard operator to get me the number, and my call was answered by a female voice in French. Monsieur Ferencz was not there, she said, but she would relay any message. An answering service, apparently. I asked the woman to tell Ferencz to call me at the hotel as soon as possible.

"A cautious duck," Delahaye said. "He doesn't like people to know where he hangs out."

The return call came within five minutes. Evidently the service had been able to contact him or had instructions to do so. Ferencz, in his way, was well organized.

"I've decided," I said, "to discuss the matter further with you."

"Good. When?"

"Well, later this evening?"

"All right. Ten o'clock. You know the Pont Royal Hotel?"

"On the Rue du Bac?"

"Yes. Further down, on that same street, is a small bar. Les Amis is the name. If you'll be there at ten, I will join you. The police, of course, are not to know about this. Is it understood?"

"Understood," I said.

"Just the two of us, as associates."

"All right."

"Ten o'clock, then," he said, and hung up.

Ten o'clock was four hours away. I had time to look through the letters Marie had brought and get something to eat.

Delahaye, in a low voice, was giving Gazin instructions. He turned to me.

"It's arranged," he said. "Gazin will be there. Give no sign of recognition. A car will be outside the bar with two officers. We'll pick him up as soon as he joins you."

"Then what?"

"That's all. I'll be in touch with you in the morning. Don't worry. We'll make it appear as though we were tailing you."

I didn't like it. I didn't like it at all. It wasn't my line. But if Ferencz did have information that could be useful to me, Delahaye was far better equipped to get it out of him than I was, and there was the advantage of not having to trade what I knew of Caryl and her movements.

"One other thing," Gazin said, as both were about to leave. "Should he appear suspicious and not approach you, give me a sign, so I'll know him."

"A kiss on the cheek?"

Gazin took it straight. "Signal to the waiter," he said.

When they were gone, I went through the letters, four of them written in German and signed "Grete." Clearly I was onto something. But I couldn't read the scrawled handwriting, other than the dates. Marie called the hotel desk to ask about a translator and found that no one would be available until morning. There were also two letters written in Hungarian, one from Budapest and the other mailed from London. The one from Budapest was signed "Laszlo"—her brother, obviously. The date showed it to have been written in May 1968. The other must have been from her relatives in England.

The French clippings I was able to read. They were cut from newspapers published in Marseilles and Nice, and the dates on them were in April 1968. *Englishman Dead in Car Crash,* one of the headlines read.

She had kept the clippings about the accident that had killed her former fiancé. Sentimental value, I supposed. But something in them riveted me. The police were investigating, because of suspicious circumstances. I read the text more carefully. An Englishman, Ian Cameron, a British film director, had been found dead in his car on the coastal road between Saint-Tropez and Nice. The car had gone out of control on a bend, crashed to some rocks some fifty yards below, and burned. A certain disfigurement of the body was the cause of the police investigation.

"My God," I said, almost involuntarily.

Marie's voice was concerned. "What is it?"

I had come across another headline: *Police Reveal Murder of Englishman.*

A sick feeling gripped me. One more for the list of what Caryl had *not* told me. She'd said that Ian, her fiancé, had died in a car crash. But she had held back the fact that it was murder.

Through several of the clippings, the details emerged. It had been ascertained that the victim had died prior to the accident. It was theorized that someone in the car with him had faked the crash. The perpetrator was unknown, nor was there any indication of a motive for the killing.

Police Baffled: the last headline in the little pile.

In the text of this clipping, I found Caryl's name mentioned. The Englishman's fiancée, Caryl Batory, was in a Saint-Tropez hospital, still in shock. The sea expedition, a marine documentary, that was to be made by Cameron under the aegis of the marquis de Carenne, owner of the yacht *Pantagruelle,* was now canceled because of the death of the director. All associated with the expedition had been questioned, but no clues to the killing had been found.

"You dropped one," Marie said.

I looked down. It was the smallest of the clippings, no more than an inch long. A counterfeiter had been arrested in Marseilles. I knew the name before I read it. Zoltan Czepel had been picked up at a small hotel; in his room were found forged traveler's checks. He was in jail, awaiting trial. That was all. But Caryl had saved that clipping, too, placing it with the others about Ian. Her way of saying there was a connection? But what kind? Had she and Czepel planned the killing of Ian together? Or, was it her way of pointing to Czepel?

At a quarter to ten I took a taxi to the Pont Royal Hotel on Rue du Bac. It sped me there, across the Seine, in ten minutes. I felt queasy about this, taking a man unaware, probably submitting him to some pretty rough questioning. Ferencz had offered me a kind of quid pro quo, in good faith, for all I knew. He wanted Zoltan, I wanted Caryl, Delahaye wanted Ferencz because he appeared to have knowledge about the Marcel group—all very tenuous. It seemed to me I was wasting time. Couldn't I have arranged it better? Groping, I thought, always groping. Questions raised that led to more questions.

I had a few minutes, and I sauntered along the Rue du Bac, looking for the police vehicle that would be not far from the bar.

I saw it, parked innocuously enough on the far side of the street, one man inside at the wheel, another looking under the raised hood, as though seeking the cause of engine trouble. A little obvious, I thought. Ferencz, if he was at all suspicious, would notice that, too.

The bar was on a corner of a small side street. The name, Les Amis, was lettered on a window. The interior was dim. When I entered, I saw Gazin standing, his back to me, at the zinc bar, a glass of beer in front of him. There was a mirror above the bar, and, in all likelihood, he saw me. I looked around, saw no one who resembled Ferencz. A *fille d'joie* sat at one of the iron-legged tables and eyed me with invitation. I took one of the tables and seated myself so that I could see the entrance. There were perhaps a dozen persons, all told, in the bar. A waiter approached me. I asked for beer, and he brought it to me.

At a few minutes past ten, the door swung open and Ferencz came in. His glance swept the room and rested on me. Then he came toward me, and, as he did so, I rose, as though to greet him. Gazin swung round at that moment, and, with what seemed almost like a bound, came toward us, barking, "Police." Ferencz shook his head sadly at me, then said to Gazin: "Your *carte d'identité,* please."

Gazin reached in his pocket, and, as he did so, I saw a flash of metal. Ferencz made a sweeping gesture, a curving movement that brought the knife in his hand beneath Gazin's chin. The room seemed to freeze. What was happening was unbelievable. I had to put it together . . . the look of utter surprise on Gazin's face . . . the wide, deep gash across his throat . . . the blood spurting . . . and slowly, slowly, Gazin toppling to the floor. My own knees went weak. I clutched the back of a chair for support. The prostitute shrieked. And I caught a glimpse of Ferencz running, disappearing through a back door. It was only then that my presence of mind returned enough for me to run to the front entrance and yell to the men across the street. One of them stopped tinkering under the hood of the car and raced to the bar. The other followed. The bar patrons were gathered around Gazin's prone form. I saw enough. Gazin's eyes were wide open, staring, still with that look of surprise. He had not expected to die.

Later, hours later, I was in Delahaye's small office on the third floor of the police headquarters on the Rue des Saussaies. I had been taken there by the two plainclothesmen, but only after a police surgeon had arrived, determined the cause of death, and allowed Gazin's body to be removed. I'd had to wait outside the office, while Delahaye completed a conversation with several other officers, some uniformed, some in plain clothes. One remained behind when I entered. He took a seat behind a small desk on which was a stenotype machine.

Delahaye looked tired. His eyes were sunken more deeply than ever in fat folds of skin. His large stomach sagged and strained the buttons of his dark gray jacket.

He looked up at me, almost covertly, but I knew it was to hide his feelings of chagrin, remorse, sorrow, anger.

"Mr. Parrish, I must ask you to repeat all you know about this man, Ferencz, after which you will please give us your movements after I and . . . Gazin . . . left the Plaza Athenée. That would be a few minutes after six o'clock this evening."

The officer at the desk began clacking away on the stenotype machine. I spoke carefully, my voice accompanied by the dull, clacking sound. I described my entire day, my arrival from Budapest, the meeting with Ferencz. Delahaye sat on the edge of a larger desk, listening with a glum expression. He knew it all, but it had to go on the record.

After the first shock, during the waiting, my mind had cleared. I knew that Delahaye would try to connect Caryl with the murder of his associate, if only as one lead to follow. I wasn't going to get her into this. And, it was for that reason, and because of my instinctive feeling that she could in no way be part of something so ugly, that I explained Marie's presence in Paris as business. She had brought me some office papers, I said, that required my attention.

I also stated very clearly, for the record, "You asked me to meet with Ferencz, although it was against my wishes."

Delahaye directed his remarks to the stenotypist. "Because this man, Ferencz, made mention of the Marcel group, it was my plan to question him. I take responsibility for the decision. I requested the subject to meet with the suspect and arranged for Gazin to be at the beforementioned bar, Les

Amis. . . . Please continue, Mr. Parrish."

I described the happening in the bar.

"When," Delahaye asked, "did you first notice the knife in the suspect's hand?"

"I saw a flash of metal," I said, "and didn't realize at first it was a knife."

"Can you describe the weapon?"

"Not really. It happened so fast. I saw the movement, and the blood. He ran, that is, Ferencz ran to the rear of the bar. . . ."

"Which," Delahaye interrupted, "he had apparently reconnoitered in advance. The rear door led to a WC, which had a window leading out on Rue Mal Fleurs. It has been learned that the window was open or was opened by the culprit, and by that means he made his escape. The entire area was combed, and no witnesses were found to indicate the direction he took. One passerby stated he heard the sound of a motorcycle starting. . . ."

I gave Delahaye a quick glance, and he nodded soberly.

"It is possible," he added, "that the culprit made his escape by such means."

Delahaye sniffed a few times, as though to clear his sinuses.

"Is there anything further you can remember from your earlier conversation with Ferencz?"

"I've given it all to you," I said.

I wanted desperately to push from my mind the recurring image of that slash across Gazin's throat, but it kept forcing its way back and, with it, a similar image: the man, Caryl's fiancé, found in a car wreck, his throat slashed. But to bring that up, to have it on an official statement, with further consequences for Caryl—I couldn't do it, not until I knew more than I really wanted to know.

"One more thing," Delahaye said. "I have here a photograph—a wire photo, actually. Can you identify this subject?"

The face was a bit blurry but recognizable. A number was

placarded just below the face, younger than Ferencz, but definitely him.

"That's Ferencz," I said. "I'm positive."

Delahaye looked at the stenotypist and said in a flat, dull voice: "Mr. Parrish identifies as Ferencz the former prisoner known as Zoltan Czepel."

20 LONDON AND PARIS, OCTOBER 1960

Letters from Zoltan came infrequently, mailed from different places. He was traveling a lot, he would say in the letters, written sometimes in Hungarian and, after a while, in English, as though showing off to her his command of languages. He was doing well, he claimed, and was back in the banking business, but not small stuff this time. As soon as he could, he would come to see her, and he assured her of his continuing love.

Living in London had not proved up to her expectations. Her uncle, Josef Nadasy, was a perpetually tired man in his fifties who worked as a silversmith in a grimy factory in the Lambeth district and had a nagging cough that never seemed to let up. Her aunt, Judit, a blood relative on her mother's side, spent most of her time scrubbing and cleaning the small two-story row house in Richmond. A chronic complainer and worrier about money, Aunt Judit had quickly scotched her ambition to renew her ballet training. Instead, she was sent to a secretarial school that offered quick courses in typing and shorthand. She would have to pay her part of the expenses, she was told, for food did not come cheaply, and, if she weren't there, her room would be let out to someone else.

She found a job in Bermondsey at an estate agent's office, typing up leases, eviction notices, and various other forms. Luckily, the English she had learned during her school years in Budapest helped her to accommodate quickly to living and working in London. It was a thing she was good at by now—learning languages.

But she also realized that she was hardly better off, and perhaps worse off, than if she had remained in Budapest. She thought often of returning, but letters from her brother Laszlo discouraged her out of the notion of ever going back, and the memory of that flash and sharp explosion at the border crossing still haunted her. Now and then she went to movies or the theater with a young rental agent in the estate office, who would take her to a pub afterward for beer, and whose breath, when he took her home, was so foul that she refused him so much as a kiss at parting. An assistant manager who was married wanted to take her out, but she knew that wasn't a good idea, considering the gossipy atmosphere of the office.

When Zoltan finally arrived in London, it was almost as though he had come from the clouds to rescue her from a dreary existence. She found him, sitting in the small living room in the Nadasy house, when she came home from work one gray late afternoon in October. Her aunt Judit, after a disapproving sniff, left them and retreated to the kitchen.

His clothes were impeccable, and his lean face was more darkly good-looking than ever. He had the look of success about him. His dark gray flannel suit with a faint vertical stripe running through it appeared to have been fitted to him by an expensive tailor. When he shot his starched white cuffs, gold links appeared.

"I'm taking you to Paris," he said, after she gave him a fervent greeting.

He held her off from him and looked her over with approval.

"You're beautiful," he said admiringly. "You're really beautiful. Put on your best dress. We're going to dinner."

He took her to the Savoy Grill, a place she had never been before. Even her best dress looked second-rate when she compared herself with the expensively dressed women at the other tables. Zoltan improved matters when he pulled out a gift for her. It was a chain-link gold necklace with a heart-shaped pendant studded with tiny rubies and diamonds.

He told her over dinner that he was connected with a big businessman in Paris whose name was Bernard Halmos. He was a kind of broker, whose trade was international. "All sorts of things," Zoltan said vaguely. "Consignments of this and that. He's a middleman. He can use a receptionist who knows languages."

"But I don't know French," she said. "Just a few courses I took in Budapest."

"You'll pick it up," he told her confidently. "And I'll bet the pay is four times what you're getting here."

He wanted to know her passport situation, and she told him she had obtained an international passport from the British, designed for refugees, though it was not good for travel in any of the eastern countries.

"We both want to stay away from those, anyway," he said with a grin. "Don't ever tell anyone, but you know how many passports I have?" He held up a hand showing three fingers. "I need them for business," he explained.

She agreed to go with hardly any hesitation, though she wanted to know how she would arrange it with her aunt and uncle. She gave them half her small salary each week.

"I'll take care of that," he said.

Her aunt Judit made only one small gesture of protest. "Your brother wouldn't like it," she said, "going off with that Zoltan."

But the opposition came to an end when Zoltan handed her an envelope containing a hundred British pounds.

Within a week, she had her first view of Paris.

Compared to London, the new city sparkled with life and beauty. At night the Arc de Triomphe glowed as though lit from within. Zoltan, after picking her up at the airport—he had left ahead of her—took her to a small apartment just off of Avenue Kléber. "It's not mine," he explained, "but I have the use of it when I'm here in Paris. You can stay here until we find you a place."

The apartment was cozy and comfortable. She had to walk up four flights to get to it, but once inside she felt she was in a little world of her own. Whoever had furnished it had been Russian. Little icons were on tables and on a mantel over a fireplace. The bedroom had a wide bed, with a pink quilted cover, and it was the softest she had ever slept on. Lovemaking with Zoltan was like a luxury now, ever so leisurely and fulfilling. He would stay with her here, he said, whenever he was in Paris. They couldn't think of marrying yet—he had so many big deals looming in the future—but when they did marry, they would be fixed for life. They would have all the good things.

"What are the good things?" she asked him. She hoped he

would say having love was one of the good things, if not the best of all.

But he replied: "Money, and a handsome villa somewhere, and good clothes, and jewels, and perfume, and good wines, and the best food. Sun when we want it and snow in the winter and not having to take shit from anyone."

It sounded nice, but she thought she could do well enough without all those things, as long as she had someone to love.

Bernard Halmos, whom she met the next day, was tall, heavy, in his late forties, almost entirely bald. Some grayish brown hair remained at the sides of his head and that was all. His manner was somewhat gruff, but he was immaculately turned out and gave off an odor of musky cologne. It turned out that she wouldn't be a receptionist right away, but she would be very helpful to him, he assured her, because of her knowledge of English and German. He gave her a desk in an office with four other young women. Correspondence in German and English was her special responsibility. An older woman, whose name was Madame Clamart was her supervisor, and treated her with almost fond politeness.

That, she gathered, was because Halmos and Zoltan had business together. Zoltan visited the office a few times and always was immediately closeted with Halmos in a large inner office. Her monthly salary was given to her in advance, and, when she calculated it in terms of pounds, she was surprised at how much it was. Zoltan stayed only a week in Paris, but during that week he found her a pleasant little studio flat not far from Parc Monceau, a lovely part of Paris. The studio was on the ground floor of the inner courtyard of a five-story apartment building. It was almost like having a little house of her own.

Five evenings a week she took French courses at an institute on Avenue Mac-Mahon, and she studied the language religiously on weekends after Zoltan went away on one of his trips. He gave her the address of an apartment in Zurich where she could contact him if need arose. So much of his business was confidential, he said, that he didn't like to talk about it, not even to her.

But she was happy, happier than she had ever been. The

lovemaking, when Zoltan would reappear, became necessary to her, and at times was like a fever of need. There were times when she could hardly wait for him to come back.

The strange thing about her job was that she never quite knew what kind of dealings Halmos was engaged in. The letters spoke of shipments and arrangements for payments through this or that bank in Hamburg, or Cologne, or Geneva. But the shipments were invariably identified with numbers, such as "Allotment 2365 B/Cologne, refer to letter of August 7, 60 concerning lot 7721L." They made no sense to her. The clearest it ever got was when a letter would come saying, "Shipment received, discount in effect." And, really, that made little sense to her either.

She once asked Madame Clamart what the goods were that Monsieur Halmos dealt in; she was told that they had to do with what were called job lots, and might involve anything from shipments of woolens to consignments of automobile parts, but that she shouldn't concern herself with such matters, because it was all too complicated. It was not long after she made the query that she was taken away from her desk and given a new one in the receptionist's office. There she answered the telephone, greeted visitors, and worked a small switchboard, which wasn't difficult. Some of the connections on the switchboard were to what she gathered was a warehouse outside of Paris. The separation of mail was her responsibility, too. Much of it, she found, although she didn't open any of it, had addresses of banks in Switzerland, West Germany, and Italy.

Her own salary was invariably paid in cash, French francs. She also learned that she had none of the benefits of French working people. This was because she did not yet have a working permit, and she was advised by Madame Clamart that it would be better not to apply for one, because, in that case, her salary would have to be reduced. Halmos, when he came in, would greet her in a friendly but rather distant way, and it occurred to her that it was for Zoltan's sake that he had given her employment. But when one day she greeted him in her newly learned French, he smiled and gave her an approving pat on the shoulder.

She had worked at the office for four months when one day

Zoltan came in, after a three-week absence, and told her he was taking her to Switzerland for a vacation. "Don't worry," he said. "I'll fix it with Halmos."

And that was the first of her many vacations with Zoltan, who had stretches of time when he didn't have to do business. On that first one, she went with him for two weeks to Saint-Moritz. They stayed in a pleasant hotel called the Schweizerhof, and she learned to ski, and life had never been fuller.

Only one cloud remained. One night, after lovemaking, Zoltan asked her to see if she could find some cigarettes in the pocket of the jacket he had worn earlier, and, in looking for it in the closet, her hand brushed against something hard in another jacket. Curious, she felt inside the jacket, and there, in a holster attached to one of the sleeves, was a pistol.

"You still have a gun," she said to Zoltan reproachfully.

"Well," he said with a lazy smile, "I carry a lot of money on me sometimes. Just a precaution, if anyone tries to get it from me."

But she didn't like it. She didn't like the idea of a gun being around with them all the time. It reminded her too much of what had happened at the border crossing.

21

I slept late. It was a knock on my hotel room door that woke me. Marie stood there, regarding me critically.

"What is it?" I asked, my voice still hoarse from sleep.

"You look terrible, Steve," she said. "Are you all right?"

"I guess so."

She handed me the morning newspapers, left outside my door, and a sheaf of typewritten notes.

"What are those?" I asked.

"The translator came early," she said. "I knocked before, but you didn't wake up. Anyway, she's done them—the German letters, not the Hungarian ones. Want me to find someone who does Hungarian?"

"Not yet," I said. "Have you read the papers?"

"No, why?"

"Just wondered," I said vaguely.

I was alert enough to know that the best thing would be to get Marie out of Paris quickly, out of range of a murderous Zoltan Czepel.

"I want you back in New York," I said. "Make a plane reservation for today."

"Oh," she said, sounding disappointed.

Nothing, I saw, on the front pages of the *Tribune* or *Le Monde.*

"I was hoping," she said, "to spend a couple of days in London."

"All right," I said. "But get there fast."

"More trouble," she said, pressing her lips together.

"Yes," I said. "But I'll tell you about it later, after I've read the letters and had some coffee. Meanwhile, make that reservation to London, on an early plane."

She hesitated, then said, "O.K., I'll order your coffee."

Still in pajamas, I read the neatly typed translation of Grete's letters. Marie had arranged them in sequence. Three of them had been written in 1959 and mailed to a London address from different cities—Vienna, Munich, Hamburg. In them, Grete seemed merely to be reporting that she was working in different cafés, saving her money until she could afford to quit and open a shop of some kind. A fourth was mailed to a Paris address in the seventeenth arrondissement, a simple note saying she was now a hostess in a café in Heidelberg, where she was thinking of settling for a time. She had made a few friends, and she advised Caryl to get around more and not depend so much on Zoltan. I wasn't learning much.

A fifth letter seemed one of condolence. It had been mailed to a Hotel Metropole in Marseilles and was undated. "You must start a new life and forget about Zoltan," one of its sentences read. "He has brought you no good, and he is getting only what he deserves." The letter apparently referred to Caryl's arrest and the jailing of Zoltan in London. Again, little I didn't know, other than pinpointing Caryl's whereabouts in 1963 in Marseilles.

It was the last letter that gave me something relatively useful. It was recent, postmarked, February 5 of this year, from Berlin. I noticed my fingers shaking a bit. The waiter knocked at that moment, and I let him in with my coffee and croissants. I gulped some of the coffee black.

I read: "I am so happy to hear that you have at last found the man you want. Now the past is over, and you can begin to live as you should live. . . ." I thought, with a deep relief: that clinches it, it was something she wrote to her friend, something she must have meant. "Things have gone well for me, too. I am working in Berlin now (your letter was sent on to me from Heidelberg) and I have a partnership in a nightclub, where I act as the hostess. I doubt you will want to visit me there, so what I suggest is that we arrange to meet in Saas Fee if you are coming to the Continent. Remember the time we spent there so long ago? I still go there each year in March for three weeks of skiing (it keeps my hips and legs firm) and maybe we could have our reunion there. . . ."

And that explained why Caryl had headed for Saas Fee, though without me.

"But perhaps you will not want your husband to know that

your good friend once stripped herself for the benefit of old men and leering tourists, so, if you come together, we will just say I am an old friend from Vienna, now in business for herself in Berlin. In any case, I am happy you are forgetting all the bad things that happened in the past. As for the bad one, nothing has been heard of him. And, be assured, if he ever came to me, I would tell him nothing. Of course, if you did not want me to meet your new man, I would understand."

The letter was signed, "Lovingly, Grete."

And still no last name. But I knew this much, that Grete, a blonde woman, was a hostess in a Berlin nightclub. And I knew where I was going next.

22

I gave the doorman of the Parkhotel Zellermayer my bags and registered at the desk. I was known here. Twice before I had made trips to West Berlin, and each time had stayed at this pleasant hotel, adjacent to a small park where nursemaids sat on benches and gently rocked children in their carriages. My room was in the new wing, and with it came a gleaming, efficient bathroom.

Mark Eisler was the man I wanted to see. He was an Israeli who had done that rare thing—settled himself in West Berlin and flourished. He owned three nightclubs, a travel agency that arranged tours to Spain and the Balearic Islands, and an export business for certain Rhine and Moselle vintages. It was through this last that I had gotten to know him. If you knew Eisler, you were invariably well entertained, and there was probably no one in Berlin who knew the nightclub scene better. I found him in one of his offices, in the back section of the Saddle Club on the Kurfürstendamm.

He was tall and dapper, no older than I. He wore a turtleneck of pale blue cashmere, and a darker blue blazer with gold buttons, also cashmere. His shoes were polished cordovan Italian. He greeted me like a best friend who had been missing too long and immediately brought out a bottle.

"Schnapps," he said. "The best."

I downed the golden, mellow brandy, and told him I had some problems, delicate problems, and could use his help.

"Anything," Mark said, spreading his arms wide. "Ask it, my friend."

His eyes, though, set in the benevolence of his smile, were wise and shrewd.

"I need to locate a certain woman. Her name is Grete."

"Our phone book," he said, "lists perhaps twenty thousand Gretes. Could we narrow it down a little?"

"Well," I said, "figure her to be thirty-five, blonde, probably once a stripper. She now runs some kind of club here. Possibly she once used the name Gretchen, when she was a dancer. But she's a hostess now."

"Much simpler," he said. "You have described Grete Kellner, whose club is no more than half a mile from here. But may I ask what you want with a former stripper—except the usual?"

"Information."

"Legal business?"

"In a sense," I said.

"Her place is called Joie et Plaisir, touristy of course. It's on the Schleuterstrasse, just up from the Ku-damm."

"Would it be open now?"

"Not before nine."

"But she has a home address?"

"Let's see. . . ." He picked up a telephone book and scanned the listings. "Three Grete Kellners," he said. "But one lives in a working section where our Grete would certainly not live. Another is a Frau Kellner, and I have not heard that our Grete has a husband. So, it would be Grete Kellner of Soorstrasse 60, which is close to Sender Freies Berlin, our radio and television facility, a fairly good district. A taxi takes you there in ten, fifteen minutes. Unless you prefer to telephone her. I can have my secretary get her for you."

"No," I said, "I think I'll go there directly."

I had stood up, and now he stood up, too. He surveyed me smilingly, knowing I had told him next to nothing but discreet enough not to inquire further.

It was six o'clock. I sent up a mental prayer that I would find Caryl living with Grete Kellner at Soorstrasse 60, and stopped a cruising Mercedes taxi. I was let out at a building in one of the older apartment blocks; the stone facings of the buildings, all four stories high, had recently been painted gray. The entry to number sixty was modest, with bell buttons beside each name. There was the name. Kellner. My heartbeat quickened. How near was I now to Caryl?

I hesitated, then pushed the button opposite her name. I waited, nothing happened, neither a voice over the intercom or a clicking that would indicate that the lock on the door had been released. I tried the entryway door. It opened. I found myself in a hallway near an elevator.

I took the elevator up the second floor. Her apartment was listed as 2C. I found the door and pressed the bell button on it. I heard a tinkle inside, then a sound of movement. Footsteps approached the door, and it opened a crack. A gray-haired woman's face peered at me.

"I'm looking for Fraulein Kellner," I said.

The woman surveyed me, hesitant. From inside, I heard another woman's voice asking in German who was at the door.

"Tell her," I said, "it's Steven Parrish. I must speak to her."

The woman at the door spoke to the woman inside. My smattering of German was enough for me to know that she was telling Grete Kellner that I was an American gentleman, asking to see her.

The answering voice came plainly in English: "Tell him to go away."

"I must speak to her," I insisted. Through the open space I called loudly: "I must speak to you, Miss Kellner, about my wife, Caryl. I'll bring the police if you don't see me."

I waited; the response didn't take long. A blonde woman's face replaced the other. The features were chiseled; the eyes, wide and blue, studied me.

"What's this nonsense about the police?" she asked me, in nearly perfect English.

"I know very well you've been with my wife," I said.

"And what makes you think that?"

"You were seen with her in Saas Fee."

"I was, was I? Who told you that?"

"Is she here now?" I demanded.

She gave a toss of her head and opened the door wider. "Well, come in. She said she thought you'd be here sooner or later."

23

"Sit down, please," Grete Kellner said.

She had taken me through a hallway to a sitting room that seemed all soft sofas, chairs, and rugs that covered other rugs. Heavy draperies over the windows kept any last light of the day from entering the room. There was a faint musty odor, as though the room had had no airing.

I took one of the chairs, covered in burgundy-colored velvet, and sank deep down in it.

"Can I offer you something?"

She had on a long, loose dressing gown of gold-figured silk that had fallen slightly open at the neck. I had a glimpse of creamy flesh, of cleavage. Dittersdorf, in Saas Fee, had mentioned that her "magnificent bosoms" had caught his eye. They caught mine, too.

I said no thanks, and she seated herself on a couch opposite me. The dressing gown fell open at the knees, and I saw cream-colored, shapely legs. She was a full-bodied woman, but not plump. Her much too golden hair fell, long and straight, to her shoulders, outlining her face. Her eyes were blue, very large. Her red slippers had white puffs.

She felt in a pocket of the dressing gown and pulled out a packet of English cigarettes—Rothman's—offering me one.

I shook my head.

She lighted her cigarette, tossed the match into what looked like a small Grecian urn, and appeared to be examining me.

"Well?" she said. "You like my breasts?"

"What?"

"You're staring at them."

"Oh," I said, embarrassed and nettled at the same time. "Sorry."

She shrugged.

"Don't worry. I'm used to it. Anyway, if you're looking for Caryl, she isn't here."

"I won't take up your time," I said a little stiffly. The musty air in the room was being replaced by the scent of her perfume. She wore too much of it. "Just tell me where she is."

"How would I know that?"

"She was with you."

"Where?"

"Saas Fee."

"All right, I met her there, yes."

"And she came to Berlin with you?"

I had made it more of a question than a statement, and a look of knowledge came into her eyes. Then she released a stream of cigarette smoke and smiled broadly.

"So, this talk of police was a joke. You don't know anything. You're guessing. Why have you come to me?"

"I have a letter you wrote to her—from Saas Fee."

"Yes, I wrote a letter. I congratulated her on her marriage. A little too soon, yes?"

"Maybe not," I said, irked by her knowing expression.

"Still," she said, as though being philosophical about it, "it's better to find it out sooner than later. The longer you know someone, the messier it gets. Weeds grow. You can't get through them."

It was like pushing the stop button on the tape recorder too late. "Find out *what?* What did she find out, or what did I?"

"The mistake," she said, as though it was obvious. "But with marriage that happens ninety per cent of the time."

"Exact figures, of course."

"Well, look around you, at all your married friends. Are they happy? Maybe they pretend it's not so, but secretly, just as often not so secretly, they're dying to make love with someone else. I have made an actual count. Nine out of ten husbands have wanted to sleep with me—oh, they loved their wives, you understand, but marriage does get boring. You don't ask, do I accommodate them? Sometimes, maybe. And the wives . . . Anyway, never mind. Caryl has left you. Maybe she didn't like sleeping with you. Whatever it is, she did you a kindness. A clean break. No weeds."

"So you don't know," I said.

"You can't be too unhappy," she said. "I see you're still looking at my breasts."

"It falls open. The gown, I mean. Maybe you ought to pin it."

She gave me an amused stare. "I don't care. I've shown them since I was sixteen. Anyway, what's the good of telling you what she may have said? To hurt your feelings?"

"Tell me."

"She said she shouldn't have married a lawyer."

"Did she say why?"

"I understood what she meant."

"I don't."

"Naturally, you wouldn't. So careful never to say anything but the proper thing, fussy, self-important, no humor."

"Did she say those things?"

"Not exactly."

"So, let's disregard that, and get to the real reason why she's running away from me."

"You *do* sound like a lawyer," Grete said petulantly. She tapped the side of her head. "I can figure it out. She has a knack, Caryl has, for choosing the wrong men. So, for once, before it's too late, she's being sensible. I'll tell you what she told me: that you're jealous, that you couldn't forgive her past mistakes, that you are the worst kind of self-righteous American."

"She told you all that?"

"Most of it. I don't remember the exact words."

"If she told you that, she lied to you."

"To me? I'm the one she always trusted most."

Like the lawyer I was, I abandoned that line of questioning. "How long was she here with you?"

"Two days."

"And she left."

"Yes."

"Why?"

"She didn't tell me."

"Where did she go?"

"She didn't tell me that, either."

"So she trusts you more than anyone else," I said. "She doesn't tell you why she leaves, or where she's going."

"Just as well," Grete snapped, "considering all these questions you ask. I'm not the kind who pries into someone's personal business. She wanted to be free, so I helped her."

"How?"

I saw from her expression that she had let something slip out.

"I gave her a little money," she said, but it was an evasion. "She seemed afraid of you, so . . ."

"Of me?" I took a shot at it. "Or Zoltan Czepel?"

She nodded, as though she should have known it all along.

"So, you know about him. You're jealous of him. That explains it. There are pieces of my past I'm not proud of, either, but I certainly don't like people bringing it up to me. What I've done I've done, and it's finished. You should not have bothered her about that. She was so young, she didn't know anything. . . ."

"I didn't bother her about it," I said. "I didn't know about him then. So it couldn't have anything to do with Zoltan."

"You brought him up," she reminded me. "Anyway, this is boring. You won't learn anything from me that you don't know already. So, must we keep talking about it?"

"Grete," I said, "Caryl has given you a story, or you're giving me one. Anyway, I'm going to find her."

"Naturally," she said, with a toss of her head that shook her long blonde hair, "your side of it would be different. It's always that way. My advice to you is to forget her. She doesn't want to be your wife anymore. You're a good-looking man. There are others. You're tense. You should relax. You could try a doctor, or . . ." She suddenly looked demure. ". . . another woman."

Her dressing gown had fallen open again. Deliberately? If it hadn't altogether struck me before, it did now—she was available. Why not? Why not try that way?

It was as though she knew the notion was in my head.

"Allow me to offer you a brandy," she said. "We can have a little talk about other things—more pleasant things."

I caught a glimpse of a golden brown nipple.

"No," I said, confused, tempted to see what she was leading to, and at the same time wondering if there was some kind of trap here, something I wasn't yet aware of. "Your dressing gown . . ."

"Oh, yes," she said. "Careless of me. We hardly know each other, and already you know what I look like. But not bad, wouldn't you say?"

"Very nice," I said. "But I'm the kind of American who likes to take an attractive woman to dinner."

"You're offering me dinner?"

"Yes."

"Too bad," she said. "But I must go to my club soon. Perhaps you'd like to see the show?"

"Perhaps," I said. "What time does it begin?"

"Ten o'clock," she said. "And also at twelve and two."

"Tell me one thing," I said. "Is Caryl here, in Berlin?"

"I've already told you," she said. "I don't know. And, if I did, I wouldn't tell you. Now I'll tell you something else. When a man offers me dinner, I don't like for him to talk about other women. Understood?"

I stood up and held out my hand. She shook it.

"Thank you," I said.

"I may see you later?"

She seemed almost anxious that I come to her club.

"Very likely," I said.

I had time to kill. I entered one of the glass-enclosed cafés on the Kurfürstendamm and sat at a table that gave me a view of the sidewalk. A light drizzle had begun to fall. Lingering over a plate of wurst and a glass of dark beer, I gazed at the people passing by. Sooner or later, if one sat long enough, one would see almost everyone in Berlin. It was possible Caryl was still in the city. I was half in hope that I might see her.

It was nearly ten when I left the café and headed for Schleuterstrasse, which was a few streets away. The drizzle was still falling, and I turned up my collar against it. Dancing lights on one of the signs spelled out *Joie et Plaisir.* A signboard next to the entrance, had photographs of the entertainers. One of them showed Grete in top hat, dinner jacket, and black satin shorts that revealed full, shapely legs.

"The show begins in a few minutes," the doorman told me. "Very interesting entertainment."

I had already gathered that from some of the photographs; it was not too difficult to see that the performers were transvestites. Although bare, the arms and legs were decidedly muscular, knees a bit too knobby.

Inside, the place had a look of seedy elegance. The murals were painted caricatures of top-hatted but otherwise nude figures that might have been male or female. The banquettes against the walls had soft, velvet-covered seats. Near the entrance was a bar, attended by two muscular barmaids; a couple of men seated on stools gave off odors of exotic shaving lotions, and they gave me melting glances as I passed by. Most of the seated patrons, however, seemed to be tourists. Grete Kellner was nowhere in sight. A five-piece band at the side of a small, raised stage played something resembling a can-can.

A waiter led me to a table quite close to the stage. The din of the music was almost painful.

"Champagne, sir?"

"Whiskey and soda," I said.

"The minimum includes a bottle of champagne," he said. "You'll find it less expensive. Forty marks covers everything."

"Scotch."

"It's the same forty marks."

"I'll still have scotch."

He left after a shrug and was back hardly a minute or two later with a weak scotch and soda.

After a loud fanfare from the band, the lights dimmed, and Grete appeared on the spotlighted stage, dressed as in the photo display. She welcomed her guests in German, French, and English, and promised extraordinary entertainment. First was Christine, "straight from a triumph in Paris."

Christine was tall and stringy, and wore a blonde wig. Close to the stage as I was, it was easy enough to notice that "she" shaved not only her legs and arms, but her face. "She" danced about a bit and sang a suggestive French song, holding her hands to her well-stuffed brassiere.

When Grete returned to the stage after the number, she noticed me, and her nod of recognition included a mischievous wink.

"Ladies and gentlemen," she said, "we are honored tonight by the presence of a gentleman from New York—who is looking for a wife." The spotlight swung around to me, and patrons began applauding. "Does anyone have a wife for him? Yes? No? Well, perhaps one of my girls will do. Mademoiselle Fifi comes next. She dances beautifully. If you like Mademoiselle Fifi, if you think she'll make you a good wife, tell me, and I'll arrange it, sir."

My face must have reddened, and my neck was perspiring under my collar, but I managed a smile and a wave to Grete, who tossed her hair as she left the stage.

I stuck it out until the show, six acts in all, ended. Then I ordered a bottle of scotch from the waiter and asked him if I could invite Grete Kellner to my table. When he returned, he said that Fraulein Grete would join me soon.

I waited. A half hour went by. I drank some of the whiskey. Close to another half hour elapsed before Grete finally appeared in a clinging short dress of white satin.

She seated herself beside me, close enough for me to feel her soft thigh against mine.

"So," she said. "You enjoyed the show?"

"Interesting," I said.

"My girls didn't appeal to you?"

"Not my type."

"You'd be surprised," she said, "how many straight gentlemen hang around to ask for dates with the girls."

"Do the girls accept?"

"Sometimes."

"And I suppose the gentlemen are in for quite a surprise."

"Oh," she said, with a laugh, "I could tell you stories. Fifi took this nice American to her place, and she explained about her operations. Do you know what he said? He said, 'When it's that close, it doesn't matter.' What would you do?"

"I think," I said, "I would politely excuse myself."

"So you are stuffy, after all."

"A little bit," I said.

"You didn't mind the joke I played on you?"

"I suppose I minded, but if it gave you pleasure. . . ."

She took my hand and squeezed it. Go with it, I thought. She was not Caryl, and she had a tartish quality, but she was frank in her sexiness. Through the years, I guessed, she had sat with men, and plied them with drinks, and maybe suggested favors to come, all part of her profession. And, for all I knew, I was expected to pay, too, eventually. But if she had her purposes, I had mine.

I added, squeezing her hand in return: ". . . but I much prefer you to Fifi."

"You're still inviting me to dinner?"

"It's not too late for you?"

"The night has hardly begun," she said.

She crooked a hand at a waiter, who quickly came over.

"This gentleman's bill is on the house," she told him.

She kissed my cheek and got up.

"After the next show," she said, "I'll join you. Be patient, my nice American."

24

Outside, the drizzle had stopped, and the air smelled fresh and clean at this early hour of the morning. Parked near the entrance was a yellow Porsche; on its top were clamps for holding skis. My head began to clear.

"Get in," she said.

She drove through the empty streets, shifting gears like a racing driver. We went along the Kurfürstendamm to the Gedachtniskirche, where she turned into a wide street that skirted the Am Zoo railway station. In the Savignyplatz she stopped at a café called the Zweibelfische. "It means 'onion fish,' " she explained.

At the end of a long, narrow room, surprisingly noisy and crowded at this hour, was a bar. A jukebox blared out "I Want to Be Loved by You," sung unmistakably by the disembodied Marilyn Monroe. A room to the left had tables, most of them filled with young people.

A distracted-looking waitress, threading her way between tables, brought us bowls of onion soup, encrusted with a layer of melted cheese.

"You like this place?" Grete asked. "There's not much choice at this hour. Most of the people here are Marxists. It won't close until everyone stops arguing and goes home."

"Are you a Marxist?" I asked.

She leaned her head back and let out a peal of laughter.

"No," she said. "I'm a decadent capitalist. I like money, lots of it. These people here know about the Germans. They're Germans, too, but they don't trust the other Germans. I like them for that. But did we come here to talk politics?"

"No," I said.

"Are you rich?" she asked.

"Not very."

"But some," she said. "Your life is disturbed now, but you still have a look of comfort about you. You had what is known as a good upbringing, yes?"

"I suppose," I said.

"I wish you'd relax more." She said it almost petulantly. "If we were somewhere alone, I would relax you. You know how?"

"I can make a couple of guesses."

"I was thinking of a massage. I'm good at that. I once did it, you know, for a living." She made a wry face. "But, if you're wondering if Caryl did also, no, she did not. I taught her a nice dance, though. Too bad she was shy."

"Why too bad?"

"You knew?"

"You mean about her dancing. I heard something about it."

"She told you?"

"No."

"Strange, you learning about your wife now that she's gone. Why not before?"

"I guess she wasn't ready to tell me."

"You're still curious?"

I nodded.

"It was a club in Vienna. A strip place. She needed some work, and I gave her some dances to do. But she was too modest to take off all her clothes. Me, I never had that problem. I have something to show, don't you think?"

"Yes, I think so."

"If you'll relax and be nice, maybe I'll give you a private viewing. Maybe it would make you forget Caryl for a while."

"It might," I said, lying.

"You're not sure?"

"Not yet."

"Well, we'll see. How is the soup?"

"Very good."

"Tell me the truth," she said. "What do you think of me?"

"You're a beautiful woman." It wasn't a lie.

"That's all?"

"I don't know you well enough yet. . . ."

"I must tell you something." She had lowered her voice and was leaning forward. "I must shock you a little. Sometimes I prefer girls. Well, does it shock you?"

"Only because it seems a waste."

"Ah," she said, "such a straight man. But, sometimes, a man appeals to me. You do. What kind of lover are you?"

"Didn't Caryl say?"

"I didn't ask her. But you're wondering now about Caryl and me. I can see it in your eyes."

It was true. I'd begun to wonder, enough to have a sinking feeling.

"No," she said. "Caryl isn't that way. I'm very good at telling. I never make a mistake. There was a time when I grew sick of men, and I tried women." She patted her bosom. "What I have appeals to certain women, too."

"Caryl knows about that?"

"She may have guessed. But Caryl is discreet. She wouldn't have said anything."

"Maybe that's why she left?"

"No. You're the reason she left. She said you might find a letter I sent her from Saas Fee. You did?"

I nodded.

"She's smart, and you're smart. Anyway, she's changed. If you saw her, you probably wouldn't recognize her."

"Why not?"

"She changed the color of her hair, and. . . . But I'm telling you too much. No more."

"Your girls," I said, knowing it was time to change the subject. "How do they . . .?" I patted my chest.

"Oh," she said. "That I can tell you about."

In the next several minutes, I learned more than I ever needed or wanted to know about hormone injections, hair removal, creams, and lotions. Grete took considerable amusement in telling me about it. Finally, she stifled a yawn. "I must have my sleep. Now I'll go home and sleep till the afternoon. Where are you staying?"

"The Parkhotel."

"So, I'll take you there, my lonely American."

In the Porsche, after she had stopped at my hotel entrance, she gave me her hand.

"Good night. Or, good morning. How long will you stay in Berlin?"

"A while longer."

"To look for Caryl?" I saw a mischievous glint in her eyes.

"And to see more of you."

"So, your broken heart is not altogether broken?"

"Maybe it's repairable," I said.

"We'll see." She inclined her head toward me. Her soft lips opened wide. "Not now," she said. "It's much too late, and I'm tired. I'll call you."

"Good night," I said, my lips still wet from her kiss, and got out of the car. As I waited for the porter to let me in, I heard gears shifting as the yellow Porsche zoomed around a corner.

I told myself in those fretful moments before drifting into sleep that I had flirted with Grete because she had taken the lead and flirted with me, that she had been almost deliberately provocative and that I had merely responded as any normal man would. Yet, I knew, undeniably, that I had been aroused by her. *I'm free, after all,* I told myself. And perhaps it was true that Caryl had deserted me. In any case, I was left high and dry. No, that wasn't the reason. I had to hold onto it. Sooner or later, if I persisted, Grete would tell me more. That was why I must see her. Not because of the kiss.

I slept until noon, then ran a tub; while I was soaking, I heard the telephone ring. Grabbing a towel and drying myself, I answered.

"Steve? Grete here."

"You're up early," I said.

"Already you know my habits."

"Well, you told me."

"Did I? Anyway, I'm awake, and I've been thinking of you. I feel something. Do you?"

"Yes."

"We're not children, are we? So, would you like to come here?"

"When?"

"Now?"

"I'll be there," I said.

Hell, I thought, it's sex. Why not? If I were to find Caryl, would I tell her? Yes, I thought, play it straight.

She let me in herself, in the same gold-figured dressing gown.

Hardly had she closed the door behind me when she was in my arms, her lips seeking mine. Then she took me by the hand and led me to her bedroom. On her dressing table were large bottles of perfumes, cleansing lotions, nail polishes, and a picture of a young woman. The shades and drapes were drawn, although some daylight managed to filter through. The girl in the photograph was young and pretty, with close-cropped hair. "For Grete," the scrawled writing said, "with my undying love."

Grete removed her dressing gown. She was truly magnificent. *All's fair in love and pursuit,* I thought, and pushed everything else from my mind. Her lovemaking was slow and somehow graceful at first, but then she grew fiercer, and I became hungry, too. She gave little moans and cries, she took bites of my neck, my arms, my shoulders. With one last, loud cry, she reached her climax. Both our bodies were wet.

"Ah," she said, like a woman who had just finished a satisfying meal, "that was good." As though in confirmation, she got out of bed, giving me a view of shapely buttocks, and returned with a bottle of German brandy and two glasses.

She smiled teasingly as she sipped beside me in the bed. "Did I make you forget her?" she asked.

I thought it best to nod my assent.

"It does seem strange," she said.

"What does?"

"That she should want to leave you. You make love so nicely. I really don't understand it."

"Then you agree there has to be more to it?"

"Than wanting to be free of you?"

"Yes," I said. "To go to these lengths, to run off, to ask your help, to change her looks. All because of me?"

"Maybe there's more to it," she agreed grudgingly.

"Like serious trouble," I said.

"But it's her own business," Grete said defensively. "Otherwise she would have told me, or you, or both of us. She was very certain about it. She wanted you to forget her. I'm a help—yes?"

"Yes," I said.

"Now you must go." She sat up and cupped her hands under her breasts, as though to give me a last enticing display. "I must take a little nap and get ready for tonight. When I finish at the club, I'll come directly to your hotel room. Agreed?"

"Agreed."

Later that afternoon, I dropped in at the Saddle Club, on the chance of finding Mark Eisler there. He was in his office.

"So," he said, "your business here goes well."

"Quite well." I didn't elaborate.

"Anything else I can do for you?" he asked. "Female company perhaps?"

"No," I said. "But a client of mine wishes to find someone. For the sake of hypothesis, let's say it's a woman. She comes to West Berlin, but wishes to change her identity. What would she do for identification, to get a job, for travel purposes?"

Mark gave me an ironic smile.

"She's in the right place for that," he said. "All it would require is a little money. For instance, at the railway station, the Bahnhof-Zoo, you can always find people who will sell you false documents. The going rate for a British or American passport is 750 marks. For 500 marks you can buy your identification card, the *Behaelfsmaessiger Personalwausweis.*"

Would Caryl have known that, I wondered, or would Grete have told her?

"I can find those people at the Bahnhof-Zoo?"

"The particular ones? Difficult. Naturally they don't have names. But . . ." He gave me a shrewd glance. ". . . if you want to buy some, I can help."

"It's not for me," I said quickly.

"You make me curious, Steve. I can be trusted, you know."

"I'm speaking hypothetically," I said. "Forget I asked."

Mark insisted that I have dinner at the club and see his new show. I was given a good table, a bottle of champagne, and an unobstructed view of some "artistic" striptease. The girls, this time, were genuine.

I remained awake after I got back to my hotel at about 1:00 A.M. I kept the room radio going so as not to fall asleep. Three o'clock came, and then, slowly, another hour passed. Grete, then, had thought better of it and decided not to come. I had dozed off, and wasn't sure if I dreamed the light tapping on my door. I got up and opened it.

"You see," Grete said. "I'm here. Don't bother turning on the light."

Her clothes rustled as she removed them in the dark. Her perfume, Caryl's perfume, filled the room. Her soft body came next to mine. I closed my eyes and closed my mind, too.

25

She was still asleep, snoring faintly, when I ordered a late breakfast for two, speaking softly into the telephone. I studied her face, noticed faint lines around her eyes, the first signs of aging. Suddenly, her pale blue eyes opened wide.

"Cigarette, please," she said. "And coffee."

I lit her cigarette for her, and, a moment later, a youthful maid entered the room with a tray. She placed it down with a hastily muttered *"Bitte,"* and scurried from the room as though in fear of impairing her morals.

I poured Grete coffee.

"I suppose," I said, "she would have gone to the Bahnhof-Zoo for her documents."

"Who? What documents?"

"What we were speaking about yesterday," I said. "If she went to all that trouble to change her looks, she'd also need a new identity. Berlin's a good place for that, isn't it?"

"Why do you speak of those things now?" Grete said crossly.

"Just trying to get it clear in my head," I said. "Both of you left Saas Fee in such a hurry, to come to Berlin."

"My vacation was over. I had to leave. She came with me."

"But didn't she notice her picture in the paper?"

"Why do you talk about this? It's too early."

"I'm trying to understand it," I said. "She knew that people might recognize her from the picture. Am I right about that?"

She held out her cup to be refilled.

"You sound like a detective," she said. "Not a lover. Don't I please you?"

I assured her that she did.

"This talk about Caryl does no good. She has her own life now. She wishes it that way."

"And a new name," I said.

"Yes, another name. And you won't get it from me, because I gave her my word."

"I'll have to get a legal separation or divorce sooner or later," I said. "You can see the trouble I'd have. Suppose I wanted to remarry?"

"She's gone a week and already you want to marry again?"

"I'm thinking of the future. I'd have to serve her with papers. What if I wanted to marry you?"

"For that bargain, it would take two," she said with asperity.

"But you see the problem."

"Send your damned papers to me," Grete said. "I'll see that she gets them." She sighed when she realized the slip she had made and added lamely, "I could try, anyway."

"You know where she is," I said with certainty. "I'm not asking this because of myself alone. There's someone else involved. He wants to find her."

"Who?"

"Zoltan."

"He's away. In prison. You're lying."

"Zoltan is free. I saw him in Paris. He murdered a police officer there."

The change in her expression was sudden and startling. The color drained from her face; I saw fear in her eyes.

"When?" she said.

"A few days ago."

"My God! He knows you came here?"

"It's possible. I tried to throw him off the track, but he seems to have ways."

He had that address book of mine for one thing; and Mark Eisler's name was in it.

"Did he also know Caryl was with me in Saas Fee?"

"I don't think so. But how well do you know him?"

"Well enough to stay away from him."

"Caryl didn't mention him?"

"No. Why should she?"

"That's what I'm trying to find out."

"So you make love to me for that."

"No," I said. "But we both should know what this thing involves. . . ."

She suddenly threw aside the sheet that was covering her and scurried to the closet for her clothes. "You should have told me that. If I'd known, I would never . . ."

"I tried," I said. "The first time we talked, I tried, but you didn't want to listen. Caryl has got to be warned. You understand that, don't you?"

"I understand nothing!" She almost shrieked it at me. She finished dressing, combed out her long blonde hair, ran a pink lipstick across her lips, and moved toward the door.

"Don't go," I said, gripping her arms.

She shook herself free. "Finished," she cried. "I don't want to see you again. Go away from me."

"Where?"

"Anywhere. He'll kill you. You think he won't? If he comes to me . . ." She shuddered.

"What? You'd tell him where she is?"

Her eyes held both anguish and a kind of fury as she stared at me. "I don't know," she murmured, as though exhausted. She pulled open the door and half-ran down the corridor.

I mentally kicked myself for having overlooked something important. I should have warned Mark Eisler to give out no information about me, if anyone inquired. I got him on the phone.

"Mark," I said. "I'm not in Berlin."

"Where are you calling from, then?"

"I mean, I'm here, but I don't want anyone to know."

"Strange you should tell me that just now."

"Why?" I felt a premonitory clutch of apprehension.

"A half hour ago, a French detective paid me a visit."

"Delahaye?"

"No. Gonnard, he said his name was. Félicien Gonnard, Paris Sûreté. He showed me his card. Wondered if I had seen you lately. Wanted you for a few questions. I told him you had dropped in at the club and that if you came back I would ask you to get in touch with him."

"You told him I was in Berlin?"

"My dear friend, I don't fool around with the police, French or whatever. Half the time they already know the answers to their questions. I didn't lie, you have indeed dropped around, but I didn't tell him where to find you. That way we're both protected. What crimes have you committed, by the way?"

"Would you describe the man?"

"Oh, medium height, cropped black hair, middle thirties, those dark glasses the French police like to wear. Not a bad-looking fellow. I have his card here. Wrote a telephone number on it. You want it?"

"Yes, give it to me."

He was silent.

"Mark?"

"That's funny," he said. "It's a five-digit number. We no longer have five-digit numbers—all changed to six and seven.

"Mark," I said, "do you have protection? Bouncers, that kind of thing?"

"Certainly, why?"

"Make sure they're around if he comes back."

His voice turned cold. "I don't like this, Steve."

"Neither do I. I'm sorry. He's a fraud. I'm getting out of Berlin. I'll tell you more some day."

I hung up. My hands were trembling.

Zoltan was in Berlin, prowling around. How long would it take him to go down the list of hotels and check those I would be likely to be in? The Parkhotel Zellermayer was off the beaten track, but not that far off. He'd try the Bristol-Kempinski, the Berlin Hilton, the Schweizerhof, the Savoy. And Grete's nightclub. I called the club and asked for her. She wasn't there, and they didn't know when to expect her. Perhaps late in the evening. I tried her home telephone. No answer. I called several times, at intervals of five minutes. Still no answer. But, fearful of Zoltan, perhaps she was not answering. I packed my bags and checked out of the hotel, leaving a forwarding address for a hotel in Stockholm. That was in case Zoltan came visiting. But my intention was to go back to Paris, where I would have the relative safety of Delahaye's protection. I sent him a telegram, a brief message: "Our mutual friend last seen in Berlin."

Then I took a cab to Grete's apartment house. One last chance she'd tell me where Caryl had gone. And to warn her.

In the cab I wrote out a note which, if she were not in, I would slip under her door: "Leave Berlin." She would fully understand the implications of the message. At Soorstrasse 60, I asked the taxi driver to wait for me and not to worry if I were delayed. There would be a generous tip. I went directly through the unlocked foyer door to the elevator. Another thing she could do was get the lock fixed on that door. On her floor, I rang the bell.

No answer. I pressed the bell again. My ear against the doorjamb, I listened for sound of movement inside. I heard nothing, but my nostrils caught the scent of perfume. And the hallway, too, held a faint, lingering odor.

"Grete," I said urgently. "You're there, and I must speak to you. You know why."

The doorknob turned. She opened the door a crack and reluctantly let me come in.

"Well," she said, cold and unfriendly, "what is it I know?"

"He's in Berlin," I said. "It's definite."

"You've seen him?"

"He visited Mark. He knows I'm here."

She motioned me to follow her into the living room, where the blinds were drawn, and only faint daylight penetrated through the slats. A cigarette smoldered in an ash tray. She was wearing the pink dressing gown, and I noticed she was now careful to prevent her breasts from being exposed.

"So what do I do?" she asked. "Invite him over for a drink?"

"I think you've got to leave Berlin."

"Impossible," she said. "I couldn't leave for a week. You forget, I put the show together, I deal with the agents."

"Close it down for a while."

"And the rent?" she said. "The canceled contracts, the help? You think I'm that rich? You think I can throw away thirty, forty thousand marks?"

"I'll help out," I said, "if you take me to Caryl."

"Now you're offering to pay. I was waiting for that. It's a trick, isn't it? There's no Zoltan. With a murder charge on his head, he wouldn't show himself. Anyway, I talked to Caryl."

"When?"

"Twenty minutes ago."

"So you know where she is."

"All right, I know where she is. I told her you were here, I told her what you said about Zoltan. She's through with both of you. I promised her neither of you would get anything from me."

"Can't you realize," I said, surprised at the almost abject pleading in my own voice, "that I'm trying to protect both you and her? She's got it wrong, you've got it wrong. But at least she has a gun."

"Caryl?" She sounded incredulous. "What would she do with a gun?"

"She's frightened," I said.

"She told you she had a gun? You saw it?"

"She left bullets for it behind."

"And what would she do with a gun without bullets?"

She was being stubborn, I thought, not stupid. And time was being wasted reasoning with her.

"These were extra bullets for the gun. Let's get to her and find out why she has it. You know she's a gentle person, don't you?"

"She wouldn't harm a fly."

I had the momentary wish that Delahaye was here, so that he could hear Grete say the words.

"Come with me," I said. "Take me to wherever she is. Even if you don't take me to her, come with me. Now."

"She doesn't want you," Grete said, tonelessly. "Neither you, nor Zoltan. I promised her."

"Then will you get out of Berlin, somewhere safe?"

She shrugged.

"What's the use? If he could find you, he could find me."

"And you won't tell me?"

She simply stood there, shaking her head.

"I'm sorry," I said. "I'm sorry about all this."

She turned her back on me. I saw her shoulders heaving.

In the hallway I pressed the elevator button. The cage was in use. I didn't wait, descending the stairs instead. The taxi was still outside. I glanced up and down the street, but saw no one. "Tempelhof," I told the driver.

At the terminal, I was told there would be a two-hour wait until the next flight for Frankfurt, where I could connect for Paris. Time lost, not only the two hours, but backtracking to Paris, where my hope was that Delahaye, somehow, would aid me in finding Caryl. Perhaps I was wrong in not informing him of my trip to Berlin. He was a professional, and I was an amateur. I had black coffee at the bar, by now habituated to casting wary glances at whoever came near. My unease increased. I shouldn't have left Grete. I remembered the sudden, upward flash of the knife in the Paris bar. Hell, I thought, there's still time. I checked my bags.

The taxi ride back to Soorstrasse 60 took only fifteen minutes. Damn it, I thought, she's got to come with me, if only for her own sake.

On her floor in the apartment building, I didn't like what I saw—her door was slightly ajar. My steps grew cautious. The door was open because the lock had been forced and ruined. Dully, it struck me that I shouldn't enter but should run for police help. I heard inside the faint sound of moaning. I swung the door open slowly, as quietly as I could. The moaning came from the living room. It was more like a series of sighs now.

Grete was lying crumpled up on the rug. Her face was bruised, her blonde hair matted with blood, as though she had been struck with a heavy instrument. Was someone else in the room or the apartment?

Her eyes were slightly open, staring upward.

"Grete," I said.

She moaned.

"I'll get a doctor," I said. "You'll be all right. Was it him?" It seemed to me I was calm, surprisingly so, almost as though I had expected this.

I saw the look of recognition in her eyes. She was conscious enough to know me.

"Heidelberg," she mumbled thickly. "La Jeunesse."

"You told him?"

"Heidelberg," she mumbled again. "Old quarter. Dresses. He . . ."

Her eyes closed.

I got up and went to the phone. The cord had been cut.

I bent down to her, spoke in her ear. "I'll be back with a doctor."

But she didn't hear me. I bent my head to her breast to hear the heartbeat. But already the touch of her body was cold. I picked up her limp body and placed it on her pillowed couch. Her gown fell open. I closed it over her white breasts.

At Tempelhof I changed my Paris destination to Heidelberg. I still had to make the change at Frankfurt, and, if Zoltan was headed for Heidelberg, he would be on the same plane. Unless he used other means. At the information booth, I checked it out. It was possible to reach Frankfurt from East Berlin's Schonfeld Airport, and to get to Munich by train. There was also the autobahn, if one went by car. I kept a watch on the departure gate and also on the availability of police and guards should Zoltan appear. The plane to Frankfurt was announced, a BEA flight. I made sure to be the last to go through the gate. No sign of Zoltan. Of course, I thought, he wouldn't be so obvious as to take this flight. And whether he went by plane, car, or train, I had a good chance to get to Heidelberg ahead of him.

PART THREE

26

I had never fired a weapon in either anger or self-defense, but I badly wanted one now. I'd had some army training during a draft period of eighteen months. At Ford Meade, Maryland, where I was assigned, I'd gone through the usual basic training courses with World War II–type small weapons—the M1 rifle, the thirty caliber carbine, and an ugly police pistol familiarly called the grease gun. It fired a clip of twenty forty-five-caliber slugs. After a month of maneuvers in South Carolina, I spent my remaining time of service in the Judge Advocate Department at the Pentagon.

I remembered all this on the plane as though mentally preparing myself to do battle with Zoltan, if we should meet face to face. During my college years, I had joined the wrestling team and wasn't too bad at it. I had lost more than I had won, but I had learned the holds and still remembered them. But what use would a few hand holds and arm locks be against a genuine certified killer? A psychopath? The record was unfolding.

One: He had fired point-blank at a border guard. Motive, escape.

Two: He had killed a consular attaché in Milan: Hired job?

Three: Apparently the killer of Ian Cameron. Motive, jealousy? Insane possessiveness? Possibility of collusion on Caryl's part? Grete's words, some of her last: *she wouldn't harm a fly.* Rule it out.

Four: Ruthless killing of Gazin.

Five: The brutal beating of Grete. Whatever he had hit her with, it had been again and again. Method of killings, therefore, whatever came to hand.

How, then, to prepare for him?

How much of that record had Caryl known, and how much more was there besides? Caryl knew enough to arm herself. Where had she picked up the gun? In Paris? Or had she brought it with her? Wouldn't it have been detected, if so, at the Kennedy Airport security gate? The BEA Viking was nearing Frankfurt when it occurred to me. Zoltan would certainly travel by car or train, rather than fly. Armed, he wouldn't take chances on having his weapon or weapons discovered. Therefore, I was ahead of him. I calculated it would take him at least ten hours of driving, with delays at checkpoints, before he could reach Heidelberg by car. I hired my own car, an Opel Manta, from Hertz at the Frankfurt airport.

I reached Heidelberg by way of the autobahn in less than two hours. It was evening when I arrived. Now, how to find something called La Jeunesse in the old quarter? I checked in at the Europaischer Hof, a large, modern hotel not far from the main train station. The telephone directory listed a dress shop called La Jeunesse on Hauptstrasse, which turned out to be a busy street in the old quarter, both sides lined with shops, bars, and restaurants, most of which catered to tourists and American soldiers stationed in the area. I found the shop. Its one display window, protected by a vertical iron grating, showed dresses, blouses, skirts, and slacks. The door was locked and was also protected by an iron grating. I could dimly make out racks of dresses and some display cases inside. I looked for the name of a proprietor on the door and window but found none.

What would Caryl be doing here? Selling dresses. How close was I to her now? Heidelberg was not that large a city, although its environs stretched out quite a bit along the banks of the Neckar and up into the hill areas dominated by the old castle and the new buildings of the university.

Back in my hotel room, I tried the shop's phone number, on the chance that it was connected to the owner's residence. No answer. Nothing to do but wait until morning.

And, by that time, Zoltan could be in Heidelberg. I had a small pocket knife for paring fingernails. Not much of a weapon for defense or attack, and my mood was such that I fervently wished for something more dangerous. Zoltan was getting to me, no doubt about it, and maybe that was what he wanted—to get me to where I was ready to face him in the open. Careful, I warned myself. He was a lot better at it.

The police? I could go to them now, give them the story, and set up Zoltan at the shop. He'd think of that, too. Meanwhile, the police would probably regard me as a strange and suspicious character and would hold onto me for questioning.

No, I had to get hold of Caryl and get her away from here as fast as possible. I had the car. It was a good one and had hummed along the autobahn nicely. I had taken it up to a hundred and thirty kilometers an hour.

There was nothing to do but wait out the night, with Zoltan coming ever closer to Heidelberg. But wouldn't he have to sleep, too? I tossed and turned and hardly slept at all.

Before leaving the hotel in the morning, I picked up the *Frankfurter Zeitung* at the newsstand in the lobby. The story was there. My German was lacking, but Grete's name, and the name of her nightclub, Joie et Plaisir, leaped out at me. It was on the second page. I folded the paper and took it with me. In the Opel, I cruised slowly past the boutique. It was eight thirty, and none of the shops was open yet. I parked the car on a little side street, just past La Jeunesse. A café across the street from the shop was open for breakfast; its menu even offered scrambled eggs and bacon and American-style hamburgers. A table near the window gave me a vantage point from which to watch the display window of La Jeunesse, still covered by an iron grill. Sooner or later, someone had to come and raise the grill and open the shop. I ordered coffee and drank it black. My stomach couldn't have held anything more substantial.

Minutes ticked by. It seemed to me that each minute brought Caryl closer—and also Zoltan. I kept the paper raised to my face, as though I were reading it.

A few minutes past nine, an old man in work clothes came along, dangling a set of large keys, and unlocked and raised the iron grillwork. A few minutes later, a woman, fortyish, in a brown suede coat, unlocked the entrance door and entered the shop. The proprietress, evidently.

I left change for the coffee on my table and crossed the narrow street. A bell tinkled as I opened the door of the shop.

The woman had removed her coat and was now behind a long glass case arranging colorful blouses in neat piles. She looked up and gave me a nice smile. She had a pleasant face, that of a woman who had once been very attractive. Now there were lines around the corners of her mouth and creases in her forehead.

She had guessed me to be an American, for she said in English: "May I help you, please?"

"Yes," I said. "But not for a purchase. I'm looking for someone—your new assistant. Will she be coming in?"

I knew her answer in advance.

"Karin? She's no longer here."

"You're sure her name is Karin?"

She shrugged. "I didn't know her well. She left after working with me only a few days. Why are you asking?"

"She's my wife," I said.

Her eyes widened. "But she's not American. She has a German work permit."

"Can you tell me where she's staying?"

"She was with me, until . . ."

"Until when?"

"Yesterday," she said reluctantly, as though she were telling me something she perhaps should not.

"Did she say where she was going?"

She shook her head. "Perhaps you should explain?"

"Yes, I'll explain," I said.

I'd have to alarm her, I knew, and there wasn't time to waste. Almost involuntarily, I glanced out the display window to the street. The traffic had increased, and people were walking by. No one had yet paused at the shop window to look at the display, or at us.

"You're acquainted with Grete Kellner?"

"Of course."

"And she recommended Karin—my wife—to you?"

"She didn't say she had a husband."

"I'm sorry," I said, "but you probably haven't seen this morning's papers." I unfolded my copy of the *Frankfurter Zeitung* and pointed out to her the item about Grete's murder.

She read it and gave a gasp.

"I don't read German well," I said quietly. "How did she die?"

"You knew—before?"

"Yes, but not how."

"She was beaten—badly—blows to the head—and kidneys. . . ." She put her hand to her mouth.

"I'm not here only to find my wife," I said. "But you're in danger, too."

"Me?"

"I'll tell you," I said. "But there isn't time now. Grete telephoned yesterday?"

"Yes."

"She spoke to my wife?"

"Yes."

"How soon after that did she leave?"

"Almost at once. She made some telephone calls. . . ."

"Do you know to whom—or where?"

"No. You said . . . why am I in danger?"

"Because the man who came to Grete, who killed her, will come to you. You see, he's looking for my wife, too."

"Oh, this is terrible. I don't know what to do. What am I to do?" Her voice had taken on a hysterical edge.

I said, as soothingly as I could, "What is your name?"

"Helga Netzer."

"Frau Netzer," I said. "The first thing you must do is close your shop. Lock it tight. Will you do that? Will you trust me?"

She stared at me searchingly, then nodded. Then, quickly, she went to the entrance door and bolted it.

"Is there a back door?"

She nodded.

"That, too," I said.

Behind a partition there was a small work space with two sewing machines and a desk. In there, I told her what I knew. It took awhile, because she kept interrupting with questions.

"But why did your wife leave you?" she asked.

"I don't know the answer yet," I said.

"Was she afraid of you?"

"I don't think so."

"But why does she keep running from you?"

"It's not me," I said. "It's Zoltan."

"But couldn't you help her?"

"I want to. For some reason, she won't let me."

"If you knew about this Zoltan, why didn't you help Grete?"

"I tried. I called the police, but it was too late."

"Then we must call the police now."

"We will," I said. "But first, we must wait for Zoltan."

"You're sure he's coming here?"

"Yes. He wouldn't have killed Grete until she told him where Caryl was."

"She changed her name. Why?"

"To disappear. For some reason, she wants a new life, and a new name. What color is her hair?"

"Blonde."

"Dyed," I said. "Or a wig." I showed her a snapshot of Caryl. "What last name did she give?"

"Bohn. Karin Bohn. Grete, poor Grete, only explained about her that she had lost her fiancé in an accident; and wanted to forget, and needed work badly in a new place. I needed an assistant. . . . I gave her a room in my apartment, while she looked for one of her own. She was very quiet and seemed sad. But she was very honest. She paid me for the telephone calls—thirty marks."

"That would be out of the country, then."

"Yes."

"For long distance," I said, "is there a way of finding out who or where she called?"

"The telephone company would have receipts for calls like that. They'll come with my next bill, perhaps a week."

"Where did she call from—here, or your apartment?"

"The apartment. I could call the Centralezelle of the Post Office, where they have records of all operator calls."

"Would you do it?"

She nodded.

"But first," I said, "could you call the workman who unlocked the grills and have him replace them? It would be best if your shop seemed closed."

"Why?"

"Because, if Zoltan comes, he'll hang around waiting for it to open. Once we see him, we can call the police."

"Yes," she said. "I'll do it."

While she made the calls, I went to the shop proper and looked for vantage points from which I could see outside without being seen. There were several dress racks on wheels that could be moved around. I arranged two of them so as to form a kind of barrier between the window and the shop interior. By peering between the hanging dresses, I could see out through the window. I was glad to see the old man appear and cover the display window with its iron grill. The street was now choked with slowly moving cars. Frau Netzer came out of the workroom and joined me behind the clothes rack.

With a short nod, she said, "You seem to know what to do."

"I'm getting experience," I said.

"What is your business in America?"

"I'm a lawyer."

"I think you're a nice man."

"Thank you," I said gravely.

"I have her calls," she said. "She made two. One to Avignon and the other to Marseilles. Both to the same person—the marquis de Carenne. Do you know the name?"

I had to think a moment before I remembered. The name had a familiar ring, but where had I come across it? Yes, in those French news clippings Marie had brought. He had something to do with Ian Cameron. A ship that was to be used for an expedition. His ship.

"He's someone rich," I said, "who owns a ship."

She looked at me blankly.

"I believe Caryl knew him," I said.

I tried to visualize the clipping. The marquis de Carenne, owner of a yacht called—what? Some odd name. Caryl's trail led now to him, to Avignon or Marseilles. Once rid of Zoltan, I had a new trail to follow.

I asked Frau Netzer, "Is there a place you can stay for a while, not in Heidelberg?"

"Why?"

"For your safety. I want you out of this. I don't want . . ."

"I understand," she said quietly. "I have a married sister in Innsbruck. I could go there. You think it necessary."

"Yes," I said. "But only if we don't catch Zoltan. Maybe even if we do. You see, he's clever. He disguises himself. Even if the police caught him, he could fool them. I think you should go to Innsbruck."

"He would be looking for me?"

"And me," I said. "Everyone I see, he seems to see."

She was close enough so that I felt her shudder. Suddenly, not thinking, I put my arm around her shoulder.

"It will be all right," I said. "I know enough now. I didn't before. We'll be careful. You wouldn't have a gun here, would you?"

She gave another shudder and shook her head.

Just then a shadow fell across the grill that covered the window. I was barely able to see someone at the edge of the window. I changed my position behind the dress racks, crouching, to see him better. He was medium height and wore a leather jacket, a knit wool skiing cap, leather boots, and the wide, dark glasses used by skiers. I could make out his face distinctly. I found myself gripping the woman's hand tightly.

"That's him," I said. "I'm pretty sure."

We watched as he crossed the street and entered the same café I'd been in earlier. He took the very same table, one from which he could survey the street and the shop.

"We'll get him," I said, "if he stays there long enough. Call the police. Give them the name of the café and his description. Tell them he's wanted by the Paris police for murder. And that he's armed and dangerous."

She nodded, her lips tight, her face pale, and rose stiffly from her crouching position, her head low. Losing her balance slightly, she caught hold of the rack to steady herself, and, ridiculously, the movement caused the other rack to slide away from us. I got hold of the rack and moved it back to hide myself again, but Zoltan had apparently glimpsed enough to cause him alarm. I saw him get up hurriedly from the table and leave the café. On the opposite side of the street, he walked rapidly to his left, not glancing back. I went to the window and peered up the street. Zoltan was getting into a blue Volkswagen. He had probably sensed an ambush. He drove down the street, and I lost sight of the car. I felt a sense of dismay. I had been counting on catching him. We'd had the chance.

"What do we do?" Helga Netzer asked, apologizing with her eyes.

"We get out of here," I said.

27

The door at the rear of the stockroom opened on a brick-paved passageway, the walls on each side narrow and high. At the end of the passageway was Neckarallee, which wound toward the Neckar River a few hundred yards off. The car was where I had left it, with a traffic ticket on the windshield.

"Where's your apartment?" I asked Helga in the car.

"On Bruckenstrasse. It overlooks the river, east about two kilometers."

"I'm taking you to your sister's," I said. "You can't be in Heidelberg with him on the loose. How fast can you pack some clothes?"

"Fast," she said, tight-lipped.

I followed her directions to the apartment house, a new concrete-faced building with small terraces, but sped right on past it.

"Why didn't you stop?"

"You didn't see it?"

"See what?"

"The blue Volkswagen parked near the building."

"There are lots of blue Volkswagens," she said.

"I'm not taking chances."

Two blocks further on, I U-turned and headed west in the direction of the autobahn.

"She must have given him your name," I said.

"Poor, poor Grete," she said, and when I glanced at her, I saw tears in her eyes.

She was a handsome woman still, her blonde hair streaked with gray.

"How did you know her?" I asked.

"I used to have a shop in Vienna—many years ago. Grete bought her clothes from me. We became friends. When I moved to Heidelberg, she visited me often. You see, my clothes come from Paris, Rome, Düsseldorf. It's—it's . . ." Again the tears flowed.

"Hard to believe," I said.

It was for me, too. Not so many hours ago, Grete's body had been close and warm against mine. I closed my mind to the thoughts and regrets.

We reached the autobahn, and I took it in the direction of Karlsruhe.

"We must try to think like Zoltan," I said. "He'll watch the shop and your apartment house for a while. How long? He'll be on the alert for the police. Then he'll realize you're not in Heidelberg. Would your neighbors know you have a sister in Innsbruck?"

"He'll inquire?"

"We can be sure of it."

"Yes," she said, "but my sister uses her married name. No one would know that."

"You're certain?"

"She has visited me in Heidelberg. I must have introduced her to a few people. Perhaps I gave her married name, Ansbach."

"Then you might not be safe at your sister's, either. Could she find you a place to stay?"

"Her husband, Karl, is a ski instructor. He could find me a place in the mountains."

"When we get to Innsbruck," I said, "you'll tell your sister and your brother-in-law everything. Get in touch with the police. Tell them everything, too. Have them put a watch on your sister's house. Then notify a man with the Paris police, Delahaye. Remember the name."

She nodded. "What will you do?"

"I'm going to Avignon—to look up this baron de . . ."

I found myself gripping the steering wheel tightly. The name of the marquis de Carenne's yacht had flashed suddenly into my mind. It had been in one of those clippings.—the *Pantagruelle.* It was to have been used for the filming expedition of Ian Cameron's. Caryl, looking for a safe place, had thought of a ship. Ships leave no tracks. Presumably, because of her relationship with Ian, she knew the marquis well enough to call on him for help.

"You think she will be in Avignon?" Helga asked.

"She's never where I think she is," I said. "I've got to try to think ahead of her, the next step, the one beyond that. Does your telephone bill come to your apartment?"

"Yes."

"And of course the long distance calls would be listed."

"Oh, yes."

"Have you called your sister the past few weeks?"

"No."

"That's a help," I said.

"He'll go through my mail?"

"It's possible," I said. "I'm trying to think of everything. The marquis's name will mean something to him."

"Why?"

"He was in that vicinity about five years ago," I said.

"She told you that?"

"No. I wish she had."

"I could take the train from Karlsruhe," she said suddenly.

"Why do that?"

"Because you're anxious to go to Avignon."

"No," I said. "The first thing I do is to make sure you're safe with your sister."

She said pensively, "If it were me, I would never have run away from you."

We didn't reach Innsbruck until nearly eight in the evening. A heavy snow had fallen the day before, and, once off the autobahn, it was slow and careful going. I stopped in the center of the town and picked up several German newspapers and gave them to Helga.

"See if there's anything more on Grete."

There was.

"They're looking for you," Helga said.

"I expected they would."

"If the police question me?"

"Tell them everything, as I said. And call Delahaye in Paris."

Helga's sister lived on a quiet residential street with pleasant houses set apart from each other.

I waited in the car until someone came to the door and greeted Helga. Then she came running back to the car.

"Be careful," she said.

"You, too."

I reached out my hand and, with a wan smile, she took it and gripped it hard.

"I will see you again?" she asked.

"I hope so," I said. "I very much hope so."

She turned and ran back to the house, where her sister waited in the doorway. When she was inside, I drove off.

It was a long, lonely drive to Avignon, and a new snowfall didn't help. By the time I reached Geneva, it was morning and I was dog tired. I took a room at a hotel and slept for several hours. When I woke, I got the hotel operator to put through a call to the marquis de Carenne in Avignon. It was half an hour before she got someone on the line. The marquis was not at home; did I wish to speak to anyone else?

"Anyone," I said.

A woman, probably a housekeeper, was on the line. She spoke no English. She had trouble with my French.

"Where is the marquis?" I kept asking, in French.

"Le bateau," she said.

"He's on the boat, the yacht, *La Pantagruelle?"*

"Oui."

"Where?"

She didn't know or would not tell.

I hung up and wondered where in hell, or how, I could find out where a yacht called the *Pantagruelle* was. Somewhere in the Mediterranean, surely. But where?

Right then, there was nothing else to do but to continue on to Avignon.

28 LONDON, APRIL 1963

"Anything to declare, miss?"

The British customs officer, thin-faced, with a small bristle mustache, looked at her inquiringly. Her two bags of shiny new maroon leather were before him on the long platform.

"No," she said.

"Cigarettes, perfume, gifts purchased abroad?"

"No," she said, "nothing."

"Kindly open this one, miss." With a forefinger he tapped the bigger of the two matched bags.

The bags had locks, but she hadn't bothered to turn the keys. She snapped the twin locks on the larger bag and lifted the lid for his inspection. The customs man felt around with practiced fingers among dresses, underwear, sweaters, a pair of shoes. He frowned.

"Your passport, miss."

She handed it to him, along with the customs declaration and the entry card she had filled out. He flipped through the pages of the passport slowly, studying it.

"You're a Hungarian national?" he asked.

"Yes," she said. "But—"

"I see," he said. "A refugee? Your purpose in visiting England?"

On the entry card she had put down, "visiting, for the purpose of seeing friends."

Actually, she was to meet Zoltan here. She had seen him less frequently during the previous year. He had gone away for as long as two months at a stretch. The job with the Halmos firm had grown boring; there were days on end when she would have little or nothing to do, not even greeting visitors at the reception desk, as though the firm had entered a period of inactivity. She made up her mind to seek another job, and so informed Halmos, who merely shrugged.

She scoured the want ads in the French papers and also in the *International Herald-Tribune,* where the job offers seemed most interesting. It wasn't long before she came across one that seemed made to order for her. It read:

EXECUTIVE SECRETARY: Experience administrative duties. Prefer trilingual (English, French, German) some knowledge Hungarian helpful, to assist executive of firm with international business interests headquartered in Marseilles. Translations, German to French, French to English, must be perfect. Good salary offered. Write Box 50, 410, *Herald,* Paris.

She composed her letter of application and sent it off, thinking she wouldn't at all mind leaving Paris for Marseilles. She had made few friends and those were from the Halmos offices. And she kept herself free of engagements, because she never knew when Zoltan would appear suddenly from one of his trips. Once, while sitting alone in a café, reading, a young man asked if she minded his sitting at her table, since the others were occupied, and she nodded assent. It turned out, after he began a conversation, that he was a music critic for one of the Paris papers. He was seeing a new production at the Opera-Comique that night, and he wondered, quite diffidently, if she'd like to accompany him. She would have gone had she not worried about Zoltan's reaction. He was away at the time, and, when he returned, she told him of the incident.

Who was he, Zoltan demanded. Had she been seeing him? No, she said, but she did get lonely at times, and the man seemed pleasant and nice.

"His name," Zoltan demanded. It was as though a dark cloud had come over his face. He gripped her arm and twisted it.

"I don't remember," she said. "You're hurting me."

"Which café?" he asked.

"You're being silly," she told him. "It was just that—he asked, and I said no."

"But you wanted to go with him."

"No, I didn't," she lied. "I would have liked to have heard the music, that's all."

"If I ever see you with anyone . . ." he said. He didn't finish, but his lips were pressed tightly together and creases appeared in his forehead. His hands tightened into fists. She swore to him that the incident had no meaning, and finally he relaxed. Yet, at dinner, he returned to the subject again, this time asking what she had said to the man, what she had spoken about, and had she mentioned him or his work? Of course not, she had answered. It was just a casual conversation, and anyway, she knew very little about his work. "You hardly tell me anything anymore," she said. The next day, as though contrite, and also perhaps to emphasize their ties to each other, he gave her a ring with a good-sized blue-white diamond, and insisted she wear it on her engagement finger. "If anyone talks to you, a stranger," he said, "just point to that." She gathered that it didn't mean marriage. Just as well. There were times when she had a strange kind of fear about being attached to Zoltan permanently.

She was bothered, too, by the favor he had asked her to do for him. It had filled her with misgivings. This was to take a safe deposit box in her name at Barclay's Bank on Rue du Quatre Septembre. He explained that it was needed for the safekeeping of securities used as collateral in case of forfeiture of loans or failure to deliver goods to his associates. He said that it was a standard safety measure in his business. A friend of his, Julio Alvarez, would be a co-holder of the box. He would have one key, she would keep the other.

"I don't like it," she told him crossly. "It sounds funny. And why me?"

"Because we trust you," he said smoothly. "Anyway, it's normal. The tax situation is complicated for some of the people I deal with. The French are impossible about taxes, especially with international transactions. Do it for me, please. Haven't I treated you well?"

As though to prove that last assertion, he took her out for a superb dinner at Maxim's, then to a concert at Salle Pleyel.

She signed for the box, and from time to time Zoltan would give her large, brown, sealed envelopes to place in the box. It was simple enough to do. She would go to the bank, see a bank assistant at one of the desks. He would give her a signature card on which she wrote her name. He would check it in the files and then escort her to the safe deposit vault where, left alone, she would unlock her box, place the envelopes in it, and relock it. No one asked questions. Obviously, as Zoltan had said, this was quite a normal thing to do.

But, more and more, the urge grew to lead her own life. It wasn't exactly as though she were in bondage to Zoltan, but she felt bound, in a nagging way, by invisible strings. A letter came to her. Would she report for an interview at the Hotel George Cinq, suite C? She went there, to be greeted rather formally by a Frenchman whose name was Monsieur Henri Verret. He was correctness itself. He wore a pin-striped dark gray suit, starched white shirt, with a silver-gray tie. He had a faint odor of Imperiale cologne. He explained that he represented the business interests of the Marquis Pierre de Carenne, the well-known shipper, who had real estate holdings as well. Monsieur Verret tested her English, French, and German. "Remarkable," he said. "And you're of Hungarian nationality. Perfect. The position is yours, if you will accept it."

She accepted. She was asked to report to Marseilles in a week, and Monsieur Verret wrote out a check to cover her traveling expenses and a week in a hotel until she found a place of residence.

During her last week in Paris, Zoltan returned. She told him of the job she had taken, prepared to accept his wrath. And, if he wanted to break off with her, she was ready for that, too. If that was all she meant to him, that she had to stay in one place, always waiting for him, then she could do without him.

Surprisingly, though, he accepted the news calmly.

"In a way," he said, "I prefer this new arrangement. You see, I get to Marseilles often, more often than here. So, I'll be able to see more of you." In fact, he seemed pleased that she was now so accomplished that she could win a very good job over other applicants. As a going away present, he gave her the maroon leather matched luggage.

True enough, she saw Zoltan more often in Marseilles. She had found two rooms in a small residential hotel, and there were occasions when Zoltan stayed in her suite for days at a time.

Her new place of employment was in an office tower not far from the port. The enterprises of the marquis de Carenne occupied an entire floor. She was introduced to the marquis himself, who, she had learned, left the details of his business to associates, among them Monsieur Verret. The marquis was in his early forties, tall, darkly handsome, and wore a yachting jacket with his family crest over a white cashmere sweater. She had already heard of the imposing yacht on which he was said to spend much of his time, and she had heard, too, that he liked young companions of both sexes on his frequent cruises. One of the secretaries, soon after her arrival, had said to her: "Don't be too surprised if you get an invitation to sail with him—with a face and figure like yours."

After six months with the firm, during which she did a great deal of translation of legal documents and bills of lading, she was due for a week's paid vacation.

When she was notified of this by Monsieur Verret, he almost negligently added: "By the way, the marquis is sailing to Cannes. He invites you to be his guest."

When she told Zoltan about the invitation, he erupted into one of his nasty moods. "I suppose you didn't mention your fiancé. I wouldn't mind a trip on that boat. Besides, I'm heading to London that week, and you could meet me there if you have a week off."

Rather than face his anger and jealousy, she quickly said she would, of course, prefer to spend a week in London with him. Monsieur Verret, when she told him that she couldn't accept the marquis's invitation, merely nodded bleakly. Zoltan had to leave the day before she did. He would reserve a room for her at the Savoy and meet her there. And here she was at customs.

"Would you open the other bag, please, miss?"

Again the custom's officer felt through her possessions, then he closed the bag, lifted it, and inspected it carefully.

This had never happened to her before; usually, at customs, they just marked her bags with chalk, or put stickers on them, and waved her through.

"You arrived from Marseilles?" he asked.

"Yes."

He lifted the bags from the platform and placed them to one side.

"I must ask you to come with me, miss."

"Why?"

"Just come with me, please."

He had her go to the end of the platform, come around to his side, then led her into a bare office, with only a few wooden chairs.

"Wait here, please," he said.

"What is this about?"

"Sorry to detain you, miss—it won't be long."

She sat on one of the chairs and waited, fretting. Zoltan was to meet her in the arrivals area, and, since her flight from Marseilles had landed on time, he would be wondering where she was.

It was more than half an hour before the door to the room opened and a woman in customs uniform beckoned to her. She went to another room with the woman, where, after the door was locked from the inside, she was told to disrobe.

"Why?"

"A search, madame," the woman said. "Everything off, please."

The woman had a stern face and was stocky and broad-shouldered. The search was infuriating—more than that, humiliating, for the customs woman probed everywhere on her body.

"You may dress, mademoiselle."

After she was clothed again, she followed the woman down a hallway to a larger room, where the first customs officer had now been joined by another, who appeared, from the gold stripes on his sleeve, to be his superior. On a table were her bags—mutilated, utterly torn apart. And on the table, too, along with her possessions, were six glassine bags filled with white powder.

"Well, miss," said the officer with gold stripes. "Suppose you tell us about it."

It was utterly incomprehensible to her. She assured the customs officers, the woman, that she had no knowledge of the white powder, which they told her was cocaine. Yes, the bags had seemed rather heavy, but that was because she had assumed they were made of the best and stoutest leather. They were a gift. She was shown the secret compartments in the bags; it looked as though each were especially designed to hold and conceal three packages, one on the bottom, covered by another bottom panel, and two others in the sides.

Was she meeting someone? they wanted to know.

Yes, she was. They were quick to notice her hesitation, but it was because she was sure that someone had duped Zoltan —that he, too, was unaware that the bags, when he gave them to her, held cocaine. But, no, now that she thought of it, the bags had seemed lighter when he first gave them to her. Zoltan, of course, had easy access to her room while she was away at work. And she remembered now that, when he had called her from London, he had said off-handedly: "You can use the new luggage."

First she felt sick that Zoltan would use her in this way, then furious with him, to put her through this dreadful grilling, the humiliation of it. She began to cry.

And she answered all their questions.

They kept trying to make her say that she knew the cocaine was in the bags, that she had planned with Zoltan Czepel to bring it to London. She insisted, tearfully, that it wasn't so. The bags had been given to her, a gift.

They said they would have to hold her during an investigation. She was taken in a police van, a horrible experience in itself, to a police station in London. She was booked and fingerprinted and put in a cell block with other women.

It was three days before a police matron came and told her that she was going to be set free. "Seems a friend of yours has confessed to the whole thing," the matron told her. "I'm taking you to him now."

Zoltan was behind a screen. The matron said she had only ten minutes to talk to him.

But she didn't want to talk to him. She faced him silently, accusingly.

"I got you out of it," he said. "I couldn't let it happen to you."

She said tonelessly, "I despise you."

"I'm doing this for *you,*" he said fiercely.

"For *me?*"

"They'll put me away. I could have . . ."

She turned her back on him. She told the matron she had nothing more to say. And, right then at least, she didn't care any more about what happened to Zoltan. No matter what happened to her, or him, she would never see him again.

29

I made a stop at Lyon.

A former classmate at Columbia, Dick Butler, had gone into newspaper work and, specializing in investigative reporting, had written a book about a scandalous incident that had occurred in a French province. Some of the local flour had gone bad and poisoned an entire village. Reading his book, I'd been amazed by the wealth of detail he'd obtained, in spite of cover-ups by officials all the way up in the government, and I'd asked him how he went about it. "The first thing I do," I remembered his telling me, "is visit the newspaper offices. I'll usually find someone who's a mine of information. Then I just follow up on the gossip."

Lyon had a number of newspapers, but first I visited the Syndicate d'Initiative, tantamount to the city's chamber of commerce. I was more familiar with such organizations. The woman I spoke to was helpful. I told her I was involved with wine imports to the United States and asked if she could put me in touch with some newspaper reporter who might know about some of the less publicized château wine growers of the region. I shamelessly used the name of Ben Graham as the man I represented. "Mr. Graham," she said. "But I know him. Of course the man you must speak to is Emile Despard of the *Lyonnaise populaire.*"

"A reporter?"

"No, the business editor. How much time do you have? I can arrange an appointment."

"I'm in rather a hurry."

"Let me call him now."

She put the call through and informed me that Despard would be happy to see me at once in his office.

He was a wiry little man of about fifty. His large yellow-tinted glasses over a beaked nose gave him an owlish look. He enjoyed speaking in English, he assured me—gave him the chance to practice the language.

I sat across from his cluttered desk and fabricated a story

to the effect that my client, Ben Graham, had heard something about a vineyard owned by the marquis de Carenne, who, according to rumor, produced a remarkable wine, similar to a Chateauneuf du Pape, on his estate near Avignon. I had promised Graham, I said, that I would look into the rumor during my current *tour gastronomique.*

Despard pursed his lips, looking even more birdlike.

"I know of him," he said. "Not personally. I believe he produces a bit of wine, but I have always understood it was strictly for his personal use. Since he lives in great style, yes, I assume it would be an excellent wine."

"Do you think I might contact him? At least track down the rumor to the source, so to speak?"

"I doubt if I could help you there. A fairly elusive fellow. Enjoys life to the full, as they say."

"You mean he's likely to be off somewhere on one of his yachting trips?"

"That," he agreed, "or one of his many houses. As far as doing business with him, I doubt you'd have much luck. His affairs are handled by representatives, mainly. The marquis inherited a good bit of wealth, along with that title. I must say, he has managed it very well, considering his reputation."

"As a playboy?"

"You might say that, yes."

"His title," I said. "Where does it come from?"

"Oh," Despard said. "You know these titles. People like the marquis keep to them as a point of pride, conceit. The family tree is easy enough to look up."

He reached behind him to a window shelf and selected a volume that apparently was a kind of French *Who's Who.* He found the page, and, with his finger indicating the entry, handed me the book.

The entry was large and began with the lineage of the marquis, which went back to the sixteenth century. His business address was listed as Marseilles, his main residence as the Château Benezet on route N. 570, south of Avignon, and other residences in Saint-Paul de Vence, and Santa Margherita Ligure, Italy. His occupations were listed as shipping, import-export, and brokerage; he was a member of several clubs and organizations and had been awarded the *legion d'honneur* in 1969 for his philanthropic pursuits. His birth year was 1927.

"Quite a gentleman," I said. "No wife or children, apparently."

Despard allowed himself a discreet smile.

"One might say he does not lack for company."

"Has fun on that yacht of his?"

"The pick of the crop. There may be a few news photos in our files. The usual bikinis. Handsome young men, all that. Naturally, an invitation to one of his trips would be prized. And, now and then, he holds a party aboard. Quite a social event. Unfortunately, I'm not on his guest list."

"It mentions philanthropic interests. What would those be?"

"Environmental matters, mostly. Protection of marine life, much concerned about pollution in the Mediterranean. But you know what they say about people like the marquis."

"No," I said, "I don't."

"There's a reporter on this paper who once printed a nasty item to the effect that the marquis is against pollution because it clogs his ship's propellors. But the truth is, I feel, that this fellow was denied an invitation to one of the parties. There was an actual bit of scandal once. Had something to do with the yacht, the . . . "

I helped him. "The *Pantagruelle.*"

"Yes, odd name. The feminine of Pantagruel—from Rabelais, you know. Appears that you must never use a masculine name for a ship."

"Except the military," I said.

"Quite right," he agreed. "Generals, and all that. In any event, he was about to set off on a marine expedition involving a film, and the director of the film was found dead in a car. Turned out the poor man's throat had been cut by someone he had picked up on the road. Very mysterious."

"Must have upset him."

"Oh, yes. The marquis canceled all his cruising and entertaining for the season. Our society reporter was much upset."

"About the murder?"

"I suppose more about a social event she was hoping to

cover. I once saw the ship, anchored off Cannes. At night, lights are strung from the masts; it's quite a sight. It's always there at film festival time."

"That's in May?"

"Yes, early May."

"I doubt that I'll be in France that long. I would like to see the ship, though, and, if possible, meet the marquis. Assuming he's cruising somewhere, do you think I might be able to find him?"

"Quite possible, though I doubt you'd get aboard all that easy. Unless you were introduced in some way. Did you say you were going to Cannes?"

"I could go there."

"I have a friend there, a yacht broker. I imagine he could help you more than I could."

"Would you mind giving me a note to him?"

"Not at all."

He gave me a name and an address in Cannes, on a piece of note paper.

"I wish you luck," Despard said, "but I really can't imagine the marquis being interested in a small wine sale."

"I told Graham I'd try," I said. "It would be a pleasure to sample his wine, in any case."

"If you're interested in some out-of-the-way vineyards," Despard said, with the gleam of the wine lover in his eyes behind the yellow-tinted glasses, "I could be of more immediate assistance."

"Another time, perhaps," I said.

At a service station on route N. 570 outside Avignon, an attendant told me how to find the Château Benezet. I was to proceed three kilometers to a road on the right. There would be tall hedges, and the opening that was the road would appear suddenly. Along that road for another two kilometers and I would come to the gate of the château, which was on the left.

The gate was locked.

Through the bars I could see the château looming at the end of a curving, cindered driveway. The windows of the upper two floors were shuttered. It was not a particularly handsome building, but the grounds surrounding it were well kept, and a line of tall poplars extended to what looked like cultivated farmland beyond the château in the rear.

I found a bell at one side of the gate. The clang was loud; it was answered by the barking of dogs. A man appeared from a low-lying building near the château, either a garage or a workshed, and came toward the gate, a German shepherd at his side. The man wore boots and work clothes.

He remained on the other side of the gate, peering at me.

"Is the marquis at home?" I asked in French.

He shook his head.

"Is anyone here?"

He gave an elaborate shrug, which might have meant someone was here, but in that case what did it matter to me. The dog growled, and he patted its head.

"I spoke to a housekeeper yesterday," I said.

"Madame Clairette, *oui,*" he agreed.

I asked if I could speak to her, and he shrugged again and left me waiting outside the gate while he trudged toward the main entrance of the château. A door had already opened and a woman was peering out at me.

"Qu'est-ce que, Pierre?" I heard her ask.

They exchanged a few words, and she came to the gate.

"Monsieur?" she said, with mingled politeness and suspicion.

I decided on directness, trying English on her first. "I understand my wife, Caryl Batory, telephoned here to the marquis. I must find her. Can you give me any information?" She looked uncomprehending, so I repeated the words, somewhat haltingly, in French.

"Je ne comprends pas," she said.

I asked if there were visitors staying at the château, and she said there was no one but herself and Pierre. Where was the marquis? She was not permitted to give that information. Was he on his boat, the *Pantagruelle?* She said she was sorry, she did not know.

The windows of the château seemed to stare at me emptily. The woman's stony expression clearly implied that I was not going to get through that gate.

"Merci," I said unnecessarily, and I returned to the car.

30

Michel Grignon couldn't have been more friendly. The name Despard brought a smile to his face. "You've seen Emile? How is he? You know, I once considered the profession of journalism myself, but my love of boats prevailed. I haven't done too badly, you see."

He waved his arms as though to embrace his establishment, a large open showroom in the old port area of Cannes. Pictures of sleek yachts adorned the walls. Handsome marine fittings were displayed like pieces of sculpture. Two young salesmen were busy at telephones in glass-enclosed cages. Grignon was forty, spruce, well dressed in blue blazer with gold buttons and creased gray-flannel trousers.

I had told him I wished to learn the whereabouts of the *Pantagruelle.*

"Lovely ship," he said, "lovely. Eight thousand tons, two-thousand-mile cruising range. You have an invitation to visit her, I assume."

"Well, not exactly," I told him. "I've been asked to look up the marquis by a mutual friend, but unfortunately he's off cruising. Perhaps if he puts in somewhere reachable . . ."

"But I know him!" Grignon enthused. "I could put in a word for you."

"It's a delicate matter," I said. "You see, there's a woman aboard, or so I've heard, who I'm interested in, and I'd prefer surprising her. You understand?"

"Of course. So, your problem is to find the *Pantagruelle.* Of course, if you waited, sooner or later she'll turn up here, or at Saint-Tropez. The marquis puts in at one or the other and gives a party. Naturally, everyone who's anyone wants an invitation. But you're in a hurry, I can see. She must be quite a woman."

"Oh, she is," I assured him. I wasn't doing too much lying for a change.

"What I can do," he said, "is contact Le Garde-Côtes, and simply request the ship's position. After that, it would be up to you."

I agreed that might be the best thing to do, and he made the call himself. There was a fifteen-minute wait, during which he showed me pictures of the boats he had for charter or sail. When he was called back, he jotted down the coordinates, and then, spreading a large chart out on a table, he fixed the position. The craft was about seventy nautical miles off the island of Crete and heading in a northeasterly direction.

"You have a few choices," he said. "As you can see, there are Kárpathos, Rhodes, Kos, and Kálimnos, all with harbors of adequate depth for a ship the *Pantagruelle*'s tonnage. The social activity in Rhodes would be greater at this time of the year—so, if I were you, that is where I would go. From Nice you have flights to Athens, and from Athens it's an hour by plane. Should you miss her there, you could charter a boat to the other islands or could overtake her. The *Pantagruelle* cruises at twelve knots, I believe."

He waved away my thanks and assured me it would be pleasant to do business with me, if I were ever in need of a boat.

The harbor of Rhodes was dominated by the Crusader's Castle. The water sparkled an incredible blue. Three ships of good size were anchored off shore, but none, I learned from a port officer, was the *Pantagruelle.* All three were Greek cruise ships.

I took an outdoor table at a taverna not far from the harbor, drank a glass of the local wine, and considered what to do. There was a Greek Coast Guard station here, undoubtedly, and my English-speaking waiter told me how to find it. The officer on duty didn't speak English, but a young Greek woman, a telephone operator, did. I said that I had been expecting to find the *Pantagruelle* anchored here and hoped to see someone aboard, but apparently I had been misinformed.

She checked a log.

"Yes, tomorrow," she said. "The ship is expected to put in here for refueling."

I took a taxi to the airport, retrieved my bags, and booked a room in town at the Cairo Palace. My room was on the third floor; two tall windows overlooked the harbor. The view, for some reason, made me ache with a kind of longing. For Caryl, yes, but, more than that, to have her with me here. If it weren't for the dreadful mess we were now both in, what a perfect place this would be to relax, enjoy each other, to know finally about each other all that we didn't know.

A tap on the door awakened me. My breakfast tray was brought in by a swarthy maid who, unsmiling, opened the window shutters and, with not so much as a glance at me, withdrew. Black, acrid coffee in hand, I looked out over the quayside and the blue water of the harbor. A good-sized ship, glistening white, was moving slowly in, a plume of smoke trailing from its single stack.

I dressed in a hurry and walked the few hundred yards to the Coast Guard office. Near a teletype machine I found the same young woman I had spoken to the day before. I asked her about the ship coming into the harbor.

"Yes, the *Pantagruelle,*" she said, not bothering to glance out the windows. The clacking teletype had already given her the information.

"Will she dock?" I asked, controlling my excitement. I had yet to figure out how to get aboard, but I was sure I would find a way.

She shook her head. Docking facilities were lacking for a ship that size; she would stay at anchor; a tanker had been ordered for refueling. Did I wish her to radio-teleophone for the ship's launch?

"I'd rather hire something and go out to her," I said.

"You wish to do that?" She sounded eager. "My brother has a boat. He'll give you a better price. I can take you to him now."

I agreed.

The pier she took me to was crowded with small fishing boats, cayaques, and motor launches available for charter. Her brother, who was hosing down an ancient Chris Craft of twenty feet or so, had a mop of curly black hair and a muscled chest and arms. He was about thirty. When his sister explained what I wanted, in Greek, he came toward me with outstretched hand.

"Costa Panopoulis," he announced. "I am at your service."

"I want to get aboard that ship," I said, indicating the *Pantagruelle.* Its movement had ceased, and it was now lying broadside to the main quay, about two miles away, I judged.

"The captain knows you?" he asked.

His large brown eyes studied me. One never knew what to expect from Americans, his expression seemed to say.

"No," I said.

"You won't get aboard," he said.

"Why not?"

"I know the ship. Very rich people, very exclusive. Sometimes strange people."

"How strange?"

"You know," he said evasively. He said something in Greek to his sister, who, her eyes amused, told me that some of the men on the ship were "delicate types."

"Yes, I see," I said. "But let's give it a try."

We settled on thirty drachmas for the trip to the ship. The boat had a faded canvas top for shade, but I remained in the open stern while Costa backed the boat from its slip and then guided it out into the harbor. As we came nearer to the *Pantagruelle,* I could make out figures on a rear sun deck. On closer inspection, I saw three women and four men lying or sitting as though absorbing sun. They glanced our way. None of the women was Caryl. One was blonde and thin, but seemed in her late teens. No one on the deck gave us more than a cursory glance.

Costa swung his boat expertly alongside, about midship. "You'll have to ask for the captain," he told me. "Or an officer."

A sailor in a horizontally striped shirt, wearing a black beret, peered down at us. Costa spoke to him in Greek, then in Italian, which the sailor understood. I gathered that Costa had told him I wanted to come aboard. The sailor left the rail and came back with an officer. He shook his head vigorously. "No visitors."

"It's important I see the marquis," I called up to him.

"No visitors," he said again.

"Give him my name," I said. "Steven Parrish. Tell him I'm looking for Caryl Batory. Is she aboard?"

"No," the officer said. "No such person."

"Tell the marquis," I said.

He gave a shrug and left the rail. When he came back, he shook his head. "No visitors," he said again.

"Any way we can get on the ship?" I asked Costa.

The sides were smooth, and there was no means of ingress.

"They would have to let down a boarding ladder," Costa said.

"Let's hang around for a while," I said. I felt certain Caryl was aboard the ship. Costa moved his boat some twenty yards away from the ship. We waited. The officer made angry gestures to us.

"This isn't doing any good," I said. "Circle around the ship."

I hoped that Caryl would see me and come outside. On the stern deck, the sunbathers now looked at us more curiously. A couple of them waved. One young man made a derisive gesture. The thin blonde girl held up a glass, as though offering me a drink. I began to feel foolish. A tanker approached the ship from the port area, and we hung around during a refueling operation. I heard a grinding noise.

"What's that?" I asked Costa.

"Pulling up anchor," he said. "The ship will leave."

"Can we follow her?"

"In this?" He looked dubious.

"How about a larger boat? Can we find a charter?"

"Oh, yes."

"Can you handle a bigger boat?"

He gave me an almost pitying smile.

"Anything," he said. "I'm a good seaman."

"You've got the time to follow the ship, wherever it goes?"

"Plenty of time. You have money?"

"Enough," I said.

"We get very good boat. The best."

Smoke was again drifting from the *Pantagruelle*'s stack as we returned to the quay.

31

The sea was smooth. We kept a distance of about a half mile from the ship as it cruised in a northerly course. Our boat, the *Arcturus,* was one of several yachts of various sizes in the clear, calm waters of the Aegean. Costa had taken me to a charter service near the port, where for a price of forty-five hundred drachmas a day, we rented the twelve-year-old, forty-foot cabin cruiser. It had a master cabin aft and a smaller cabin forward, where Costa stowed his gear. The *Arcturus* looked well kept and had twin diesels powerful enough to keep pace with the *Pantagruelle.* By the time we left, the larger ship was small on the horizon, but Costa said, no worry, we would soon catch up.

He outfitted our boat with enough food supplies for a week. At the hotel, I sent off a cable to Marie that I would be out of contact for a while, that I was at sea, and would cable again when I made port. Before shoving off, I made a request of Costa.

"Can you get hold of a gun?"

He looked at me sharply. "What kind?"

"A pistol. Maybe a thirty-eight revolver."

"You expect trouble?"

"It's possible," I said. "Does it worry you?"

"No worry," he said.

Later, after we had left the harbor, he gave me a heavy wrapped package. In it, I found a thirty-eight-caliber Smith & Wesson, similar to a policeman's service revolver. I placed it in a drawer in a cabinet next to the bed in the master cabin. In other circumstances, I would have relished this expedition. But I was hardly in a holiday mood. *Just get close,* I mentally warned Zoltan, *just make your move, and I'll use the gun.* The chamber held six brass-jacketed bullets. *You're doing this to me, and I'm sick of you, of what you're doing to Caryl, and of your sick head.* I actually was delighted at the thought of exploding all six bullets into him.

When we had drawn close enough to make out the outlines of the ship, I told Costa to keep it in sight but to avoid indicating our intention to follow. "Sooner or later, they'll put in somewhere. Maybe you can talk to some of the crew." I gave him Caryl's description, and he looked puzzled when I said she might be either blonde or brunette. I explained about the wig.

"Why does she not want to see you?" he asked.

"Trouble," I said vaguely.

"She's maybe a little . . ." He made a circular motion with a finger against his head.

"No," I said.

"Another man," he said, looking wise.

Since that seemed to satisfy him, I let it go.

Every now and then, Costa would speed up the engines and take us off course, then, when the *Pantagruelle* was smaller against the horizon, would take up the ship's track again. "We see them better than they see us," he said. "Many boats like this. They won't know one from the other."

The sun turned red and began to dip toward the western horizon. The last sight of Rhodes was the distant pillars of an ancient temple, high on a bluff. I watched it fade from view, almost enjoying myself.

When darkness came, Costa increased the RPMs of the engines, explaining that we could draw closer, to better keep the lights of the *Pantagruelle* in sight. I noticed that our compass heading had changed toward the west.

He made a curving gesture with his hand.

"First north," he said. "Now they go west."

"Toward where?"

"Kos maybe. The Sea of Crete. So many islands—hard to say."

"Do we travel all night?"

He nodded, but said: "When morning comes, we must refuel. No problem."

"I can relieve you," I said.

"Not at night," he said, shaking his head. "In the morning, yes."

I made us some sandwiches and coffee and then unfolded a deck chair, putting a blanket over my shoulders against the chill. Where, I wondered, would she have joined the ship? I was beginning to feel certain she was on it—otherwise, why would the marquis so firmly have forbidden anyone to come aboard? Crete, perhaps. If she had learned the ship's whereabouts from her call to the château, she could have reached Crete in a matter of hours from the Frankfurt airport. A radio-telephone call to the marquis, and he could have put in for her. The throb of the motors made me drowsy. I was shaken awake. I could see the lights of the *Pantagruelle* scarcely a mile away.

"Go sleep," Costa commanded me.

I had grown to like his rough, pleasant face. I went to the master's cabin and got into bed. I slept better, soothed by the constant drone of the motors, than at any time since Caryl had left me. Curiously, I felt very close to her, almost as though she were the extra pillow I cradled.

Next morning, when I came up on deck, I saw that Costa was guiding the boat slowly toward a landing at a cement pier. He gestured to me to look the other direction, and farther out in the harbor I saw the *Pantagruelle* anchored by a long line to the shore. White houses and villas seemed to be set on rock foundations on a bluff that rose sheerly several hundred feet.

"Where are we?" I asked.

"Thíra, also called Santorini, for Saint Irene. A party went ashore half an hour ago."

"What's the smell?"

It was a peculiar acrid odor, altogether unfamiliar.

"Volcanos," he said. "All over these islands—the Cyclades."

While he looked after the refueling, I walked along the quay to a small harbor town—a cluster of white houses, a few tourist shops, and one hotel of fairly good size called the Atlantis. Guides offered me a mule trip to Fira, a town set on the very top of the bluff. But I had caught sight of a group sitting at tables on the hotel's terrace.

I had on dark glasses against the sun and wore the dungarees and sweater I'd purchased the day before in Rhodes. I found a table where I could unobtrusively observe the group from the ship. I was given a cursory glance by a few of them, and they continued with their conversation. Three of the women were young, hardly out of their teens, their legs and arms sun-browned, much like the girls stretched out on Riviera beaches as though posing for tourist folders. All three were decidedly pretty. The fourth was middle-aged. Two of the men were young, dark-haired, good-looking, with an air of pampered indolence. The third man was paunchy, with long gray sideburns. It was the middle-aged woman who appeared to be dominating the conversation. I gathered she was arguing against taking the mule trip to Fira.

Was Caryl on board, or wasn't she? Were these the only guests of the marquis? Why wasn't she with them? The waiter brought me black coffee and some round doughy rolls. The group seemed in no hurry. Finally, they appeared to have made up their minds. They would go to Fira. That meant the ship would be in the harbor for a while.

And, as though to make this even more clear, some sailors, with round caps bearing the initials "MS/P" came to the terrace and ordered wine. I noticed one of the sailors staring at me intently, as though he recognized me. He had seen me circling the ship the day before, perhaps. Then, strangely, he gave me a faint nod. I nodded back, waiting. But he turned away.

Was it a signal?

I returned to the *Arcturus.* Costa had completed the refueling and had made himself coffee. He munched on some bread with a thick slab of some kind of smelly cheese. "You want some?" he asked.

I shook my head.

"There are some sailors up there," I said. "On the terrace of the hotel. Maybe you could talk to them."

"What do I say?"

"Find out where they're going next."

"O.K."

He was gone the better part of an hour. When he came

back, he looked satisfied with himself. He had found out that the ship was bound for Corfu, where it would put in for a few days. After that, they would return to Saint-Tropez, where the cruise would end.

"I spoke to one called Carlos. He seemed the friendliest. I told him my boss was interested in the ship and would like to see it, to go aboard. He said maybe in Corfu, it could be arranged. We go to Corfu?"

"Yes. How far is it?"

"Two, three, four days, depending on weather. Sooner if we go by way of the Canal of Corinth. If the weather turns bad, the ship goes that way."

"How's the weather look?"

With a forefinger, he pointed in an easterly direction. Just over the horizon I saw clouds gathering. Already a haze had blunted the brightness of the sun.

"Not so good," Costa said. "I'll get some sleep. I think I'll need it."

He went into the forward cabin, while I remained on deck. I wondered: was Carlos the one who had nodded to me? Was Caryl, in that way, saying she would meet me at Corfu? A breeze, actually a wind with a bit of chill in it, had sprung up. The water had turned choppy. But it was as though the wind had brought with it a semblance of hope.

32 SAINT-TROPEZ, OCTOBER 1967

The ring of the telephone awakened her. It would be Ian, of course. He was hard at work, taking meticulous pains to make sure everything would be in order for the expedition that would set off in three days, and he was often up until the small hours of the morning. Most of the crew were installed, as were she and Ian, at the Hotel de Paris, which they used as a working headquarters.

Anger, more than fear, gripped her when she recognized the voice. He was out, and he had found her. She had known that it would happen one day.

"What do you want?" she asked coldly.

"I must see you."

"No," she said. "Never."

"It would be better if you did."

"Why?"

"I need you."

"For what?"

"Go to the port," he said. "You'll find me at one of the cafés."

"I'm tired," she said. "You woke me. I told you it was over. I meant it. I have someone else."

"I think you had better see me," he said.

She knew the tone. The hardness in it.

"It's useless," she said.

"It hasn't been pleasant for me. And you owe me something."

"I can't think what."

"I took your place. Isn't that enough?"

"All right," she said wearily. "I'll see you this once."

"Walk along the line of cafés that overlook the port. You'll see me."

She hung up, dressed quickly, and walked the few narrow blocks of streets to the quay, lined with yachts. A few of the cafés, with their sidewalk terraces, were still open, but not many sat at the tables. At one of the cafés, back in a corner, she recognized Zoltan. His black hair was cropped short, and his pallor was noticeable. For a moment, only a moment, she felt pity for him.

She sat down beside him.

"I can't stay long," she said.

"Why not?"

He gripped her hand hard. She tried to withdraw it, but he held on tightly.

"I have to be at the hotel."

"For this man?"

"It's no business of yours," she said.

"I have business with you," he said. "You're coming to Paris with me."

"You're crazy," she said. "I have to be here. I'm working."

"The expedition? What do you need that for?"

She didn't answer, and, seeing the stubborn set of her lips, he let her hand go.

"I'm not asking all that much," he said almost humbly—a humbleness she by no means trusted. "I need what's in the safe deposit box. You have the key."

She shook her head.

"You don't?"

"I threw it away," she said. "Besides, there's the other one."

"Julio?" He gave a sharp, short, mirthless laugh. "He's dead. Anyway, there's your signature at the bank. They'll give you another key."

She said angrily: "You expect me to walk in, after all this time, ask for a key. . . . After the way you used me! After what happened to me in London? All for your dirty money."

"Such selfishness," he said with a mocking smile. "Five years out of *my* life and she thinks only of herself. You forget so easily."

"No, the opposite. I haven't forgotten."

"That's good," he said. "So you remember how I got you out of Budapest. How I took care of you, got you work, money, places to live. You lived well, didn't you? Paris, Saint-Moritz, good clothes, jewelry. . . . What happened to the ring?"

"It's in a sewer somewhere with the key."

"The nights," he said, more softly. "Now you spend them with this other—Cameron—is he better than me? Maybe not so good?"

"If you intend to be so disgusting, I'm leaving." She made a motion to rise, but his arm reached, gripped her wrist tightly.

"Something could happen to him," he said.

"You're filthy!"

"You don't understand." He sighed. "How do I make you understand? We're rich. Together, we're rich."

"Keep it," she said. "Enjoy it. Peddle your cocaine."

"You might try it. You might see things differently. It's excellent for lovemaking."

She said evenly but fiercely: "I was through with you long ago. I'm getting married."

"You are? When?"

She was about to say, after the filming expedition, but thought better of it.

"It's useless. There's nothing more we have to say to each other."

"No!" he cried, pounding the table with his fist. "What's mine is mine. You think you can get away with this? You think Marcel would allow it?"

"Marcel?"

"You still don't know about Marcel?"

She shrugged.

"Seriously? After all this time?" He stared at her wonderingly, then with suspicion. "Perhaps you've already been to the box?"

"You're talking nonsense. I've got to get back."

"This Cameron," he said, still gripping her wrist. "Who is he? How did you meet him?"

She remained silent.

"He's in the way," he said fretfully. "We should do something about that. You haven't told him about us?"

"There's nothing to tell."

"You feel nothing?"

"For you?" Her eyes blazed at him. "I'll tell you what I feel—emptiness. Complete, total emptiness. If you disappeared before my eyes this very second, I would feel the same emptiness."

He smiled at her, as though what she had said had passed right over his head.

"All these years, and I thought you were waiting for me. But then I heard something. Word still got to me, you see. I heard you met this Cameron, through your friend the marquis. So you became lovers. All right, I can understand it. You were human. You became interested in his work. I can understand that. But the situation has changed. I'm free again. And Marcel promised. . . . I want what's in the box. Do I make myself clear?"

"You're a fool," she said. "The police could be keeping a watch on it. On you, or on me."

"Why?" Again his eyes had turned suspicious. "Why would the police be watching?"

"Because of your record, and the one you were good enough to give me."

"No," he said. "I don't think so. It must be something else. You want Cameron to have it."

"He doesn't know! He'll never know."

"Then perhaps I should tell him."

"You wouldn't. . . ."

"I could meet the fellow, have a drink with him, acquaint him with our relationship, mention an arrest for drugs, all sorts of things."

It was as though her heart literally sank.

"Suppose," she said, "I went to Paris with you. Got what you want. Then what?"

He nodded, as though she had finally come around to his way of thinking.

"Then we might reconsider the situation."

"I'd have to find a way to arrange it."

"Would that take long?"

"No, not long."

"How long?"

"A few days. How can I reach you?"

"The Hotel Metropole. Marseilles. But I can't wait long."

"It won't be long," she said, knowing she was lying. "And then—finished?"

"Perhaps," he said. "If your mind hasn't changed."

"Oh, it won't. You can be sure of it."

"One never knows," he said. He rose from the table, gave her a last ironic smile and a wave, and left the café terrace. It was surprising how quickly he was gone from her sight, almost as though he had melted into the darkness. She hurried back to the hotel, thinking that she had bought time. In three days the *Pantagruelle* would leave port. Then, for three months they would be at sea. She would have time to think, to consider what to do. Sooner or later, she would have to tell Ian about Zoltan, perhaps the marquis, too. After all, he had befriended her before. Or, she thought, I could simply disappear. But she wanted those three months with Ian. She loved him with a love greater and deeper than anything she had ever felt for Zoltan. Emptiness? No, that was wrong. What she felt now for Zoltan was pure and bitter hatred.

They were due to board the ship in the afternoon. Ian used the morning for a quick trip to Nice. Word had come that a historian there possessed some old charts indicating hitherto unknown sea lanes used by the Phoenicians. They might provide clues to the locations of wrecks of ancient ships. He entrusted to her the remaining details in Saint-Tropez and sped off in his small open Triumph.

Three hours later, police arrived at the hotel in Saint-Tropez asking for people to identify a body found in a wrecked Triumph found between Saint-Tropez and Cannes. In his own car, the marquis took her, shivering with dread, to the scene. The car had gone out of control on the corniche and crashed on rocks below. A policeman lifted the canvas covering the body. Ian's sightless eyes stared up at her; his sport shirt was drenched with blood. She screamed. The marquis held her, speaking useless words of comfort, while a doctor injected a sedative.

She remembered little of the next few hours. The injection must have put her to sleep. She was in a white hospital room. A nurse sat beside her, told her she was in Saint-Tropez, in the hospital. She refused to take the two small pills and glass of water offered by the nurse. She forced herself to focus on what had happened, on Ian's being gone. "Please tell me everything," she said to the nurse. The nurse, no older than she was, was reluctant at first. "You should rest," she said. "You went into shock."

"I'm better now."

"The young man," the nurse said, "The filmmaker. He was dead before the crash. The police discovered it."

"How?" Caryl asked.

"A knife. The police think a hitchhiker murdered him."

"I must see the marquis," Caryl said, with set lips. She knew now. Zoltan had kept his word. She wanted him dead.

Toward evening of the same day, the marquis came to her room. She asked the nurse to leave.

"I know who killed Ian," she said. "I want to tell you everything. I want you to listen."

The marquis nodded gravely. He held her hand while she talked.

"It was the same one who put the drugs in my bags," she said. "Zoltan Czepel."

"But he's in prison!"

"No," she said. "He visited me a few days ago. He made threats. He wanted me to go with him to Paris."

"Did Ian know this?"

She shook her head tiredly.

"I'm to blame. I should have told him. I should have told you everything before. I . . . he asked me, long ago, to keep a safe deposit box for him. I put things in it, valuable things. He wanted what was in the box. I . . . refused. Actually, I said I would, but I didn't intend to."

"And for that he killed Ian?" the marquis said dubiously.

"He probably knew I didn't intend to keep my word. I was sure the police would arrest me. I thought that during the expedition I would think of what to do. But now I'm ready to tell everything to the police. He gave me his address, in Marseilles."

"We will see to it at once," the marquis said.

"The Hotel Metropole, in Marseilles."

The marquis rose, but she held onto his hand, and he remained with her.

"There's more you should know," she said. "In Paris I

worked—before I came to you—for a man called Halmos. He and Zoltan worked together, just how I'm not sure. The securities I put in the box had to do with their business. After I was arrested in London, I never went near the bank. Zoltan told me that what was in the box was still there. He wanted it badly. If I tell the police about it, what will they do to me?"

The marquis pondered. The room was silent. Then he said:

"If the contents of the box turn out to be stolen, charges could be brought against you. But there must be a way to get around that. I will consult my lawyers. Meanwhile, I'll notify the police concerning your suspicions about Czepel."

A lawyer came to see her the next morning. He had papers for her to sign. They gave him her power of attorney to examine the contents in the box in Paris. There was also a letter instructing the lawyer to notify the Paris police of their contents. Another letter contained a statement to the effect that she had merely been the bearer of the contents in the box, knew nothing of their nature or value, and that she made no claim to them.

"You would still be under suspicion, of course," the lawyer told her, "and for that reason we feel it best for you to leave the country." There was a statute of limitations in such cases, and within a few years it would expire, at which time she could return to France if she so desired.

She attended Ian's funeral that afternoon and immediately after was taken to Nice, where she boarded a plane for New York. The marquis saw her off. As she was about to go through the departure gate, he formally kissed both her cheeks and said she could depend on him for discretion. He saved the news for last.

"They have Czepel. He is being held on a theft charge. He is being questioned as to the murder. All his movements are being traced. He will be brought to justice. As for your possible testimony, my lawyers feel it would do no good. Perhaps he will confess. But it is you I care about. Ian would wish you to do as you are doing."

She flew off to what she was determined would be a new life.

PART FOUR

33

"This is my friend Carlos," Costa said. "He'll help you."

The man who stepped aboard the *Arcturus,* where we were tied up at a quay in close quarters with other boats, was the seaman from the *Pantagruelle* who had nodded to me on the terrace of the Hotel Atlantis on Santorini. He hardly bothered to acknowledge my hello but said abruptly, "Sir, you will come with me now."

We had been docked a few hours. It was afternoon. The *Pantagruelle* was at anchor out in the bay. I had sent Costa to find Carlos, and here he was with him. I had expected there would be negotiations, and I was prepared to hand over my dwindled supply of traveler's checks or, if need be, to get more money at a bank in town. But there was none of that.

"Go with him," Costa said with a vigorous nod. "He knows what to do."

Carlos was slim and wiry. He had a sharp-featured face with brooding dark eyes. He was leading me across an esplanade, on the other side of which were several resort hotels that faced the bay. He turned into a narrow, twisting street.

"Where are we going?" I asked him.

With only a brief glance at me, he shook his head, as though to say I was not to ask questions. He kept up a brisk pace. My optimism that, through him, I was to meet up somewhere, in some place, with Caryl began to fade. I was beginning to feel alarm. Suppose Zoltan had got to him first, and I was being led into a trap?

We turned a corner into another narrow street, this one lined with small shops, some with pastries displayed in their windows, others with dried fruits and nuts. From one came the strong odor of fish. When he began to enter an alleyway, I hesitated. He beckoned me, almost angrily, to follow him. We went through a wide entrance at the end of the alley, and I found myself in a dimly lighted garage. Carlos spoke to an attendant in Greek, and a car was pointed out to him. It was a black Mercedes, fairly new.

"Get in, please," Carlos said.

"What's all this about?" I asked.

"No questions," he said.

Whatever I'm in for, I thought, *I'm already in it—so, let's go.*

I took the passenger seat. Carlos, in the driver's seat, started the car without the slightest hesitation. We left the garage, went back through the alley, and in a matter of minutes were out of the town and heading west toward the hills. We passed through a small village, then wound upward through what seemed to be a vineyard area. We were obviously going farther and farther away from the harbor and the *Pantagruelle.* I began to regret leaving the Smith & Wesson behind in the cabin.

Then, in the distance, I saw water. We came to a stretch that had some newly built hotels and several luxurious villas, all of them overlooking the blue of the sea. We stopped at one of the villas, hidden behind a stone wall. Carlos got out, and, with a key, unlocked the latch of a wooden gate. Back in the car, he drove through and stopped fifty yards further. The villa was modern, of brown stone, two stories high. It had a flagstoned terrace on which were lounging chairs, some shaded by green and white parasols.

"You will stay here," Carlos said.

He rang a bell and a maid appeared, a girl of hardly more than eighteen, round-faced, olive-complexioned. She nodded her head vigorously and smiled at me as Carlos spoke to her in Greek. I heard the name Paul Barlow. Had Carlos made a mistake?

Then, with the same faint nod he had given me at Santorini, Carlos turned and went back to the car. He drove off through the gate, pausing only to close it behind him. I heard the sound of the car receding back along the way we had come.

"Please," the girl said, indicating I should follow her.

"Do you speak English?" I asked.

She shook her head, smiling apologetically.

"French?" I asked.

Again she shook her head. I shrugged and went with her.

I was led through a spacious, comfortably furnished living room to a hallway that was softly carpeted and to a bedroom. She indicated this was to be my room.

"What's your name?" I asked.

She looked uncomprehending.

"Your name," I repeated.

"Ah," she said. "Elena." And scurried away.

The bedroom had a long, wide bed, covered with blue satin and a matching bolster. The windows had blue satin draperies and filmy white curtains. A door led to a gleaming white bathroom. On the top of a bureau, I noticed an envelope. It was addressed to Mr. Paul Barlow. Either there had been a mistake, or I was to assume that I was Paul Barlow. On the back of the envelope was a crest and beneath it: *The Marquis de Carenne.* The name was in raised lettering.

I opened the envelope; inside was a note and another sealed envelope. The note was in English and read: *My dear Paul. I hope you will be comfortable. Please treat the villa as your own during your Corfu stay. Your invitation to the carnival ball aboard the* Pantagruelle *is enclosed, and I will greet you personally then. My estimable sentiments. Pierre.*

The other envelope held the invitation. Paul Barlow's name was inscribed by hand; the date of the ball was the sixth of April, tomorrow. The time was from 2100 hours; costume was obligatory.

I began to wonder if I were dreaming this whole thing. It had been a rough trip for a day and a half, and my legs had been shaky even after calm weather returned. Nor had I had much sleep. No, I wasn't sleeping now, but it was still like a dream—the taciturn Carlos, the smiling little maid, this villa which was apparently mine for the time being, or Paul Barlow's, whoever he was. Anyway, there was nothing sinister about this villa, nothing I could detect. The windows looked out on a garden, and some of the shrubs were already in bloom. At the end of the garden was a pool, large and deep enough for swimming.

All right, figure this out, I told myself. *Caryl doesn't want to leave the safety of the ship, nor would it be safe for me to be seen hanging around the town. The Marquis, her protec-*

tor, arranges for me to be brought here, a place he probably owns. I'm to wait for her here, or, it will be arranged to meet on the ship. In costume? Could that be it? The precautions were extraordinary, but why not, since if I had managed to locate her, Zoltan, too, could have done so, and could already be here in Corfu.

It made a modicum of sense, except I had no costume to wear, nothing but the clothes on my back. The adjoining bathroom, I saw, was well-stocked with towels and toilet articles. I opened the door of a closet and there it was, the costume, on hangers.

If I was to attend the party, it would be as a Venetian nobleman, circa, I guessed, seventeenth century. Opening some drawers in the closet I found accessories: a red half-mask; a false black goatee and mustache; a striped silk cap; and a jeweled dagger in a sheath. I tested the dagger's blade, and found it razor sharp.

But how would I know Caryl, if she were also in costume? Or was all this some nonsense, involving not me, but someone called Paul Barlow.

I took a hot shower, found a pair of swim trunks in one of the drawers and went out to the sunny garden. The pool had looked inviting. I let myself in, found the water cold, but pleasantly so, and swam for a while. When I emerged, I saw Elena peering at me from a window. When aware that she had been noticed, she quickly withdrew. When the sun began to decline and the air turned cooler I went inside and changed back to my clothes. Emerging from the bedroom I saw Elena at the end of the corridor beckoning to me. She led me to the dining room, where the table was set for one. Apparently Elena and I were the only occupants of the house.

On the table were two opened bottles of wine. One was a local white wine. The other was French, I could tell immediately by the shape of the bottle, a Bordeaux. Turning it to its label side, I had a twinge that came from more than its familiarity. It was a Brane Cantenac '61. Was it a coincidence? Caryl and I had shared that same fine '61 in Stowe, a long time ago, it seemed now. It had to be in lieu of a message; it *was* a message. And it reassured me. I poured myself a glass. It had reached its full, yet delicate maturity.

Well, I was being made comfortable enough. Pleasant odors reached me from the kitchen. The missing element was Caryl. If she were here now, this would be a kind of perfection. It was a month since I'd seen her last, and somehow the closer I seemed to get to her, the dimmer she grew in my memory, as though it was no longer Caryl I was pursuing, but her phantom. The wine wasn't bringing her back, only that memory of our first night together.

Elena stood at the door to the kitchen. Again she beckoned me. The kitchen had white-tiled walls, and a red-tiled floor. It was immaculate. On the stove were three pots, steam rising from them. She lifted each pot cover in turn, as though I were to make my choice. A custom of the Greeks, I remembered, for the foreigner unaccustomed to the local food. I chose something that looked like balls of chopped meat and rice. The sauce tasted of lemon. I was served in lonely splendor.

Night came. The odors of flowers drifted in through screened windows. How safe was I? Could Zoltan find me here? The thought grew, mixed with a certain fear, that Zoltan was not far away—otherwise, why all these precautions? It struck me that I was wrong in not notifying Delahaye of my whereabouts. But I had sent him a message, after all. Undoubtedly, he or his people would be tracking Zoltan. In my bedroom, I heard the sound of a door closing. That would be Elena, going to her bed. I got up and looked through the house for a telephone. I found it in a corner of a room filled with books and record albums. The marquis wouldn't mind a long-distance call to Paris, particularly if it was on account of the common enemy.

I picked it up, hoping for an English-speaking operator. The line was dead.

But that could be easily explained. The marquis wasn't planning to use the house, had not for some time, and obviously had had the phone disconnected.

My sleep was unsound. I was already awake when a knock came on the bedroom door and Elena entered with a breakfast tray.

"I want to make a telephone call," I told her.

She smiled vaguely, not comprehending. I made motions indicating picking up a telephone and dialing a number.

She smiled again and shook her head.

Was there a house nearby? After breakfast, I walked to the gate and down the narrow road several hundred yards to a villa, its entrance drive barred by a gate. The windows were shuttered. I decided against house-breaking and returned to the marquis's villa to wait. But for what? The day faded, and still no answer to the question. After I finished an early dinner, Elena beckoned to me, and I followed her to my bedroom. There, laid out neatly on the bed, was the costume. Time to dress for the evening. Whatever the rules were, there was nothing to do but follow them.

Examining myself in a mirror, I was surprised at my appearance. The black mustache and goatee gave me a distinctly fierce look. The costume fitted well. I was a seventeenth-century Venetian, outfitted for a courtly ball.

The dark had come when I heard the sound of a car's wheels crunching on the driveway. Through a window I saw the Mercedes I had arrived in. Carlos got out. I went to the door.

"We go," he said stolidly. "The mask."

I slipped it on, and he nodded.

We drove back the way we had come into the town. I heard oriental music slithering off crowded walls, smelled the not unpleasant smoke from broiling skewers of meat. Cafés spread their tables in front of a long, colonnaded street, and out in the harbor I saw the lighted masts of the *Pantagruelle.* We stopped at a pier, where several other cars were parked. A launch was waiting; in it were others in costume—a Mephistopheles all in black, a witch, a ballet dancer, legs revealed, but a mink stole wrapped around her shoulders to protect against the nighttime chill, a male pirate and a female pirate who appeared to be his companion. All wore masks—white, pink, red, black. I was greeted as though I were known by them, but it was the recognition of a participant, like themselves, in the coming carnival.

Carlos sat in the rear of the launch as we made our way

toward the ship, his arms folded, his face expressionless. Boarding steps had been let down at the side of the ship. I heard the sound of an orchestra, playing a Beatles tune. Carlos, with the pilot of the launch, gave us helping hands from the launch to the boarding steps. When we came aboard, two of the ship's officers waited at a barrier; they examined the engraved invitations slowly, and, one by one, we were let through, to be greeted further on by a tall man dressed as a Spanish grandee.

He wore a plumed hat. His black mask covered only his eyes and the bridge of his nose. His lips were full. He held my hand a moment longer than necessary.

"Ah, Mr. Barlow?" he said. "Welcome. I hope later in the evening we can have a little talk."

"I do hope so," I said fervently.

He withdrew his hand and was already looking over my shoulder to the next guest who had come off the gangway. I hesitated, but he paid me no more attention. But he was distinctive enough. Apparently he was the marquis. He was certainly the host of the party.

I saw that I was on the main deck, with a boat deck above and two decks below. A companionway, bedecked with multicolored streamers, led to large adjoining halls, the panels between them opened so that it made one space where most of the guests were gathered. At one end a small orchestra played. A long table held a sumptuous buffet, and behind it, in gondolier costume, were several waiters. Flowers were everywhere, their scent almost too sweet. A pleasant female voice echoed through the area, via loudspeakers: "Guests will feel free to use any cabins or rooms whose doors are open. Lock them if you wish." The voice was discreet, but the implication was not. Many of the guests were dancing on the polished flooring; pirates with ballet dancers, clowns with seminude female devils, crusaders with Columbines. . . . It was a gay, pretty scene but lacking in hilarity. I wandered to one of several bars, behind it two gondoliers. I was handed a glass of champagne. Tasting it, I found it excellent, possibly a Dom Perignon of a good year. A white-robed nun wearing a white half-mask caught my eye. She was just about

Caryl's height and slimness. I put the glass back on the bar and approached her.

"Dance?" I said.

She nodded.

I held her in my arms and knew at once she wasn't Caryl.

I said anyway, "Who are you?"

She answered in a British accent. "Against the rules, you know."

"Sorry," I said.

I danced with a female pirate and a belly dancer whose legs were shapely, like Caryl's. But neither was Caryl. I was sure I'd be able to tell, once she was in my arms.

I caught sight of a gypsy dancer who, as she passed by me in the arms of a Russian cossack, gave me a penetrating glance, almost as though she had recognized me. I kept her in sight, but as more guests arrived, crowding the room, she disappeared from my view. I went out on deck, wandered into a salon where a clown, a ballet dancer, a Spanish duenna, and a bandanaed cowboy were playing bridge, and out again.

The white-robed nun was leaning against the rail, staring out at the harbor. I stood near her at the rail. Lights from other large boats shimmered on the water. I said, "We meet again."

The nun turned toward me; eyes regarded me from holes in the white mask. Her voice was distant.

"Pardon, monsieur?"

The wrong nun. She moved away.

I was about to return to the ballroom, when I saw the tall Spanish grandee coming toward me along the now empty deck.

"Mr. Barlow," he said softly. "It is time for our little chat. Would you come with me?"

34

I followed him forward along the companionway of the main deck, into what looked like a sitting room, furnished luxuriously. It was apparently part of a private suite, for an opened door gave me a glimpse of an equally luxurious bedroom. Against a wall, near a painting, he pressed what looked like a light button; a door slid open, revealing a small elevator. He motioned me politely to enter it, and we rose a short distance. The door opened into an exercise room, equipped like a small, compact gym. There were the kind of tumbling mats on the floor familiar from my wrestling days, weights, a bicycle exerciser, and a rowing machine.

The elevator door slid quietly closed behind us.

"We can speak freely here," the marquis said, removing his mask, and indicating that I should do the same. I saw a remarkably handsome face, a touch effeminate, the nose long and aquiline, brown eyes almost liquid in their softness, and the full, sensual lips I had noticed before.

"I am Pierre de Carenne," he said. "But of course your name is not Barlow."

"No."

"And it is?"

"Steven Parrish."

"Forgive the rigamarole," he said with a modest, almost apologetic smile. "But I'm sure you understand the need for strict precautions. We must guard against a very dangerous and clever fellow, quite ruthless. He is under the delusion that your wife—Caryl—holds something of his that has great value."

"Is she on the ship?" I broke in.

He nodded, a warm glint of understanding in his eyes. He was enjoying this, I felt, enjoying his role in a kind of benevolent conspiracy.

"Then . . ."

He held up a hand. "It's important for you to know, Mr.

Parrish, that you are in great danger, as is Caryl; but she believes, and I do also, that you are in the greater danger."

"I'm already aware of that."

"I must say," he said, "that I am filled with admiration for your persistence, your courage, and your . . . shall we say, detective work? Ever since you inquired at the gates of my château, I have been aware of your movements. I have been given information about two killings done, apparently, by Czepel. I should also tell you that I received word he made inquiries about the movements of this ship."

"Where?"

"Nice," he said. "Within twenty-four hours of your own inquiries. I can't guarantee that he isn't on this ship. I hope not. But with so many guests . . . Each invitation was delivered by hand and signed for, yet . . ." He gave a troubled shake of his head. "Caryl wanted you to know all this. She left you less for her sake than for yours. Yet, when she glimpsed you off Rhodes, her resolve never to see you weakened. So finally we arranged to give you a signal."

"A bottle of very good wine," I said.

"An excellent vintage," he said. "At any rate, I have honored her wish to see you again, though I can't say I think it wise. Until this Czepel can be gotten hold of and given what he deserves, both of you would be better off separated. I'd advise you, Mr. Parrish, to return quickly to New York. No reason for Czepel to follow you there. As for Caryl, I can offer her more security than you can. But I doubt you'll accept my advice."

"No," I said.

"Then I suppose I'll have to help both of you. I've already sent a message to Paris police headquarters that Czepel may be in the vicinity of this ship."

"Any reply?"

"Yes, from an Inspector Delahaye. He is on his way to Corfu."

"He thinks Caryl is tied up with Czepel."

"Then I can certainly disabuse him of that notion. But I can see you're anxious to greet your wife. She's waiting for you in Cabin A-4, two decks below."

"Thanks," I said, my voice husky. "Thanks, very much."

He shrugged, his expression almost bored now that he had done his favor. He opened the door, switched off the light, and glanced out.

"There are stairs near the stern," he said. "Two flights. Oh—three quick knocks on the cabin door, twice."

We replaced our masks, and I left him at the elevator. I hurried along the deserted boat deck, apparently closed off for the party, and found the stairwell.

At cabin A-4, I rapped smartly three times, twice.

From inside the cabin, a chain bolt was released. The door opened just enough for me to see the white-masked face regarding me. "Take off your mask, please," a familiar feminine voice said.

I removed it. The door opened wide. A white-robed nun gripped my hand and pulled me inside the cabin. Once the door was closed and rebolted, the nun rushed into my arms. In a kind of sob, she said my name. I crushed her lips closed with mine. Then, gently, I removed her mask. Tears made her violet-blue eyes glisten.

I said, not knowing for the moment what else to say, "Don't ever leave me again."

She tried to smile, but more tears came. We sat together on the bed, and for minutes, it seemed, we merely held each other close, straining against each other, as though to be completely sure that this was real, and we were together again.

"Why?" I asked. I repeated it. "Why?"

She held me away from her, examining me gravely.

"Why did you follow me? I didn't want you to."

"You knew I would," I said.

"Not at first. I thought you'd . . ." She didn't finish the sentence, and suddenly smiled. "Your mustache and goatee become you. I saw you in that silly boat at Rhodes, going round and round. I saw you from this porthole."

"I felt you were watching me."

Her white garments made her seem almost perversely desirable. And she had returned to her original hair coloring.

"Pierre—the marquis—told me a boat was following. I

didn't have the heart to . . . Anyway, he said he would arrange for me to see you."

"You mean he arranged this party?"

"No, he has one every year. But the costume, an invitation in another name, and making sure that it *was* you. He's been so kind. He told you about Zoltan Czepel?"

"I already knew. In fact, I've met him."

I saw the alarm in her eyes.

"He *has* been following you."

"I thought I'd thrown him off, but the marquis seems to think he got on my trail again." I wondered if the marquis had told her about the kind of bloody trail Zoltan had left.

"The policeman in Paris," she said hesitantly, as though she was hoping, praying, I was not involved in it, "and Grete?"

"Gazin was the officer's name," I said. "We didn't know it was Czepel. Grete I could have saved, if she had listened to me."

She covered her face with her hands. When she looked at me again, her eyes were wet.

"I don't know what to do," she said. "I bring trouble, death. You must go away from me."

"We're staying together," I said.

"Don't say that, until you know."

"Know what?"

"What I'm going to tell you."

"Not now," I said. "Not just yet."

I took her in my arms.

The lovemaking was desperate, as though there might never be another chance. Our costumes were in a single heap. The bed was made for one, but it gave us all the room we needed.

"I met two nuns," I said, "in the same costume. Which were you?"

"The one who spoke to you in French. The other was Pierre's English secretary."

"If you knew it was me, why didn't you . . ."

"Steve," she said with a sigh, "you still don't see the danger you're in. If he finds us, he'll do to you what he did . . ." She couldn't say it.

I finished for her. ". . . to Gazin and Grete and Ian."

"You knew that?"

"Guessed it. Zoltan killed Ian, made it look like a car crash. And once he showed up in Paris, you thought I'd get the same. You left, thinking you'd save me. I'd have preferred facing it with you. Why couldn't you tell me about Ian before?"

"I didn't want that threat hanging over you. It was a risk, marrying you, but once I took it I wanted it to be a normal life, at least for you. I'd always told myself that if Zoltan ever came near me again, I would leave you."

"So it would have happened anyway, if not Paris, somewhere else?"

"Yes," she said.

"Well, that's changed. It's Zoltan or us."

"You don't know how clever he is."

"He can't be all that clever. He can't show himself, not with half of Europe looking for him. If he does, we'll make sure this time."

Suddenly, she seemed to remember something. "Helga," she said. "You saw Helga!"

"I got her away. She's safe. Even I don't know where she is. I mean, she's in good hands. There's something you don't know." I had to tell her. I wanted everything out in the open. "I made love to Grete."

She was shaking her head, and I was puzzled.

"Not so," Caryl said.

"It's the truth."

"*She* made love to *you*. I asked it of her. I asked her, if you came to Berlin and found her—I knew I'd left letters from her in my apartment—to keep you there. I asked her to make you happy, at least for a while, long enough."

"So that I wouldn't follow? Feel guilty, even try to forget you? And there I was, complimenting myself on my charm and attractiveness. And all the time she was doing you the favor. But why the lies?"

"What lies?"

"About my ill temper and possessiveness and bad American habits."

"Those were *her* lies, I suppose. I told her the truth. Even that you were a marvelous lover. I'm sure she was pleased to . . ."

"Try me out?"

"Don't say that. She was to be a gift of love."

"You're really extraordinary," I said. "I was right about you."

"Right?"

"That there's only one like you. Do you still love me?"

"Didn't you get your answer just a little while ago?"

"Yes," I said. "But I'll need more."

"Now?"

"Now."

And afterwards, again we talked.

"What exactly happened in Paris the day you left?" I asked.

"He found me. Through my own mistake. I called Halmos. . . ."

"Who's Halmos?"

"It's so complicated." She sighed. "It's such a long story."

"I want to hear it all."

"You won't like it."

"I don't care."

It must have been an hour or more that we talked, though I mostly listened. Those months and years that she had been reluctant to fill in for me were now explained. She was amazed at how much I already knew, or had at least had guessed. She was curious about her brother in Budapest and wanted to know precisely what he had said. Yes, she said sadly, he had been right about Zoltan all along, but she had been too young and rebellious to listen to him. So many things had gone wrong for her after leaving Budapest, but always she had tried to set them right. Zoltan was her curse.

The sounds of the party intruded on us, seeming to seep through the cabin door, as the hilarity grew louder.

"I should never have brought you into my life," she said.

"I'm in it now," I said.

She shivered. "He followed you," she said. "He followed me. He could be very close. He could be on this ship. How would we recognize him?"

"How would he recognize us?" I said, pointing to our costumes lying in heaps on the floor.

35

She had obtained the gun long before meeting Steve. The marquis had written her that Zoltan had been sent up for a ten-year term, with little likelihood that he would get time off, but that didn't end her fear of him. Just in case, just in the event he ever came looking for her, she intended to have it handy. She had it with her, in her handbag, at all times, even when she saw Steve for the first time in his office. It was only after the marquis had written her to the effect that she need have no further worries about legal difficulties in France, and inviting her for a trip on his yacht in the spring, that she had consented to marry Steve. But she had no intention of accepting the marquis's invitation. The past was to remain buried as far as Steve was concerned.

She felt some of the old dread when Steve insisted she go with him to Paris. But she supposed it would be all right, just for a couple of weeks. In any case, she had the gun, buried deep in a hidden pocket of her handbag. She placed in it a steel comb and brush set, to account for whatever might show up on airport security equipment. The gun, a twenty-five caliber Beretta, was small but lethal. She hid bullets for it in one of her suitcases. A guard at the airport opened her handbag, saw the steel comb and brush set, and passed her through.

Once in Paris, she was bothered by his having to leave her alone on occasion. Being there again after so many years brought back sharply memories of the time she had spent working for Halmos and living with Zoltan. She grew dizzy on occasion; maybe it came from a constant wariness, the searching of faces of passersby, almost as though she expected sooner or later to see someone from the old days, even Zoltan himself. Once, in a crowd, she thought she saw him, and she grew almost faint from terror.

She had to be sure he was safely locked away, she had to *know.* While Steve was away at a meeting, she phoned the

Halmos offices from a bar and asked for Zoltan Czepel.

"Who is calling him?" asked the woman who answered.

"An old friend," she said.

"What is your business with him?"

"I've been wondering where he is."

"We can't give out any information here," the woman said. "You'll have to identify yourself."

She rang off quickly. On the street she felt faint.

While Steve was having lunch at Fouquet's, with a couple of free hours before she was to meet him in the hotel lobby, she decided to buy herself a pair of sturdy walking shoes. She found what she wanted on the Rue Saint-Honoré; went a bit further to the Rue Royale, thinking she might pick up some nice French gloves; then, with time still left to kill, stopped in a small bar not far from the Champs-Elysées for some coffee. That faint feeling had come again.

Chilled, frozen, she knew at once that the man in the leather jacket, wearing dark glasses, was Zoltan. Somehow he had seen her and followed her. It was the moment she had been expecting all along. Despairingly, she knew it was that call to the Halmos offices that had alerted him to her presence in Paris. She unclasped her handbag, felt deep in it for the gun. Could she do it? In nightmares she had envisaged this moment, pointed the gun straight at him, and pulled the trigger. Now she thought of Steve. If she did it, it would be for him; she would lose him, of course, but he would be safe from Zoltan.

He came directly to her table, sat down easily in the chair opposite her, and smiled.

"Well," he said. "Isn't this a coincidence?"

The chill turned into cold hatred of him.

"Is it?"

"I heard you were looking for me."

"No," she said.

"But you called Halmos."

"You couldn't have known it was me."

"Who else?" he asked, with an expansive gesture of his arms. "You're married now, I hear. Tired of him already?"

She didn't answer.

"I'll have some coffee, too," he said, with a glance at her cup. He beckoned to the waiter.

She couldn't help asking. "How did you get out?"

"Oh, it took time. But I have good friends. They hired lawyers. I was a model prisoner, totally reformed. Unfortunately, I'm out of cash. My life-style is not satisfactory. So I thought: who is in the best position to help me? I thought of you, my old love. I made inquiries. I heard you were in New York. I heard you were married. Then, conveniently, you came here, to Paris—the perfect place to help me."

Her fingers found the stock of the gun.

"I'm not having anything to do with you," she said.

"Why are you hiding your hand?" he asked. "Something wrong with it?"

That flustered her. "Looking for a handkerchief," she said. She let the gun go and brought out a handkerchief, dabbed with it at her lips, though they were dry.

"You mustn't be afraid of me," he said almost gently, as though he could look into her mind. "I only want the best for you. It's always been that way. I don't think you realize it, but we're rich, the two of us. All it takes is a little trip to a bank on the Rue du Quatre Septembre. You wouldn't go there before. I think you will this time."

His lips smiled, but his eyes behind the dark glasses were hooded.

"No," she said. "There's no reason to go there."

"No reason?"

His smile vanished and he brought his face close to hers.

"You still don't know what's in that safe deposit box, in your name? I have some news for you. Negotiable securities, worth close to a million dollars when you placed them there, but more now. You see, the dollar goes down, but the securities have gone up. You want to deny me my status as a millionaire?" His voice got lower, uglier. "I was a long time in that prison. I didn't stay there for nothing. It was always promised to me, that fortune. You see, I kept silent, never involved my associates. I'm a solid, trustworthy fellow. So I'm to be repaid."

"It's too late," she said.

"Too late? Why too late?"

"The police knew about the box, long ago."

"How would the police know? You told them?"

She didn't answer. She didn't want him to know that the marquis had helped her.

"It's not possible," he said, but he looked worried. "I would have heard. I was assured . . . I don't believe you. You couldn't tell the police. Why would you tell them about stolen securities? Then you'd be involved, an accessory. You can't lie to me!"

"I'm not lying."

Then he smiled again.

"I see it now. You don't want that husband of yours to know, that Mr. Steven Parrish who I found registered at the Plaza Atheneé. A man of taste, I take it? Knows what the good things in life are? Appreciates a beautiful woman. Hmmm. We might have to do something about him. Tell you what. You need to think about it a little bit. Until tomorrow morning, at nine o'clock, when Barclay's Bank opens its doors. I think you'll meet me there. By the way, whatever happened to that former fiancé of yours? What was his name? Ian?"

Her hand moved toward the handbag again.

He said expansively: "I'll give you the choice. You can come with me, after nine o'clock, or just open the box, turn over the securities, and rejoin that nice husband of yours. I'll take you back, you know. You've hurt me, but never say that your lover, Zoltan, doesn't forgive."

He got up.

"Nine o'clock. Barclay's Bank."

He sauntered out.

The gun was almost out of her handbag, but by that time he had left the café. She heard a motorcycle start up, speed away.

Panic-stricken, her mind revolved around the possibilities. If she met Zoltan at the bank, he would know soon enough that the securities were gone. And the police would know soon enough that she had been there. If she stayed with Steve, he would be killed. She was utterly sure of that. There was only one thing to do. She had to get away. From everyone. She had to disappear.

She left the bar, and, on the Champs-Elysées, stopped a cruising taxi. Knowing Zoltan, he would be keeping an eye on her.

"Drive fast," she told the driver. "Anywhere. There's someone following me."

The driver was willing enough, even seemed to enjoy the assignment. He careened around corners, took her into areas of the city she had never seen before. Finally, she recognized the Place de la République. "When you see an empty taxi," she told the driver, "hail it. I'll change into it."

Her driver gestured to a cruising taxi, which stopped at a curb. After transferring to the second taxi, she asked the driver if he knew of a small rental car agency. She could be too easily traced through one of the large ones.

Later, at the wheel of a Peugeot, heading toward Place d'Italie and southward from the city, she became more self-possessed. By now, Grete, who had written her in New York, would be at Saas Fee, a long day's drive from Paris. The route there led through Geneva, where she could buy appropriate clothes. Why not? She was a free woman again. She had to be. Zoltan would have no reason to harm Steve if she were no longer in his life. She drove fast, almost recklessly.

36

"The Beretta—do you have it with you?" I asked.

"No."

"Where is it?"

"When I had the chance, when I couldn't bring myself to use it, I threw it away."

"Where?"

"In Geneva. I tossed it into a sewer."

Was she lying? I looked into violet-blue eyes and received only an innocent stare back.

"I have one," I said. "I left it on my boat. And if I have to, I'll use it."

Her eyes clouded.

"No," she said. "I don't want that—not at all. It's why we must separate. Sooner or later . . ."

But, at the moment, I was thinking of something else, something that came to me while she was relating her story.

"This Halmos you worked for—could he be Marcel?" I asked her.

"It's possible," Caryl said. "But I don't think so. Zoltan spoke of them as two different people."

"He might have wanted to throw you off."

"No, Halmos worked for someone else, I'm sure of it. It was more as though he was in charge of a . . ."—she sought for the words—". . . a communications center. Letters, packages were always going through his office to other places. And Zoltan didn't seem to be working for him. It was more as though he was his equal."

"Even so, Halmos still has to be a key figure in that organization. If we can get that information to Delahaye, promise him your cooperation in identifying him, indicate his connection with Zoltan, the whole ring might be cracked."

"And your wife would go to prison," she said tonelessly.

"No," I said. "Your freedom, dropping of any charges, would be the price Delahaye would have to pay."

"You trust him?"

"Enough," I said. "He wants the Marcel group, he wants Zoltan—not you. It makes much more sense for us to stay together. We're going to Paris."

"How?" she asked.

It seemed simple enough. If we got to the *Arcturus,* it was hardly a day's trip to the port of Piraeus. From there, a taxi to the Athens airport, and in three hours we could be in Paris.

"I'll call Delahaye from Athens," I said. "He'll meet us at Orly and give us the necessary security."

"And you think Zoltan would let us get there?"

"If he follows, all the better. Isn't it time you let me handle things?"

I felt surrender in the way her body relaxed against mine. Her arms came up and grasped me tightly to her.

"You won't run away again?"

"Never." I almost didn't hear the word, her lips were so close to mine.

After we were dressed again in our costumes, she left me in the cabin and went to find the marquis. All I wanted, I had told her, was a small boat that could get us back to the *Arcturus.* It seemed a long time, but it was hardly more than ten minutes before she was back. "He has a seaman," she said, "whom he can trust to take us to the *Arcturus.* The launch will be waiting for us in half an hour. We're to go directly to the gangway. He wants us to have our masks on, so that it will seem to be two guests leaving early.

A little later, as we made our way through the ship's corridors to the gangway, the mood of the party had shifted. The band still played, but the guests had separated into small groups and twosomes. We almost stumbled over two youths dressed as harlequins who were embracing on the landing of a staircase. At the gangway, which still had its barrier and was guarded by two sailors dressed as masked gondoliers, we found the tall Spanish grandee waiting for us.

"All will be well," he said, as I shook his hand and whispered my thanks. "I wish you both happiness," he added. "Call on me again, if I can help."

The launch bobbed at the side of the ship; another seaman, also dressed as a gondolier, was waiting ready at the wheel. I got in first, then helped Caryl into the launch. The marquis gave us a kind of salute and gestured to the seaman, who gunned the motor and moved us into the darkness.

With my arm around Caryl's shoulder, we sat together at the stern of the launch, the late night breeze against our faces. "It won't be more than fifteen minutes to the quay," I told her. "If Costa isn't there, I'll leave him behind. I can handle the boat."

She pressed my hand, as though to say she now was putting all her trust in me.

I waited for the lights of shore to grow brighter, but, if anything, they seemed to get farther away. Our pilot was taking a roundabout route. I went forward to make sure that he knew where we were to go.

"Why . . ." I said—and was unable to finish, because, at that moment, the sailor turned and raised his hand, and it was only afterward that I realized it held something blunt, and whatever it was came crashing against the side of my head.

I heard voices, their voices, in the blackness. I opened my eyes, cringed them shut again when I felt the fierce throb on the right side of my head. Instinctively I tried lifting my hand to the pain, but could not. It came to me that my arms were tied to my sides. The rope that bound me wound around my body and held my legs and ankles together, too. I lay on the hard decking of the launch.

"The problem," I heard Zoltan say, and he seemed to be speaking reasonably, "is how to dispose of Mr. Parrish."

The launch was in motion, cutting through choppy waves. I could tell that much.

"What do you want from me?"

Caryl's voice, desperation in it.

"Don't you know? I ask so little. Simply tell me the truth—what happened to the box?"

"Your securities are gone, long ago. I told you that in Paris."

"Marcel told me otherwise."

"Whoever Marcel is, he's lying."

"Then tell me what you know."

"I want my husband safe," Caryl said.

"I would prefer being rid of him. Perhaps you, also. I'm not interested in making deals."

"Then *what?*" Caryl's voice rose.

"Tell me," he said.

It was a painful struggle, but I managed to lift my head enough to see both of them in the forward part of the launch. Zoltan was at the wheel. The launch's running lights were enough to see that he steered with one hand, holding a gun on Caryl with the other. I felt a vast hopelessness.

"All right," she said. "This is the truth. You'll see how useless all this is. When Ian was killed, I was in the hospital for a while. The marquis came to see me. I told him—everything. About you, about the safe deposit box. I signed a power of attorney to him, so that he could turn it over to the police."

Zoltan laughed.

"You thought he would turn it over to the police? You believed that?"

"Why wouldn't I?"

"You're a fool," he said. "We'll go back there, you and I, and face your marquis together. This time I'll get the truth. But first—"

He cut the motor.

"No!" I heard her scream.

"We'll simply tie the anchor to him and drop him over. He'll never know. A pleasant death for him."

"I lied to you," she said with desperation. "The money is still there."

"No," he said. "Parrish is a bother. He's in the way."

He was near me now, and I heard the clang of something metallic. I closed my eyes, stayed still.

I was being rolled over, bound again, this time by what had to be an anchor line.

Caryl must have come at him, clawing at him, for I heard him grunt and shove her. She was on the decking beside me. Then, a sharp report, and Zoltan's body fell on top of mine. I felt something wet, Zoltan's blood, dripping on my neck. I opened my eyes and saw Caryl leaning over me. "Steve," she cried, shaking me. "Steve!"

She pushed Zoltan's form away from me.

"Find his knife and cut the ropes," I told her. "I'm all right."

Tears were rolling down her cheeks. "Pig," I heard her say. "Pig, pig."

But she found the knife and freed me, not that it helped much for a while. I could hardly move. Zoltan lay motionless on the deck, face upward, his eyes closed. Blood streaked his face. The bullet from Caryl's Beretta had hit the left side of his skull. I felt for a heartbeat. He was alive. Just as well, I thought.

"Keep the gun on him," I told Caryl. "We'll take him to shore and turn him over to the police. If he moves, if he so much as threatens . . ."

"I'm not afraid anymore," Caryl said. "If you tell me, I'll shoot him again now."

"Where was it?"

"The gun? There was room for it, under the habit."

"Will you never learn to tell the truth?" I tried a reassuring smile, but it hurt.

The motor was still running. I thrust the control into forward gear and headed toward shore, toward the quay.

"Is he conscious?" I asked her, glancing back for a moment.

I saw her prod him with her foot.

"He's bleeding a lot," she said.

"I'd just as soon have him alive," I said. "It will save us trouble."

37

At the wheel of the launch, I tried making sense of it all. How had Zoltan taken command of the launch that belonged to the marquis? Our pilot was supposed to be a trusted seaman of the marquis. And he had turned out to be Zoltan, possibly in league with the marquis. And I had heard him say to Caryl: *You thought he would turn it over to the police? You believed that?* And then he had told her that they would face the marquis together.

"Caryl," I said.

"Yes?"

I turned and saw that she had her pistol stuck right against the temple of the unconscious Zoltan. She was taking no chances, and I admired her nerve. It helped mine.

"When you signed that power of attorney over to the marquis—did you read it?"

"No," she said.

"And all you had was the marquis's word that he had cleared you?"

"Yes," she said grimly.

"Are you thinking what I'm thinking?"

"That Pierre arranged for Zoltan to be in this boat?"

"Yes, but more than that. Zoltan was telling you the truth—that the contents, whatever was in the safe deposit box, was never turned over to the police."

"But he assured me . . . he wrote me . . ."

"If the police had gotten to the box, it would have been in the files."

"What files?"

"At Interpol—the fact that you had voluntarily turned it over, made no claim, didn't know precisely what was there. And, whatever *was* in it would have been listed as recovered—with your cooperation. Also, that it would have given the police some leads to Halmos, or Marcel, or both."

"You're confusing me," she said.

"There was no reason for Delahaye to hold any of that back from me. Don't you see?"

"You think that the marquis wanted it for himself?"

"More than that," I said. "I'm beginning to understand it now. That Julio Alvarez you mentioned—well, Delahaye mentioned the name, too. When he was killed, they—the Marcel people—needed you to get into the safe deposit box. You were their insurance. Now, see if this adds up: Zoltan claimed to have been promised what was in the box—by Marcel. I'd think as a price for his taking the jail term in London. And he had to get you out of it to keep you from talking, all too innocently, telling what you didn't exactly know; but you had important names, and that would have gotten the authorities onto the Marcel group and its manner of operation. Do you see?"

"I think so," she said dubiously. "But if Zoltan was promised . . ."

"Marcel had to renege on that. He had to figure that the police would be keeping an eye on Zoltan, that if he or a confederate went near that box, he could be picked up, and the box opened. By the same reasoning, you couldn't be allowed to run around loose. So he keeps a friendly eye on you while Zoltan is in jail, except you complicate things by falling in love with Ian. I'm afraid Ian was set up by Marcel, after Zoltan's release. Then he makes sure to have your power of attorney and gets you out of the country. And he makes sure that Zoltan is sent away again for a long term. Who was in a position to arrange all that?"

She remained silent.

"The marquis," I said. "The marquis is Marcel."

"But he was so . . ."

"Kind," I said. "Kind enough to have Zoltan here on the launch, to take care of me, dumped somewhere out to sea. I wasn't even at his party; I came as Barlow! Never saw me. Everyone in costume anyway. What Zoltan didn't know was that he wasn't going to last for long, either. You, too, Caryl. The marquis is good at arranging accidents."

"But he could have, all along!"

"He needed you as bait for Zoltan. Zoltan never knew you

had transferred the safe deposit box. So he'd be on your trail. If anything happened to you, anything at all suspicious, Zoltan would have guessed the marquis's hand in it. Your marquis does things very neatly, keeps his hands clean. He's the rich playboy, having a gay time cruising all through the Mediterranean, the Aegean, stopping to pick up God knows what contraband. No wonder they can't trace it. No borders to cross. Everyone on board having a marvelous time. Guests who are rich and respectable. He waits until I catch up with you, then gets the word to Zoltan. So he has all three of us together. He even got in touch with Delahaye. In case Zoltan slips through his fingers, the police will get to him. Now he assumes Zoltan has done the job. What next?"

She studied Zoltan's inert form.

"What will we do with *him?*"

"Better if he stays alive. We'll take the *Arcturus* and get away from here."

I speeded up the launch, giving the *Pantagruelle* a wide berth. Dawn was still a few hours away. The *Arcturus* wouldn't be noticed slipping out of the harbor. And Costa would have refueled by now.

"So," she said, "when I left Halmos, it was arranged that I would work directly for the marquis."

"Marcel," I said. "You went right to the top."

I found an empty slip at the pier near the *Arcturus.* Before leaving the launch, I bent close to Zoltan. The blood on his head wound was beginning to clot, indicating there was still some life in him. It would be simple enough to kill him, I thought. I took the Beretta from Caryl and considered putting one more bullet into his skull. But the shot would be heard. And it would be cold-blooded murder. The police would find him soon enough. He was in no condition to travel. I gave him a kick to make sure. No movement. He was still unconscious. Maybe he'd die. O.K., I thought.

The *Arcturus* was dark. Costa had either gone ashore or was asleep.

I helped Caryl on board and called: "Costa."

No answer.

I felt for a light switch for the main cabin, located it near the steps that led downward from the control console on the open stern deck. The cabin lights worked off auxiliary batteries when the boat was not underway. When I found the switch, it gave off only a wan light, but it was enough to see two men standing in the main cabin. Both held pistols and they were pointing at us. One of the men was Carlos.

"So," he said, softly, "it's you, Mr. Parrish. I expected . . ."

With a wave of his pistol, he motioned us to come into the cabin. Caryl's hand clutched mine tightly. Was it possible to make a run for it? On the other hand, it was Zoltan he more likely was waiting for. Caryl's gun nestled in my pocket, but he had motioned me to raise my hands.

"We would prefer not to shoot," Carlos said, again with a menacing wave of the pistol. "But I have my orders. No wrong moves, please. Kindly tell me where Czepel is."

The other man came forward and half pulled, half shoved us into the cabin.

"What's this all about?" I said, with all too transparent bluster.

But, with a sinking sensation in my chest, I already knew. Zoltan had been expected to make use of the *Arcturus.* So, Carlos and his accomplice had been planted here to dispose of Zoltan—and Caryl. Alternatively, should we have somehow thwarted Zoltan, this was the precaution. The marquis meant business. He had chosen his time to act. I can't say that it came to me rationally in that order, for my mind was desperately concentrating on getting the gun in my pocket into my hand. At any rate, Carlos left me little doubt.

"We will take a little trip out to sea," Carlos said. He said something in Italian to the other seaman, who picked up two lengths of rope and came toward us.

He wouldn't shoot here, I thought. The harbor police would descend on us.

"Run!" I yelled to Caryl.

I doubt that she would have moved, but, as though to prevent it, the seaman grabbed her and pinioned her arms behind her back. She struggled, and for a moment he released her, but only to land a blow on her face. It was as though a red film blurred my vision; no gun was going to stop me. But before I could spring at the seaman, the red film turned to blinding white light, as though the interior of the boat were being lit up by a dozen searchlights. They *were* searchlights! Several people were clambering aboard. Carlos pointed his gun at the entrance to the cabin. Shots rang out, but they weren't his; he seemed to crumple slowly, and lay there before me on the cabin floor. His open eyes held a look of vast surprise.

The other seaman simply froze and held up his hands. Two Greek policemen entered the cabin, both with guns, behind them a slim, mustached man in plain clothes, and, behind him, the fat, welcome figure of Delahaye.

38

I'm not sure I've got it sorted out, even yet, for it was all taking on a nightmare quality, with one occurrence fading, almost without seeming connection, into another. Questions I needed answers for were intermixed with imperatives requiring action. And through it all, my head throbbing; and I only now remember that I dipped a handkerchief in water and held it against the darkening bruise on Caryl's cheek, doing this while very quickly the Greek police removed the inert form of Carlos after hustling off the other seaman. And Delahaye regarding me solemnly, as though waiting for me to completely catch my breath.

"So," he said finally, almost with a note of humor, "each of us requires explanations."

"Yes," I said. "But it had better wait. Czepel is out there."

"Where?" he barked at me.

"In the launch we came here in. We—that is—I shot him." The last was a lie, but Delahaye, I realized, still had his suspicions of Caryl, and I didn't want her involved in investigations of who shot whom and why.

"He's dead?"

"Unconscious."

Delahaye gestured to the Greek plainclothesman, and we all scrambled out on the pier. I led them to where I had tied the launch. But it wasn't there.

"I tied it here," I said lamely.

I heard the Greek officer barking orders, and suddenly the searchlights came on, sweeping the waters near the pier with powerful beams. Not too far off, I heard the sound of a motor, a familiar sound, receding. One of the searchlights was already tracking the sound. Just how far off it was, it was hard to tell, seven or eight hundred yards.

"There!" I shouted.

The launch was illuminated, as though trapped in the beam. Behind it was a thin white wake, pointing like a phosphorescent arrow directly at the *Pantagruelle,* outlined by its lights and masts, also strung with lights.

"Who?" Delahaye asked me, opening his arms wide in a gesture of exasperation.

"Czepel," I said. "Either that, or someone got into the launch."

"You don't shoot very well. His condition allows him to run a boat?"

"He wants the marquis," I said. "Now it's the marquis he wants."

Caryl huddled against me on the pier while Delahaye and the Greek plainclothesman consulted off to one side. Then both approached us.

"Lieutenant Petros has two of his men aboard the ship out there, in costume. He took the precaution after I notified him of the probable circumstances. There is a way to board the ship without being noticed, and he wishes—as I do—for both of you to come with us."

"Can't you handle it without us? She's been through a lot."

"You can furnish the identifications we lack." Delahaye said with asperity.

"I'll go with you," I said. "But she should be gotten to a safe place."

"No," Caryl said, almost fiercely. "I won't go *any*where without you."

"Who is he, anyway?" I asked, indicating the Greek officer.

"My liaison, of the Greek security police. An excellent man."

Petros was already quietly giving orders to one of his men. Soon enough, a police launch was approaching us. I suddenly realized I was anxious to go with them, to get aboard the *Pantagruelle,* to finally once and for all track down not only Czepel, but the marquis, the nemesis behind him. If his plans had worked, neither I, nor Caryl likely, would be alive at this moment. It was more than anger that filled me; it was a deep sense of outrage. Was there time to get to the cabin of the *Arcturus* and get the thirty-eight in the drawer of the cabinet?

The answer came as Delahaye beckoned us to follow him.

"We'll use your yacht for a change of clothes," he said. "Both of you had better change, too."

From the police launch, which was now lengthwise against the pier, a bundle was brought out. We returned to the *Arcturus.* The bundle, when unwrapped, held a variety of costumes. Petros officiated. Delahaye was given the cassock and round hat of a French country priest. Petros took a cossack horseman's outfit.

In the master cabin, Caryl became Columbine and I turned into Pierrot. But the thirty-eight was missing from the cabinet drawer. Carlos, probably, had seen to that. I still had Caryl's Beretta and, checking it, I found it contained five small cartridges. I was by now dubious of its stopping power, but it would have to do.

When the four of us got under way in the police launch, a pilot at the controls, the explanations came out.

"We had your yacht under surveillance," Delahaye said, "after being notified by the Coast Guard at Rhodes. Frau Netzer was kind enough to put me on your trail."

"I told her to."

"And I assumed as much. The marquis was of help, too—that is, he apprised us that Czepel was in the vicinity. But then you disappeared. The only thing to do was keep your yacht under surveillance, while Petros had his two men working the ship. Meanwhile, we picked up your man."

"Costa," I said. "Is he all right?"

Delahaye nodded. "We kept him out of sight. We saw those two characters board your yacht and realized something was up. Perhaps you can explain what it was?"

"The marquis helped us get away from the ship," I said. "And it turned out Czepel was running his launch. He knocked me cold, tied me up, but I came to, managed to free myself enough to get off a shot."

It was a bare-faced lie again, but apparently he believed it.

"How could it happen," Delahaye asked, "that Czepel would be in the launch that belonged to the marquis?"

I had the feeling he already knew the answer.

"It makes sense," I said, "if the marquis is Marcel."

He nodded benignly, just as an actual country priest might have nodded, filled with native wisdom and understanding. "Please explain," he said.

Both he and Petros listened to my theory that the safe deposit box had contained something of great value, and that he had not intended Czepel to get hold of it. That he had planned to dispose of all three of us. "Carlos," I said, "was to kill Czepel and Caryl, assuming Czepel had taken care of me in the launch. The bodies were to be dumped out at sea. The plan had to be revised when I showed up instead. But it was basically the same plan."

"You think the ship contains contraband?" Petros asked, a glint in his eyes.

"Suppose among the guests," I said, "were his operatives? It's an international guest list."

"The ship will be quarantined," Petros said grimly. "Within twenty-four hours every inch of it will be searched."

"But meanwhile, Czepel," Delahaye reminded him softly. "I want him badly. You are still armed, Mr. Parrish?"

"I wish I had something more lethal," I said.

"I meant for your self-protection. I want him alive. And the marquis."

Petros had left us and was at the launch's radio. I heard a crackle of static and several beeps. Then he twisted a dial and spoke rapidly in Greek. He returned to us.

"Better," he said, "to have reinforcements. The guests will have to remain aboard. Meanwhile, my men on the ship have been alerted for our arrival."

When we were within a few hundred yards of the ship, the launch's motors were cut down to a purr. The sound of music and laughter came to us clearly from the *Pantagruelle.* We moved ahead slowly, cautiously, without lights, and crept along the port side of the ship, the side opposite from that where the guests had boarded, and from which Caryl and I had departed not much more than an hour before. The night had turned murky from a predawn mist. We nestled near the bow of the ship and cut the motors completely. Petros flashed twice with a pocket lantern. Above us, not far from the waterline, a hatch opened, from its cavity an answering double flash. A rope boarding ladder was dropped into the launch. Petros went up first. There was just enough light to see him beckon us to climb the ladder. I began to have more respect for Greek police work. I went up the ladder, only six steps, and helped Caryl into what seemed to be a small cargo space. Delahaye was last, puffing from the exertion of climbing. The pilot remained with the launch.

We stood together in a huddle. Petros clicked on his lantern, and I was able to make out his two men, wearing the same gondolier costumes as the ship's crew. They had rough faces and looked well able to take care of themselves. Petros spoke with them in Greek, then turned to Delahaye.

"They noticed one of the ship's seamen come aboard, claiming he had fallen while transporting guests. He had a head wound."

"And where is he?" Delahaye asked.

"There is a nurse somewhere on board. Apparently he was sent to her."

"Then we must find the nurse," Delahaye said. "If his head is bandaged, it won't be too difficult to spot him."

I spoke up.

"The marquis has private quarters. An elevator connects directly with an exercise room. A door opens out to the boat deck, forward, port side. If Zoltan located the marquis, and there was to be a showdown, wouldn't the marquis take him there—as he did me?"

"You can find the place?"

I nodded.

"Then let's go there. Petros and his men will go first to the nurse, then come to the boat deck. Agreed?" he asked Petros.

"Agreed," he said.

"Can't we leave Caryl here?" I asked.

"No!" She caught hold of my hand and gripped it tightly.

"Let us coordinate," Delahaye said to Petros. "Say, twenty minutes exactly, on the boat deck, where Mr. Parrish has indicated. When will your reinforcements arrive?"

"One half hour."

"Good. We wish only a capture. Remember, Mr. Parrish,

you are here only for identification purposes. What is the costume of the marquis, by the way?"

"A Spanish grandee. And he's tall."

"It is time to put on our masks," Delahaye said.

I had an idea of where the quarters of the marquis were, but wasn't altogether sure of how to get there. Caryl knew, though. "I've spent enough time on this ship," she said wearily, but with the hint of a smile. She's game, I thought. I remembered that first time we'd gone skiing, and how she had sped down the slope ahead of me. Purposefully, she led the way.

The door to the marquis's quarters was locked, but that proved no hindrance to Delahaye. From beneath his cassock, he took out a ring full of keys and little tools. In less than a minute, he had the door open. When he returned the keys to his pocket, I noticed the handle of a police revolver tucked into his belt.

He poked his head inside the living room and seemed to be sniffing.

"No one here," he said.

"The button to the elevator is over there. It's next to a painting, a Juan Gris."

Oddly, it was only now that I remembered the painting was a Gris. I'd hardly paid attention to it the time before.

The button was there all right. I pressed it, and the panel slid open.

"Once you're up there, it opens automatically," I warned Delahaye.

He held up a hand to his lips, motioning for silence, then stepped inside the elevator. He beckoned to me. I stepped inside, too. I could hear voices, faintly but distinctly, speaking in French.

"You have an instinct for violence," I heard someone say, in French.

The marquis.

". . . but it would be wiser to control it. I tell you, she lied to you. She took the securities for herself. In any case, I agree that it's coming to you. I shall arrange it."

"A million, American."

Caryl, who was beside me, started. Czepel's voice, certainly.

"Very well, a million American."

"But now, tonight."

"But how—"

"Or its value. There's plenty on this ship right now."

"Too early . . ."

The marquis again.

". . . how do I know what is here?"

"If not in cash, then securities, jewels."

"Cocaine, perhaps. That could be arranged."

"No more of that! I'm finished with drugs! You framed me, didn't you? First in London, then in Marseilles. But it won't happen again. If I thought you had anything in mind . . ."

"Stop waving that knife. You'd never get off this ship alive. Don't you think my people know you're here? Anyway, you want to take care of the woman and her husband. I already helped you once. I can do so again."

"Do I get the million tonight?"

"Tonight."

"And if there's any more funny business . . . this will be poking into your side."

Delahaye glanced at his watch.

"Twenty minutes," he whispered. "Let us rise."

He took out his revolver and pressed the elevator button. I had the Beretta in my hand. I heard the faint whine made by the elevator, and, with it, the sudden ceasing of the voices above. They had been alerted. And the elevator door would slide open. I felt a sudden chill. Tension more than fear. Oh, I'd use the Beretta all right! I knew it. All it would take was the sight of Czepel. Delahaye wanted him alive. I knew I wanted him dead.

39

The elevator door opened, and with surprising, even extraordinary quickness for his bulk, Delahaye sprang into the exercise room, his revolver held straight and stiff before him. I held Caryl back in the confines of the elevator and peered out, my own gun pointing and ready to fire. But the room was empty. The door leading to the boat deck was open. We went to it, and I saw the tall figure of the marquis held firmly by Petros and his two men. They had removed his mask. He made no struggle, held himself stiffly, with dignity.

"The other?" Delahaye barked.

"There was only this one," Petros said.

"You didn't see the other one?"

Petros looked bewildered.

Caryl! Still in the open elevator. I dashed back into the exercise room, its door banging closed behind me. With relief, I saw Caryl at the elevator door. "Stay there!" I said.

I looked around the room. I had been in gyms enough in my college days to know that there would be a locker for storing equipment, medicine balls, weights, mats, the like. A closet perhaps. And, sure enough, there was one. Two thin metal doors at the far end on my left. I approached those doors slowly.

I put my lips close to the doors and said: "Come out, Czepel. Hands up. You're in there. I know it. I can smell your stink. Come out, Czepel. But one little move, and this gun goes off. You haven't a chance."

I could hardly believe it was my own voice saying the words. It was as though some other personality had me in its grip.

"All right, Czepel," I said. "In five seconds I shoot through the door. One . . ."

The doors burst open. He came at me so fast it was like a whirlwind that seemed to lift me off my feet and toss me heavily onto one of the tumbling mats. That long-ago, but familiar, odor of canvas and perspiration. I glimpsed his arm, the hand upraised with the knife, and I knew what to do. The toe of my shoe caught him in the groin. That gave me time to get an arm lock on him, and I had the strength to toss him on his back. The Beretta was six feet away; I had lost my hold on it when he came at me. I scrambled for it, as he scrambled to his feet. Dimly, I heard Caryl shrieking. I got the gun, and he weaved toward me, the knife outstretched. A few feet away from me, he leaped, and I squeezed the trigger. I saw a splattering of blood on his shoulder as, deflected, he landed against my leg. I shot again. This time, the stomach. He was wheezing, attempting to rise. I took a deep breath and shot three more times, aiming at the heart. He lay still, the knife still gripped in his hand.

As I looked up, I saw I had an audience. A cossack, a French priest, and two gondoliers.

"Mr. Parrish," Delahaye said sadly. "Was this necessary?"

I didn't answer.

I went to Caryl, who, sobbing, came into my arms.

Soon enough, the loudspeakers of the ship were stridently ordering all guests and crew members to assemble in the ballroom, by orders of the Greek security police. The loudspeakers continued booming through the companionways for several minutes. The gay clamor slowly ceased. The music stopped playing, and the motley crowd moved bewilderedly into the ballroom. Caryl and I stayed with Delahaye, but we were onlookers now. The reinforcements had arrived, at least twenty uniformed police. They herded stragglers into the ballroom and lined them up by twos. The loudspeakers warned that a search was underway. Anyone attempting to avoid the search would be confined and held for questioning.

"You've had a difficult night," Delahaye said, surveying the scene with grim satisfaction. "Your presence is no longer required. We will meet again in Paris."

"Why Paris?"

I was about to say that Caryl had no liking for Paris, when I realized that he wanted the whole group, and Caryl obviously could be helpful in rounding them up. She had mentioned offices there, and someone called Halmos. It was to our distinct interest to get them all.

"I'll see that your stay in Corfu will be short," he said, "even though you killed a man."

"Self-defense," I said.

"Quite clearly, self-defense," he said nodding.

"In Paris," I said to Caryl, "you won't disappear again, will you?"

"No," she said solemnly. "I promise.

40

On our arrival in Paris, we were met by Delahaye and three French officers in plain clothes. A soft-riding Citroën sped us from Orly to the city proper.

"Any preference in hotels?" Delahaye asked me.

"The Plaza Athenée," I said.

Caryl gave me a wan smile. She was looking better and had powdered over the discoloration on her cheek. My headaches had lessened, although the bump on my head was still the size of a small egg. We had spent an entire day at Corfu making statements. I had sent Costa back to Rhodes with the *Arcturus* and a substantial tip. We had a police escort with us on the flight from Corfu to Athens, where, at the airport, we were questioned again by some Greek security officers; but in view of statements made by Delahaye and Lieutenant Petros, appearance in court would not be required.

"I took the precaution," Delahaye informed me during the ride to the Plaza Athenée, "of having Halmos picked up. Evidently, word of some kind had reached him, because he was in the midst of packing his bags. They were also in time to forestall the destruction of his records."

We might have simply arrived from a holiday in the Aegean, so restrained and polite was the greeting from those at the lobby's desk when we reregistered. However, Monsieur Caille soon appeared to express his pleasure at my wife's safe return. Delahaye, still with us, took him aside for an explanatory chat. The gist of it was that guards would have to be on twenty-four-hour watch outside our room during our stay; any of the hotel's personnel entering our room for any purpose would have to undergo a thorough security check.

The hotel sent Caryl's bags to the room, and Delahaye allowed her an hour to change and freshen herself. She ended up looking lovely and elegant in a pink wool suit. Then, with Delahaye and one of the plainclothesmen, we made a trip to

Barclay's Bank on the Rue du Quatre Septembre. The manager of the bank had been alerted in advance and we were immediately closeted with him. Within a few minutes, the bank's records pertaining to her safe deposit box were produced. One was a copy of the power of attorney she had signed back in 1968 allowing its use.

"Of course," she said, remembering the name on the power of attorney. "Henri Verret. The one who hired me to work in Marseilles."

Verret, it turned out, had visited the vault in May 1968. He apparently never used the box again, for a year later the rental on the box had been allowed to lapse.

The records also showed that, prior to 1968, the vault had been visited by Caryl and by Julio Alvarez.

"Who has the box now?" Delahaye asked.

The bank's records showed that the box was now held by a Mrs. Hedley-Smith. The manager knew Mrs. Hedley-Smith personally; she kept London and Paris addresses, was seventy-three years old and a widow.

"I must ask to examine it," Delahaye said.

The manager said that it would be quite irregular without a court order.

"If you wish to waste my time . . . ," Delahaye said, with an oblique glance at him.

"But I suppose that won't be necessary in this case," the manager added. "I will take the authorization on myself."

When Delahaye returned from the vault, I asked him, "Anything?"

"Antique jewelry," he said grumpily. "Old brooches and bracelets."

After leaving the bank, we had another trip to make, this one to police headquarters on Rue des Saussaies.

"I will require your identification of Halmos as the one who employed you," Delahaye told Caryl, "and all you know of his activities, including his relationship with Czepel."

Caryl looked at me inquiringly.

"Tell them what you know," I said.

We followed Delahaye to a plainly furnished interrogation

room. We were asked to wait. A few minutes later, a tall, heavyset man in his fifties was escorted in. "This is quite irregular," I heard him say, in French, to his police escort. "I must insist that I be allowed counsel." Then he gave a start of surprise, for he had recognized Caryl. His gaze turned my way, and he regarded me somberly.

"Do you know this man?" Delahaye asked Caryl.

"Yes," she said quietly. "Hello, Mr. Halmos."

The good warm weather had come, but although we had two of Delahaye's men with us whenever we ventured outside, he thought it advisable we remain inside most of the time, while the investigation and roundup of the associates of the marquis continued. The marquis was being held in confinement in Marseilles, the case against him entirely secure, with charges that included attempted murder as well as smuggling, illegal possession of currencies and securities, along with stolen jewels and a considerable quantity of cocaine and heroin that had been picked up during the search of the *Pantagruelle.* Several guests at the costume party were being held, as well as the ship's entire crew.

In Marseilles, Henri Verret had been questioned and, after being confronted with the power of attorney signed by Caryl, had confessed to disposing of the box's contents for the benefit of the marquis—in return for a lighter sentence. Halmos maintained his innocence for a time, but Delahaye finally brought us word that he had cracked and given the police the list of names they wanted. The entire ring had been tracked, and although court cases would continue for several months, the activities of the Marcel group were at an end.

When, one morning in late April, I read the headlined story in the *International Herald-Tribune,* which meant that the police now had the case completely in hand, I knew that we could soon go back to New York. Our names were not mentioned; Delahaye had kept his word that our role would not be divulged to the press.

Delahaye came to see us later that morning.

"You are free to leave," he said. "We've got the whole

bunch. Your depositions are all that will be necessary. But there is still one little detail. A charge remains on our books against Mrs. Parrish."

Caryl looked at him gravely.

"Unlawful possession of a firearm," Delahae said. "You remember the box of cartridges for a twenty-five caliber Beretta you found among her possessions and turned over to me. You see, I entered that on a charge sheet."

"But she had no gun, as it turned out," I said. "She happened to find the bullets, put them in her bag, and forgot to mention it to me."

"Yes, I see," he said. "You're saying that bullets are harmless without a gun to put them into."

"That's right."

"But you had a gun."

"I turned it over to the Greek police."

"I only mentioned it," he said, "to let you know that the charge has been dropped. A small thing, in view of the help you have given us. I wish you a pleasant journey home. You will have your security until you are on the plane, but I doubt that it's necessary."

He turned as though to leave, then, near the door, turned back to us. His eyes seemed to have become watery. He sniffed, brought out a handkerchief, and wiped his nose, as though a cold might be coming on. "I owe both of you a personal and profound debt of gratitude," he sniffed again, "as Gazin would have said."

We shook hands. He took Caryl's hand in his and bent to kiss it.

"Bon voyage, Mrs. Parrish."

When he was gone, Caryl sprayed Cabochard on her hair, behind her ears, and in the cleft of her bosom.

"Would you mind," she asked, "if we went and bought me a pair of shoes? Something pretty, for evening wear? I know a little shop on the Rue du Faubourg Saint-Honoré."

"So do I," I said.